Praise for *The Immigrant Princess*

"The rich gifts and tragic history of Cambodia impose a complicated burden on Sophea Lim, whose quest for love, career, and independence run counter to the duties and proprieties her mother and grandmother have taught her. Thoughtful and humorous, *The Immigrant Princess* takes us on a fascinating ride into Cambodian history and immigrant struggles. An engrossing, compassionate portrait of one family's attempt to make peace with a painful past."

~Jessica Levine
Author of *The Geometry of Love*
a *Booklist* Top Ten Women's Fiction Title for 2015

"Variny Yim's enchanting debut novel about three generations of strong Cambodian women living in the United States is a compelling story of what happens to the children of refugees in a land of opportunity. Yim's vibrant characters tackle complex issues such as survival guilt, familial obligations, and the tug of war between traditional values and modern Western life; their experiences demystify the travails and triumphs of so many people who have had to reinvent themselves outside their countries of origin."

~Nassim Assefi, MD
Doctor, Writer, Curator, Activist, and Author of *Aria*

"East meets West and traditional values are turned upside down as three generations of Cambodian women adapt to life in 21st century America. In *The Immigrant Princess*, author Variny Yim deftly manages to evoke both worlds with a lighthearted touch as her characters realize the importance of remembering the truth of their history and heritage, while embracing life on these shores. A fun and spirited read."

~Barbara Graham
New York Times Bestselling Author of *Eye of My Heart*

"In this poignant first novel, Variny Yim creates a complex world of memory, loss, and triumph in a three-generational Cambodian family of four remarkable women. The story unfolds as this refugee family, having fled political instability in 1974 as the Khmer Rouge seized power in Phnom Penh, relocates to Washington DC, and learns to negotiate American culture. The two sisters, now college educated with demanding careers, navigate between traditional responsibilities to their Cambodian mother and grandmother and their own expectations as successful Cambodian-Americans. Caught in a cross-cultural maelstrom of traditional values that establish the perfect daughter as 'obedient, quiet and humble,' these two sisters manage to transform the tragedy that haunts so many Cambodian families into mutual understanding among three generations."

~Teri Shaffer Yamada, PhD
Chair of the Dept. of Asian and Asian American Studies, CSU Long Beach
Cofounder of the Nou Hach Literary Association

The
Immigrant
Princess

The
Immigrant
Princess

August 15, 2016

Dear Kathy,

Thank you for reading my book. Glad we can be friends after all these years Enjoy!

By Variny Yim

♡, V

The Immigrant Princess

Windy City Publishers
2118 Plum Grove Road, #349
Rolling Meadows, IL 60008
www.windycitypublishers.com

Published in the United States of America

ISBN:
978-1-941478-18-9

Library of Congress Control Number:
2015952948

Cover Design by Cynthia Frenette
Author Photos by Warren Mattox, Mattox Photography & Mark Swirsky

WINDY CITY PUBLISHERS

For MAILE and NAPALI
Who give me joy, love, and laughter every day

In memory of my courageous father,
YOUVAING YIM

December 1974
Phnom Penh, Cambodia

"You must do this for the children," Vaing Lim whispers into his wife's ear. Chanthavy resists her desire to sob in public and finds comfort in the masculine arm wrapped around her slender waist.

"I don't want to leave." She strokes his face with trembling fingers. "Please let us stay here with you, or come with us now. It's not too late."

Vaing wipes a tear off Chanthavy's face and leads her toward the Phnom Penh International Airport sign that sits near the entrance. A warm December breeze blows through a group of American and French expats gathered at an outdoor café, which sits like an oasis amidst all the airport hustle and bustle. One Frenchman with round John Lennon glasses and cigarette-stained teeth sips a café au lait between bites of a butter croissant.

In front of the airport entrance, two male soldiers stand guard and fidget with their rifles. Chanthavy calls for her five-year-old daughter, Sophea, who is playing hopscotch near them. One of the soldiers, about fifteen years old, stares at the beautiful woman dressed in a gold sarong and mutters under his breath, "Spoiled, rich bourgeoisies."

"They say she's King Norodom Sihanouk's favorite niece," the other young soldier responds, referring to the country's exiled monarch. "Love them or hate them, that family has been a part of Cambodia's history for over a century." He adjusts the rifle on his back.

"Your father says this civil war is breaking our country," Vaing says. "Ever since General Lon Nol overthrew King Sihanouk in 1970, we have had no peace. The king has aligned himself with the Khmer communist group. I hear they have been recruiting heavily from the villages and their forces are growing every day. These are unpredictable times in our beloved country—"

1

"Enough, please! At night, I have to shield my ears from the police sirens and bombings," Chanthavy interrupts. "As soon as the sun rises, I have to listen to you and my father lecture me about war and bloodshed. It's all so boring to me. I yearn for the days of music and laughter at the palace."

"My darling, I don't think you understand how serious the situation is," Vaing pleads. "It's no longer safe for you or our family to be here in Cambodia. Your father says the smell of more death and blood is in the air. You must leave the country now, before it is too late. With King Sihanouk ousted, this is not a good time to be part of the royal family. There is anger and unrest among the masses. This is a time of revolution and upheaval in our country. People want change."

"If that is the truth, then why are you not coming with us?" Chanthavy says. "We are your family, and you have a responsibility to take care of us. I am not able to be on my own, let alone take care of our children by myself." She touches her stomach, fuller than usual with a four-month baby inside.

"You are not going to be alone," Vaing reassures her. "You will have your mother, and also Sophea." He glances at their daughter, who is walking ahead with her grandmother. "I would like nothing more than to leave with all of you, but I cannot abandon my parents and younger siblings. They need me. Please try to understand."

"I don't understand, and I don't think I will ever understand how you can choose them over us—we are your family, too." Chanthavy is indignant until she sees her husband's frown.

"Cambodia is known as the Land of Smiles, and now my beloved husband's face is more solemn than the statues at Angkor Wat," Chanthavy says. "I'm sorry, I don't mean to hurt you. It's just our lives are changing so fast, and I am scared."

Chanthavy had recently taken a trip with her mother and daughter to visit the sacred temples of Angkor Wat in the small town of Siem Reap. Many of the great temple cities near the town of Siem Reap were constructed during the reign of Jayavarnman II and his successors. It was known as the "Age of Angkor," which means "capital city" or "holy city," and more than a million people had lived there. Cambodian kings built complex waterworks and grand temples, and their kingdom reigned over mainland Southeast Asia, including modern Cambodia, Laos, Thailand, Vietnam, and parts of Malaysia and Myanmar.

"Remember these temples," her mother had said. "Capture an image in your heart and hold on to it. We don't know when we'll be able to come back to our home."

Little Sophea had twirled and posed with all the beautiful *Apsara* statues that adorned those ancient temples. In Hindu and Buddhist mythology, an Apsara is a female spirit of the clouds and water. Over the years, translations expanded the definition to include a celestial dancer, an enchantress, and even a sorceress. Chanthavy had been awestruck by these divine females who were also known to change shape at will. Staring closely at the beautiful dancing figures, Chanthavy felt the strength and beauty of these mystical females who had weathered centuries of war, turmoil, and change in Cambodia. She wondered if she would have the same strength.

Chanthavy is deep in her thoughts when her father, Prince Viviya Norodom, the head of police in Phnom Penh, approaches them. "I believe it's time for you to catch your plane for a much-needed vacation in Bangkok." He stares at his oldest daughter one last time and motions for another young soldier to escort the women through security. "We will see you back here in a couple of weeks." Chanthavy glances at her mother, whose eyes are still red and swollen from a night of crying.

"It is an honor for me to escort you today, your highnesses," says the soldier, slender and tan with a short crew cut. "I will not leave your side until you are safe and seated in the airplane." Chanthavy's father, also known as General Norodom, gives the young boy a handful of cash. In the traditional Cambodian manner of showing gratitude, the soldier places his two hands in a prayer-like position in front of his face and *pauns* the general.

"Thank you, we are ready to go. What is your name and where are you from?" Chanthavy's mother presses a hand on top of her tightening chest.

"My name is Sambath, and I am from Battambang." To show respect, the boy pauns her and does not look her in the eyes when he speaks.

A few feet away, Vaing squeezes his wife's trembling hands. "Even in the darkest days, know that my spirit is beside you, carrying you until we are together again. In this journey, you will find your own strength." He leans down and places his head against Chanthavy's protruding belly.

Vaing whispers to the baby, "Maybe one day you and your sister will learn the story of how a village boy from Kampong Cham was able to meet and marry a princess from the Cambodian royal family."

At that moment, Sophea demands her father's attention and runs into his arms, almost knocking him over. "Pick me up, Papa! I want to fly!" She squeals as her father grabs her two hands and swings her around midair. He then props up her small frame onto the palms of his two hands. Sophea clenches her father's shoulders to balance.

"What's wrong, Papa?" Sophea exclaims. "Why are you so weak today? I'm going to fall if you don't hold me tight. Aren't you and *Sdach Ta*—Grandfather Prince—going on holiday with us, too?"

"No, *koun*, my child, not this time." Vaing places her down on the cement sidewalk. She has her mother's big eyes and full lips and his high nose.

"But why not, Papa?" Sophea starts to spin around on her tiptoes and waves her hands in the air. "Look at me! I am your Petite Apsara! You have to come with us. Please, Papa. I will be so alone without you." She pouts and begs to be picked up again.

Vaing thinks, *An Apsara is a female deity or enchantress who has mystical powers over men. I have been under my daughter's spell since the day she was born.* "I will miss you the most, my Apsara Girl. Who will beguile me with her smile and laughter while we are apart? You must be brave, and you must promise me you will always take care of your mother and grandmother."

"I promise." Sophea kisses her father on the cheek. "We'll see you soon, Papa!" She skips back to her grandmother and tugs her hand.

At that moment, the young guard announces, "The plane is leaving. There is no more time." With that, Vaing watches his family walk across the tarmac onto the plane. As children often do, Sophea turns to wave at her father and grandfather after every five steps. Chanthavy and her mother walk arm in arm, each looking back only once at their respective husbands before entering the aircraft.

"They have each other, they will be fine," General Norodom declares to his son-in-law. "I need to head back to the police station. You can come to my house for dinner tonight." Vaing watches as the general exits with three soldiers trailing behind him.

In the terminal, Vaing's foot almost gets run over by a heavy, gray suitcase as a thirtysomething looking man pushes through the crowd, creating a path for his pretty wife and three children, "Excuse us, excuse us, this is our last chance, we cannot miss our plane!" His well-manicured left hand clenches a bundle of newly printed passports.

Outside, Vaing squints up at the sun shining in the cloudless azure-blue sky, searching for the plane that is carrying his family. The shrill of police sirens and whistles fill the streets. Just then, a taxi pulls up with the radio blaring one of King Sihanouk's songs. "Do you need a ride?" the driver asks.

Stepping into the car, Vaing says to the driver, "A singing monarch. How many countries can boast that? Despite his exile, he is still our beloved king of Cambodia. May he reign again one day."

Chapter 1
25 Years Later

Sophea's Mickey Mouse alarm clock rings at five thirty in the morning. She lies awake in her king-sized sleigh bed, soaking in the rays of early morning sun that seep through the window she leaves cracked open at night. Sophea reaches past her bare thighs and searches for her underwear, which is crumpled in a ball at the bottom of her bed covers.

She giggles, thinking about her grandmother's words of wisdom, "Your living space, including 'down there,' needs to breathe. A girl's special flower can only blossom if it gets enough fresh air." Opening a window was one thing, but not wearing underwear always felt immodest to Sophea. Still, it seemed best not to argue with her elder.

Without hesitation, Sophea jumps out of bed with the energy of a kinder-gartener going on her first field trip. *Today, I will become an executive producer at WNR-TV, Washington, DC's number-one news station!* Sophea slips on a new pair of running shoes and gives flight to her thoughts as she takes a forty-five-minute run around her neighborhood.

After her shower, Sophea steps into the bedroom, flips on the television, and surfs through all the important news channels to catch the latest head-lines. The morning's top stories are interesting enough, yet still predictable. A married, sixty-something, senatorial candidate has been caught cheating with his two year old's nanny. It is hurricane season in Florida, and residents are debating whether to barricade their homes and evacuate or stay and wait out the storm. A well-known consumer group is crying "fowl" over a fried chicken chain that misrepresented its fat content. A raven-headed scientist claims to have found a formula to fix split ends.

Sophea switches off the TV and makes her way back to her closet. She rifles through her clothes and settles on a pair of dark fitted jeans, a ruffled blouse, and a blue blazer she recently purchased on sale. She blow-dries her ebony mane until it lies loosely just above her hips.

Looking at herself in the mirror, Sophea recalls how often people mistake her for being something besides a Cambodian—Filipina, Peruvian, Native American. Someone even asked her once if she was an Inuit Eskimo. Sophea locks eyes with herself and sees, for an instant, her mother staring back.

Her gaze drifts to a solemn portrait of her grandmother that sits on top of her dresser. Chas Mai's pale white skin is peppered with age spots. She wears a short, layered salt-and-pepper bouffant hairdo typical for a Cambodian woman her age. Sophea does not remember Grandmother looking any other way, as young people never consider their elders to have been young once themselves.

The running joke in her family is that Cambodian women don't age for seventy-four years until, overnight, at the age of seventy-five, their hair turns white and they begin to wear baggy trousers with mismatched tops, knee-highs, and flip-flops. "It's an overnight Asian aging destiny that can't be avoided," they all agreed.

"Ha!" Sophea looks once more at her hair. "Not me." She grabs a gold necklace and a pair of sleek hoop earrings to finish off her "power" outfit. Sophea is relieved to see a young, fashionable woman looking back at her in the mirror. She dabs on a little foundation, bronzer, blush, eye makeup, and the last pièce de resistance—a soft peach-colored lipstick that highlights her caramel skin.

"Don't be vain," she hears Chas Mai's voice in her head. *I'm not vain*, Sophea thinks to herself, *but today is a special day*. After a moment's hesitation, she dabs a bit of gold body glitter onto her décolletage. The bottle label reads, "Let them see you shine," which is exactly what she needs this morning. "Nothing will undermine my confidence today," she tells herself.

Chas Mai's silver bouffant suddenly appears under the door frame and her familiar voice announces, "Your mom and I set our alarms early this morning so we could give you a proper send-off today." Chas Mai eyes her critically. "Pants? Dresses are so much prettier and more appropriate for work. Why do you want to look like a man when you have the buxom figure of a woman? Such a beautiful woman, too, like your mother when she was your age."

"Pants are comfortable." Sophea grimaces and then changes the subject. "Did you see the briefcase I left out in the hallway last night?"

"Yes, I moved it next to the front door so you would not forget it," Chas Mai explains. "You are very forgetful when you are in a hurry. It's chilly outside. You should also wear a hat so you don't catch a cold. None of us can afford to get sick, as you know."

Sophea looks down at her datebook and smiles. "You know, it's only August, so we're still officially in summer." Chas Mai hands her a scarf anyway.

Her mother, Cookie, crowds into the room to ask, "Are you going to eat the rice porridge soup and Chinese sausage Chas Mai made for you? You will need all the energy you can get once you are a big, important TV producer. I'm so proud of you, even though you are not exactly Connie Chung yet. *Yet.*"

"Thank you, but I'm in a hurry," Sophea responds. "I'll just grab a breakfast bar and banana."

Chas Mai shakes her head and hands Sophea a small plastic bowl filled with warm rice porridge as she kisses her beloved granddaughter gently on the cheek. "This is healthier for you than a manufactured bar of oats. Oats are for farm animals. You need to make better food choices, Sophea."

Sophea spies the bus coming and bolts through the front door, grabbing her briefcase at the last second.

"Call us as soon as you hear something," her mother calls after her. "And don't forget tonight is the *Miss Planet* pageant. We will watch that together this evening." The two women stare out the window until the bus is out of sight.

Chapter 2

By 9:00 a.m., the WNR newsroom is humming with activity. The assignment desk staff is trying to juggle camera crews for two simultaneously breaking news stories: a huge and possibly violent protest expected in front of the International Monetary Fund building and a large thunderstorm expected to sweep through the region in the next twenty-four hours. Government officials are warning that the storm will bring a deluge of rain, possibly causing downed trees and power outages to thousands of homes.

Sophea scurries to her cubicle and starts to scour the Associated Press newswire service for additional stories to bring to the morning news meeting. The mayor of Washington, DC, will hold a press conference in a couple of hours to discuss a new citywide, anti-bullying law, which seems like a promising lead. She also notes neighborhood parking concerns and updates on the U Street NW Streetscape Project.

"Sophea, would you mind stepping into my office for a minute?" says Don, the station news director and her boss. "I need to speak with you." *This is it.* Sophea rests her hands on her stomach to quiet the flurry of butterflies gathering in her belly. *Nothing is going to stop me from getting that promotion today. Don is on my side. He knows how hard I work every day. This is all I want.*

"I don't know how else to say this, so I'll just cut to the chase," Don begins. "We've offered the executive producer position to Janine, and she has accepted. We'll be making the announcement at this morning's staff meeting. I wanted you to know before everyone else."

"I don't understand." Sophea can't breathe. Her contacts blur with the beginnings of tears.

"This was a very difficult decision, because you are one of the hardest-working members on our team, and you always have a smile on your face." Don is firm. "But Janine has more experience than you. She is aggressive, demanding, and not afraid to push people's buttons. We need to keep our ratings up, or we will have to start laying off people. Sorry, Sophea. You're a very nice person, but nice doesn't always cut it in the newsroom."

"I'm being punished for being too nice?" Sophea is bewildered. "I'm calm during a news emergency. People know they can count on me to meet deadlines. I get just as many stories as anyone else here in the newsroom. Don't these things count for anything?"

"You're our newsroom sweetheart, but I'm looking for people who can be leaders," Don softens. "You have the potential to be a great leader one day, but you're not there yet. You still need to prove yourself."

"I don't understand this at all." Sophea bites her lip so hard she can feel the skin rip from underneath her teeth. "You never told me I was doing anything wrong. I thought you were happy with me." She wipes a drop of blood from her lips, as well as a tear that has traveled down her cheek.

"This is not personal," Don reassures Sophea. "Janine was just the better candidate this time around. There'll be another chance for you in the future. When you see an opportunity, pounce on it. Keep showing me that you've got what it takes."

At the morning news meeting, Sophea sulks in the back of the room, sporting a pair of dark sunglasses to hide her bloodshot eyes. "Please join me in congratulating Janine as the new executive producer of our five p.m. show," Don announces to a room full of cheering colleagues. Sophea covers her ears as her head begins to throb.

"Thank you so much to Don and to all of you for your support," Janine says, pushing a headful of golden curls behind her shoulders. "We have the best news team in this city and there's no reason why we can't win November Sweeps Month. With our combined talents and skills, I am determined to keep our station 'number one' in this market. Watch out, Washington!"

After running through everyone's assignments for the day, there are only a few drifters left in the meeting room. "Congratulations on your promotion. I'm really happy for you," Sophea lies through her teeth. Her arms feel like two lead pipes as she struggles to give Janine a hug. *Why does the pretty blond always get the promotion?*

"I heard through the grapevine that you were also in consideration for the position," Janine remarks. "Don't feel too bad. The competition is tough and this time, I got lucky. Maybe next time, it will be your turn."

As Janine turns to get her clipboard, Sophea gets a whiff of a familiar scent. "May I ask what perfume you are wearing?"

"Sure, it's Chanel Number Five," Janine answers. *Naturally, Miss Perfect would only wear that most quintessential of perfumes.*

"Yup, I figured," Sophea says, "that's what my mother always wears."

Back at her desk, Sophea dials her younger sister, Ravy. "I didn't get the job. They gave it to someone with beautiful blond hair and whiter teeth. I just want to die! She even smells like Mom."

"What happened? I thought this promotion was a sure thing," Ravy responds. "You're brilliant and you have great hair, too. Stop always comparing yourself to the blond woman in the room. It didn't get you a spot on the cheer-leading team in high school and it obviously isn't working for you in the work-place. Let's meet for happy hour after work."

Chapter 3

"Don't take this professional slaughter lying down," Ravy advises Sophea. "You're a little passive, but you always get the job done." She motions for the waiter to bring over the menus.

Sitting across the table from Ravy at their favorite Mexican restaurant, Sophea explains, "All I want right now is a virgin strawberry margarita and a big basket of chips. I haven't been to a happy hour in years since I'm usually at the station until eight or nine at night scouring the news feed and helping the night shift crew with their stories. And look where that got me—nowhere!" She drops her head onto the table and starts to cry.

"Stop that—the table's filthy. Here, eat something." Ravy pushes a basket of tortilla chips toward her sister. "Food therapy is essential in a crisis like this. I think tonight requires a multiple meal strategy. Are you in?" She plunges her hand into the pile of greasy chips.

Sophea raises her head from the table and brushes a tortilla chip crumb out of her hair. "I work so hard every day. I go in to the office early. I do my work and don't complain. I even bring everyone bagels every Thursday. I'm a total team player."

Her face turns crimson as she attempts to wave down a flustered waiter who is juggling several tables in their section. The young man rambles right past her and makes a beeline toward a couple cuddling in the corner. Sophea searches for more salsa for her chips.

"You're a total pushover," Ravy admonishes. "How many times have I told you that being a 'good girl' doesn't get you anywhere in the workplace? Tell me you didn't cry in front of everyone at work." She crosses her arms in front of her chest.

"I didn't cry in front of everyone—just my boss." Sophea eats a second chip. "I got that ugly, bottom-lip tremble halfway through the conversation."

"All our lives, we've been told to be good girls," Ravy says. "To be kind, honest, not create any waves, go with the flow, be happy, do what we are told, follow the rules. 'Be a good Cambodian girl, and don't make any trouble.' Tell me, how far has that strategy gotten you in life?"

"You're right," Sophea says. "I'm a middle-aged wreck with no husband, no children, and no promotion. I'm a loser. I need some water." She waves for their waiter, but he avoids her gesture and strides past their table.

Ravy rolls her eyes. "You're hardly middle-aged. But you are a wreck... you know why? Reality. Reality happened. Kindness, respect, and deference are all useless traits in the American workplace. They'll get you nowhere. They belong in a Cambodian pagoda with praying monks and nonconfrontational Buddhists. We both have to get over our Nice Cambodian Girl Complex."

"I'm just so depressed. Today was a disaster," Sophea continues. "My boss tells me I need to be more assertive. Mom and Chas Mai tell me I'm not respectful enough. And our waiter is ignoring me!"

Ravy stands up and motions for their waiter with her right index finger. "Ramone—is that your name? I know you're busy, but my sister is dying of thirst and we need more salsa. Either we get some service right now, or I talk to your manager and you comp our meal. You decide." She shows him Sophea's television business card. "Don't make me have to use this."

Ramone apologizes, disappears into the kitchen, and returns a few minutes later with two tall glasses of iced tea, a basket of hot chips, salsa, and a complimentary bowl of guacamole. "Now, that's more like it." Ravy holds up the business card and puts it back into her purse.

"I could get fired if anyone at the station found out that I used my journalism credentials to get better service in a restaurant," Sophea exclaims. "It's unethical! You don't think he spit in our salsa, do you?"

"Oh, relax, you didn't do anything—I did!" Ravy snickers. "A free bowl of guacamole is hardly unethical. It's not like we stole an avocado from a baby."

"Huh?" Sophea shakes her head. "Remember how Mom used to force us to watch Connie Chung when we were younger. Wasn't that every Asian girl's dream—to be like her?"

"Not mine, but I know that's why you wanted to become a TV reporter," Ravy responds. "And I'm thinking that might have been Mom's dream—not so much yours." Sophea ignores her sister.

"How about we continue your meltdown at my place? *Miss Planet* is on at eight p.m. That should cheer you up. We can pick up some Thai food."

"Chas Mai and Mom are expecting us to go watch it with them tonight," Sophea says. "It's our family tradition, remember?" She puts down an extra big tip for Ramone and follows Ravy out the door.

Chapter 4

Cookie arranges the throw pillows on the sofa in anticipation of her two daughters' arrival. Cookie's Cambodian name is *Chanthavy,* but after too many misspellings and mispronunciations by the baristas at the local coffee shop, she finally decided to adopt an easier American name inspired by the pastries behind the glass counter. *Cookie* seemed most appropriate, considering her affinity for these tasty American treats—especially the chocolate chip ones, which she can devour by the dozen.

It is half an hour until *Miss Planet* begins. Cookie claps with anticipation at the thought of watching her beloved beauty pageant. Back when she was young, Cookie and her sisters were the belles of Phnom Penh, and every day was an opportunity to impress a new admirer. Suitors lined up at their home for even a quick peek at Cookie's soft, porcelain skin and dark, velvety brown eyes.

"When you are a princess, it is true that you are always on display and all eyes are on you," her mother would lecture. "But beauty is just the initial teaser. To keep a good man, you will also need a good heart and a good head." She would then thrust a book onto her daughter's lap. "Here, read up on your family history. There are two sides of the royal Cambodian family—the Norodoms and the Sisowaths, who were brothers. You are part of the Norodom line."

While Chas Mai pushed Cookie to learn about her family tree, Cookie's father sent her another message. "Even kings and heads of states cannot resist the lure of my daughter's beauty," he would boast at parties and work functions. "With just one glance, she can weaken the soul of even the strongest man."

Her father's words were put to the test one summer day in 1966, when General Charles de Gaulle made a presidential visit to Cambodia to end the war in Vietnam. Cookie's uncle, King Norodom Sihanouk, instructed the entire

The Immigrant Princess

country to roll out the red carpet for this VIP foreign visitor. A *New York Times* article described this formidable Parisian as "one of the greatest men of our times." King Sihanouk asked his fellow Cambodians to welcome and embrace this important world leader.

Preah Bat Samdech Preah Norodom Sihanouk was not only the king of Cambodia, but he also served as the prime minister, head of state, and president during his sixty-year reign as monarch. The grandson of King Monivong (who reigned from 1927 to 1941), King Sihanouk became a successor to the throne in 1941 at the age of eighteen, when the Japanese occupied Cambodia during World War II. When the occupation ended in 1945, France (which had colonized Cambodia in 1863) reimposed its protectorate over Cambodia. The young king, who initially yielded little power, won Cambodia's independence from France in 1953. Under King Sihanouk's reign, the country officially became the "Kingdom of Cambodia."

Chanthavy recalls that those days were the "glorious days" for the Cambodian royal family. Her parents were daily, privileged guests of the king at the palace. Oh, how she loved watching her parents be a part of the royal court! There was so much dancing, music, and food everywhere. For a few years, Cambodia enjoyed peace, and Chanthavy soaked in the regal life that surrounded her and her family.

Though Chanthavy preferred to immerse herself in the royal court gossip, she could not escape her father's growing grumblings about the war next door in Vietnam. He was concerned that King Sihanouk had allowed North Vietnamese guerillas to set up base on the Cambodia border when it was not even their war. The goal was neutrality, but this could look like a direct stance against the powerful United States. Her father predicted that only harm could come out of this scenario, but he continued his steadfast support for his beloved king and "brother." Chanthavy had watched many American movies and did not understand what was happening. Biased by the likes of Elvis musicals and the Rat Pack, Chanthavy only associated America with cool rock music, nice cars, and sunny beaches. She did not understand this war next door at all.

Colorful streamers lined the streets on that glorious summer day in 1966. Cambodian and French flags flew side by side on the palace grounds. Two huge portraits of President de Gaulle and King Sihanouk stared down at the main boulevard where thousands of Cambodians prepared for one of Phnom Penh's greatest parties. A huge parade welcomed President de Gaulle, followed by a motorcade that escorted him through the streets of the capital city.

As one of her uncle's favorite nieces, Cookie was invited to be part of the special delegation that greeted the eminent visitor at the airport. "He looks like a more handsome version of Alfred Hitchcock," Cookie exclaimed when she first saw President de Gaulle coming off the airplane escorted by a small entourage and his very proper-looking wife, Yvonne. Broad-shouldered and statuesque, the general stood almost a head taller than all the Cambodians on the tarmac. It was like Gulliver visiting the land of Asian Lilliputians. He wore a chic, gray, custom-tailored suit, accentuated with what looked like a military hat on his head, reminding his audience, *I may be a statesman today, but do not forget that I led our French Resistance forces during World War II.*

When the president of the French Republic finally made his way down the greeting line to Cookie, she did not dare speak to him. Instead, she turned her chin down to the ground and looked up at him from the corner of her eyes. Cookie wanted to smile, but instead she pursed her lips together for fear that the gesture would seem too forward for a Cambodian woman her age to make to a man almost five times her senior. "Modesty and reserve is how you lure a man. A good Cambodian girl does not flaunt her assets, but only whets the appetite of a man should he want to pursue her further," she heard her mother's voice in her head.

As President de Gaulle strolled down the red carpet, shaking everyone's hands, he noticed the striking Cambodian girl with the big brown eyes, sculpted cheekbones, and perfect red pout. Her features were so delicate and inviting, he almost bumped into a crowd of children waving Cambodian flags. President de Gaulle tried to make eye contact with this beautiful woman, but she did not look up from the ground except for one slight glance. He lost his breath for a moment when their eyes connected. She reminded him of someone he knew.

Later that day, King Sihanouk hosted a huge celebration in the city's Olympic stadium. Thousands of Cambodians filled the seats to witness a historic moment between this strange white general and their beloved monarch. Because she was fluent in French, the king asked Chanthavy to read "*Harmonie du Soir*," by the revered French poet Charles Baudelaire. At the end of the poem, Cookie reveled in the energy of the cheering crowd before one of the royal advisors escorted her down to the king and President de Gaulle.

"Mr. President, may I present to you my beautiful niece, Princess Chanthavy Norodom." King Sihanouk beamed with pride. "She is the rose of Phnom Penh." President Charles de Gaulle recognized the young girl he had spotted earlier at the airport and shook her hand. Then, he whispered in French to Cookie, "You are breathtaking, and you speak like a Parisian. You remind me of Elizabeth Taylor." He then took his seat and kissed his wife on the cheek.

For the first time that day, Cookie began to understand the power she could wield over men.

Chapter 5

The refrigerator hums a familiar tune, as Chas Mai sits at the kitchen table slicing tomatoes and celery with wobbly fingers that have prepared so many meals over the years. She puts down the knife and rubs the aching bones in her fingers before proceeding again.

Where are Sophea and Ravy? She paces between the kitchen table and the small window overlooking the street below. The pageant is supposed to start soon. Chas Mai peers out the kitchen window again and squints at the incoming sunlight. *Those girls need to hurry before it gets dark outside.* Her heart starts to flutter and her breathing tightens. The thought of anything happening to her two little girls is too much to bear. She grabs a glass of warm water sitting on the granite counter and swallows. The water soothes her dry throat.

Chas Mai stirs the chicken broth on the burner and mixes in the tomatoes, celery, chicken, and pineapple chunks. This is Sophea's favorite soup, *samlor machou.*

"*Maman*, the show is about to start. Can't you just let the soup sit for a while?" Cookie yells from the living room. "I'm sure the girls will be over soon enough. And, don't worry, we are still in Daylight Savings Time. They will not be walking in the dark anytime soon."

For the tenth time today, Chas Mai prays to Buddha for the safe return of her girls. It is this daily devotional practice that fuels her days. *Please, Buddha, please take care of my daughter Chanthavy and her two girls. May they make wise choices and not forget Cambodia. Please give us all the strength and courage to live a safe and peaceful life in this new country.*

Chas Mai recalls that fateful day in the Lim household, the week after Ravy graduated with a graphic arts degree from the local community college. Though Sophea was still living at home, the house did not seem complete without all four of them under the same roof. They were eager for Ravy to move back into the house like any other good Cambodian girl and resume her role as a dutiful child.

Chas Mai had just finished cleaning Ravy's bedroom with a rug steam cleaner (which was Cookie's idea), only to be met with the words, "I love you two, but I have no intention of staying in this home." Ravy poked her pink toenails into the newly cleaned carpet. "I've always wanted to live on my own. You know that."

"We don't expect you to live with us forever, just until you find a husband," Chas Mai said. "That is how it is done in Cambodia. We thought you understood."

"I'm going to live with two other roommates," Ravy explained. "We'll watch out for one another. You don't have to worry. We'll be safe."

"What if you get kidnapped? How do you know one of them won't steal your money? What if food goes bad in the refrigerator and you die of food poisoning?" Chas Mai pummelled Ravy with questions.

"Chas Mai's right, danger lurks around every corner," Sophea teased. "If you're walking on the sidewalk, you could trip, hit your head, and end up in a coma. Beware of the tuna sandwich since you can choke on a fishbone and die. Cutting an apple can only lead to a missing finger. And our old favorite—don't ever leave your house, because you could get kidnapped or killed!" She bit her knuckles with mock fear.

"Go ahead and laugh, but I have seen and lived through more than both of you. I pray that Buddha keeps you safe," Chas Mai chided both sisters. "You are breaking my heart."

Chas Mai recalled that as a young, proper girl in her household, she would never dare speak back to her elders. They were sacred and to be respected. Silent obedience was the key to being a successful child in a Cambodian household. Though Chas Mai scolded her two granddaughters for their vocal insolence, she had begun to secretly value the importance of women speaking up for themselves. Chas Mai was an avid reader, and she had marveled at her discovery of the public library down the street, where she could devour as many free books as she could finish by the due date. *Imagine getting your hands on hundreds of free books by just showing a paper card with your name on it? Unheard of in Cambodia!* Chas Mai had used the freedom of her library card to discover the biographies of such American heroines as Eleanor Roosevelt, Rosa Parks, and Amelia Earhart. America, she had decided, was a place where even women could be heroes.

❧❧❧

As usual, Sophea defended her sister that day. "Ravy's not hurting anyone," she said. "She just wants to live her life. I'm still here." She sidled up next to Chas Mai and rested her arms around the older woman's shoulders.

"Do what you want," Cookie scolded her youngest daughter. "You have always thought you are better than us. This just proves it." She pushed the steam cleaner over with her right hand. Growing up in Cambodia, Cookie never once had to cook or clean. They had many maids and servants to take care of the house. Here, in the States, Cookie had taken up vacuuming to contribute to the household responsibilities, but she'd given up on cooking after she burned her hand boiling water. Here was Cookie, offering to steam-clean Ravy's carpet with an industrial-sized cleaner and all she got was backtalk—a slap in the face as far as Cookie was concerned. *A princess never cooks, and a princess should definitely never clean!*

"I won't apologize for wanting to live on my own," Ravy responded. "Your guilt trip and tantrums are not going to change my mind, Mom. Can we just agree to be happy?"

That entire afternoon, Chas Mai busied herself in the kitchen and gave Ravy the silent treatment. As Ravy was packing, she admonished, "You will never know how much your selfishness hurts us. I will always love you, but I will never forget or forgive you for breaking our family apart." Chas Mai's head swam with fear. She had left everything near and dear to her when they escaped Cambodia; the only thing she had was her family. That was her security. That was what helped her get up in the morning. She envisioned a tower of blocks that represented the family. If even one block was removed, the entire structure would crumble. Ravy did not understand the profound effect her leaving the family unit would have.

"Why does everything have to be so dramatic?" Ravy continued packing in frustration. "I am moving out, not trying to destroy our precious family."

"It is a fact that you are destroying our family by moving out," Cookie said. "Trust me that I will never go to your new home—or vacuum an inch of it. Never!"

Chas Mai's words resonated with Sophea in a different way. Before going to bed that night, Sophea made a promise to her mother and grandmother. "I promise you both that I will never leave you. You can always count on me to take care of you for the rest of your lives, just as you have taken care of me and Ravy."

"You are our good girl, Sophea," Chas Mai responded. "Remember when your father asked you to take care of us when you were just five? You were our Apsara girl then, and you continue to be today. Please try to talk your sister out of her rash decision." As always, Sophea felt torn between her sister's desire to live her life and Cookie's and Chas Mai's efforts to cling to their old ways.

$\mathcal{E}$n route to the Thai restaurant, Ravy's cell phone rings; it is Cookie with an urgent message. "The beauty pageant is airing in half an hour. Where are you girls? It's our family tradition to watch it together."

"Mom, we know," Ravy says. "Sophea's having an emotional breakdown, and I'm taking her back to my place for some sister bonding time. We'll come by after the bathing suit portion."

"But it's a tradition for us to watch the whole pageant together. Why are you hurting us like this?" Cookie accuses. "Did we do something wrong?"

"No, Mom, Sophea just got some bad news at work," Ravy says. "We're going to drown her sorrow in some Thai take-out. You can survive without us for a couple of hours."

"Chas Mai will not be happy about this. She has been cooking for you all afternoon," Cookie says in her most pleasant passive-aggressive voice. "But do as you please. We'll be here waiting for you as always."

Ravy looks over at Sophea with two thumbs up and a wink. "It's time for you to break away from the hens," she says.

The girls detour to a tasty hole-in-the-wall Thai restaurant near Ravy's apartment. They order stuffed chicken legs, papaya salad, chicken satay, Pad Thai, and a duck and sweet potato curry. Sophea, having just devoured an entire basket of chips at the Mexican restaurant, rubs her swollen paunch and declares, "I give us permission to nourish our bodies and souls tonight." Ravy laughs and grabs a couple of pairs of wooden chopsticks and extra hot sauce to throw in their take-out bag.

❧❧❧

"I'm stuffed!" Sophea leans back into the sofa and releases the top button of her jeans. Usually she is very careful about overeating, but tonight she threw caution to the wind and indulged. Sophea was often the target of her relatives' merciless weight comments, despite the fact that by American standards, she is considered "average." Sophea recalls one of her favorite compliments. "You're pretty, but you have shoulders like a water buffalo!"

In many Asian cultures, being well-fed and plump represents great wealth and happiness. Cambodians accept that in theory, but they still prefer their women small-boned, petite, and slender. At any Cambodian social gathering, you will often see women in their fifties, sixties, and seventies who can boast of being the same weight they were when they got married in their teens.

At one family function, her aunts were determined to learn Chas Mai's secret for growing such big girls. "What do you feed them? Why are their bones so big?"

"Enough of your silly questions," Chas Mai snapped. "I will tell you once, and then we will never talk of this again." She reached down into her purse as the women gathered around her and pulled out the secret American "miracle drug" that encouraged incredible growth spurts in her granddaughters. "They call these Flintstones Vitamin Tablets. I don't know what is in them, but you see the results of their power. You can purchase them at any American drug-store." The aunts gawked and laughed, unaware how their persistence crushed an already insecure young girl.

✄ ✌ ✄

Sophea is savoring the last bite of a satay skewer when the broadcast of *Miss Planet* begins. The annual tradition of watching beautiful women from all around the globe parade in string bikinis and sparkling, floor-length gowns had always bonded her family. In Cambodian culture, female beauty and pageantry have been revered since the Angkorian period. Known as the "Golden Age" of Khmer civilization, the Angkorian period existed from the early ninth century to the early fifteenth century A.D. It was during this time in Cambodia's history when cultural influence, political prominence, and military strength peaked.

Cookie usually led the beauty pageant commentary, squealing with delight at the glorious females who paraded so fearlessly across the stage—each representing their home countries. She would pronounce as fact, "Cambodians love beauty pageants. Don't ever let anyone tell you you're against women because you like beauty pageants. Nothing wrong with a little glamour and skin to remind us of our own femininity."

Cookie envisioned herself striding down the walkway, representing Cambodia and waving to her beloved countrymen and women. Her husband, Vaing, was so proud of having a beautiful wife. Back in the 1960s, the idea of being his "trophy wife" was actually something Cookie strived for, despite the fact that she had been raised by a mother who preferred mental acumen over physical attributes.

Growing up, Cookie was surrounded by the constant pressure of being a learned and successful young Cambodian woman before it was ever culturally acceptable. Both her parents stressed "education, education, education." It was so unlike how the other royal princesses were raised. For her, the pageant was a reprieve from the expectations that followed her throughout her life to be a proper and respectable member of the monarchy. These beauty pageants, judged by some to be trivial or deprecating, helped Cookie forget all the broken dreams that she carried in her heart when their family had left Cambodia and she realized that her years of training to become the "perfect princess" was now meaningless.

⋟⋞

This year's pageant kicks off with an impressive choreographed group dance involving a medley of Michael Jackson's greatest hits. The women do high kicks in their skyscraper stiletto heels without anyone falling. This dance number is followed by the individual announcements of all the pageant contestants, "Miss Bahamas, Miss France, Miss India, Miss South Africa, Miss USA…"

"This is a great distraction, sis," Sophea says. "There is nothing more relaxing than watching gorgeous supermodels being quizzed about world politics."

"And as we all know, the correct answer is always 'world peace,'" jokes Ravy.

About an hour into the show, Ravy suggests they take a taxi to join Chas Mai and Cookie for the bathing suit portion of the show. "While you're mourning your professional life, you should also consider a new living arrangement." Ravy starts packing an overnight bag. "You're thirty and still living at home like a child."

"Must I remind you that you deserted Chas Mai and Cookie right out of college, and they have never forgiven you for it?" Sophea replies. "You're living the life you want. You can cut me a break and keep your opinions to yourself. Living with them saves me money, so it is a financially sound decision. And, it gets them off *your* back." The sisters rush to catch a cab that has pulled over to the curb for them.

⚬ঙ৯⚬

"Where have you two been?" Chas Mai hollers in *Khmer* before the two young women even reach the front door. Though she has been in the States for twenty-five years, Chas Mai demands that her granddaughters speak to her only in their native language. "We have been worried sick about you. I made your favorite soup, but it's cold now. Your mom and I were sad that you chose not to watch *Miss Planet* with us this year."

"There's still over an hour left." Ravy places both palms together in front of her face and pauns her grandmother. The three women head into the living room just in time to catch Miss Thailand's monologue about her plans to become a veterinarian after she gets her communications and broadcasting degrees.

During a commercial, Cookie motions for Sophea to join her on the couch. "Ravy says you have lost your mind. What happened today at work?" She wets the tip of her right index finger and smooths the hairs on both her eyebrows.

"I didn't get my promotion today," Sophea says. "I'm a loser."

"It's okay, my darling. Your boss knows best. You probably are not ready to take on more work," Chas Mai offers. "Change is not always a good thing. Be happy with what you have."

"Yes, be happy you even have a job." Cookie focuses on the show. "If we had never left Cambodia, you might be dead right now." She is referring to the

Cambodian genocide that took place between April 1975 and January 1979, when approximately two million Cambodians were killed, tortured, or starved to death by Pol Pot and the Khmer Rouge during the years now known as the "Killing Fields."

"Yes, that darn death card can sure put things in perspective." Ravy snorts, annoyed. "Mom, Sophea's questioning her entire existence. Why do you always have to try to lessen our struggles by comparing them to war atrocities? It's just not fair. We get it, but please try to show some compassion here."

"Both your father and your grandfather were killed by the Khmer Rouge." Cookie raises her left eyebrow. "Don't let their suffering and deaths be in vain. And, yes, that is the perspective you must always carry with you. We are lucky to be alive here in America. Life is precious, so don't let these superficial problems get to you. They always have a way of working themselves out. Trust Buddha."

"I know. I'm sorry, Mom." Ravy softens. "I know you have been through so much loss. It's just that our problems will never have any weight with you because your scale of comparison is just too great."

"Life is hard—things are not always going to go your way," Cookie clucks. "At eighteen, I thought my future was going to be living in the royal palace eating pastries and pâté with the elite Cambodian community. Instead, I'm arguing with my daughters and missing out on the beauty pageant. I will do my best not to say anymore." She forces a smile and retreats to her seat with a bowl of fried shrimp chips.

"Come lie here next to me, Sophea," Chas Mai whispers, placing a pillow on her lap. "Your mom is only trying to help. Let's not be sad. Perhaps this is a sign that you girls should be focusing more on love than work. We could certainly use a wedding soon." At thirty, Sophea is twice the age as when Chas Mai fell in love, got pregnant, and married at the age of fifteen. This age difference is incomprehensible to Chas Mai. She will not feel at peace until her granddaughters find good men who will take care of them for the rest of their lives—a dream that did not come true for her or Cookie. After all, at seventy-five years old, she is not getting any younger, and she worries about what will happen to her girls when she is no longer around to tend to the house and make them food.

Ravy scowls and sits down next to her mom to watch *Miss Planet*. The four women huddle together, taking in the show just like they have done for the past twenty years. "Do you know that there is no Miss Cambodia on the show this year because the government won't allow it right now? They say Prime Minister Hun Sen does not like the idea of good Cambodian girls parading on stage in a bikini. What do you think of that?"

"Remind me again why I should care what Hun Sen thinks? Why do we give old crochety men so much power?" Ravy asks, unaware of the trap she has just set for herself.

Like a leopard waiting for its prey, Cookie pounces on this opening to lecture her girls again on Cambodia's confusing and complicated political history, which has been plagued by multiple coups and unsteady and corrupt government rule.

⋞ೲ⋞

"Seriously, Mom? My head is swimming!" Ravy rolls her eyes. "Was it really necessary for you to give us the long history lesson again right now? We've already heard it a million times!" Ravy's face is red. "Why can't Cambodia get its act together? The country is in a constant state of chaos and turmoil. All we really need to know right now is that Pol Pot's dead, Prime Minister Hun Sen is now presiding over a somewhat peaceful yet still politically divided Cambodia, and the monarchy has been restored. King Sihanouk and his descendants continue to reign after all these years and that makes you and Chas Mai very happy."

"It is imperative that both of you know our country's history. I am very impressed by your retention level. You may look like you are ignoring me, but you do listen to me after all!" Cookie stares at her two daughters. "I bet that if you wore some fancy makeup and waxed your mustaches, you both would make beautiful pageant contestants."

Ravy and Sophea exchange worried glances, then glide their fingertips along the tops of their mouths.

"And it wouldn't hurt if they could speak *Khmer* without such a heavy American accent," Chas Mai chimes in.

Sophea is amused at how easily her family transitions from war talk to a normal conversation. At this moment, she is just happy to lie in her grandmother's arms, surrounded by the women she loves most in this world. Sophea closes her eyes and falls asleep on Chas Mai's lap, while Cookie and Ravy continue to provoke one another.

Chapter 7

At 6:00 a.m., Mickey Mouse chuckles out his high-pitched alarm, and Sophea reaches over to press the snooze button. She is pantiless again this morning, but instead of breathing freely, Sophea feels a yeast infection coming on. Yesterday her life had turned upside down, and though *Miss Planet* and Thai food had helped temporarily, her heart still aches.

I don't want to go to work and see anyone, especially Janine, Sophea whispers to herself. Her stomach starts to churn and make strange noises. She feels her forehead for a fever and massages the back of her neck. Sophea grabs some ibuprofen from her nightstand and goes in search of a thermometer.

"You're not sick." Cookie peeks her head inside Sophea's bedroom. "Whenever you get rejected, you think you're catching the flu. I remember when you didn't get the part you wanted in your high school play and you thought you were coming down with dengue fever. You had both Chas Mai and me scared for your life."

"Mom, I honestly don't feel good. The Thai food from last night is not sitting well with me. I am burping up curry and it tastes awful," Sophea whines. "The bags under my eyes could scare children. It's just not pretty, inside or out."

"Are you ready to talk yet about what happened at work yesterday?" Cookie asks. "Why did they not give my poor Sophea a promotion?"

"Are you going to try to make me feel better or worse about myself?" Sophea rubs her temples. "I feel a migraine coming on."

"Maybe a little of both, depending on what you tell me." Cookie starts to rub Sophea's shoulders. "Just talk to me, or I'll stay here on your bed the rest of the day."

"My boss said I didn't get the job because I'm not enough of a leader," Sophea says. "Don says staying quiet and humble does me no good. I need to be more aggressive and start tooting my own horn a bit if I want to get noticed. But this goes against everything you and Chas Mai taught me growing up. I feel so lost."

"We taught you good Cambodian values. You don't earn respect by being boastful," Cookie says. "Does your boss recognize that you are a first-generation immigrant who speaks with no accent? That is no small feat."

"This is about all I can muster up right now." Sophea pulls the pillow over her head. "Can I just go back to sleep?"

"Did your boss really say it's bad to be a Cambodian, or is that coming from you?" Cookie persists. "Yes, we have raised you as a Buddhist, and one day you will appreciate it. Kindness and humility are virtues, not weaknesses. You can have a big heart and still succeed in the workplace. Just be true to yourself and the rest will follow. I believe in you, Ma Petite Apsara."

"Mom, you have no idea how hard it is to make it in America," Sophea replies. "I just feel so lost and confused. I don't know who I am supposed to be anymore. I think I am going to call in sick today."

"Oh no! I did not raise my daughter to be a coward." Cookie pulls the covers off of Sophea. "You get up and face your colleagues. Embarrassment and disappointment are not good enough reasons for you to forfeit the day. I may have never worked in an office, but I have worked as a French teacher for the past twenty years. I know how hard it can get when you feel overworked and underappreciated. We'll see you downstairs."

Sophea fumes at her mother but manages to pull herself out of bed. The cool morning air hits her bare feet. Sophea decides a little meditation will help ease her nerves. *Breathe in. Breathe out. Breathe in. Breathe out.* Sophea closes her eyes and feels the movement of her chest going up and down. *Silence. Be silent. Silence is a good thing.* Sophea wills herself to embrace the calmness she is trying to generate. *Keep quiet. One minute. You can do it.* Instead, her mind starts to wander to yesterday's events. Her right leg immediately begins to bounce nervously up and down—a habit she picked up at the age of nine.

Sophea opens her eyes and squints at the morning sun coming through the window. She walks over to her secondhand stereo system and cranks up her *Greatest Nineties Dance Hits* CD. Sophea turns up the volume until

Whitney Houston's "I'm Every Woman" resonates throughout her bedroom—and throughout the house. Singing and dancing to a song about empowering women helps ease this morning's funk.

Not even Whitney Houston, however, can convince Sophea to dress in a fancy outfit, style her hair carefully, or put on makeup this morning. Instead, Sophea grabs her comfy jeans from the bottom of a pile of dirty laundry and slips on a fitted pink T-shirt that reads LAS VEGAS FOREVER. She stares at the silver sequins outlining the words and decides the T-shirt is just inappropriate enough for work to make her feel rebellious. But she also grabs her beloved black sweater, which will cover up any sign of disrespect to her coworkers and boss.

Downstairs in the kitchen, Chas Mai greets Sophea with a big, warm bowl of leftover rice soup. At that moment, Cookie walks in and says, "Did the flu make you lose your hearing? That music was a bit loud this morning. I want you to know that it's wrong to use 'being Cambodian' as the reason you didn't get your promotion. It's insulting to me and to Chas Mai."

"Mom, please, I'm tired. I know you don't understand, but it's my truth," Sophea responds. "Can I just eat my soup in peace?"

"Peace is what we sought when we escaped the war in Cambodia and came to the States," replies Cookie. "You're ungrateful for the life you have. Stop complaining and feeling sorry for yourself. You would have never survived the Khmer Rouge with your negative attitude—"

Chas Mai interrupts. "Ravy told us there is a man who has been aggressively pursuing you over the last two weeks. Is this true? Since work is not going so well right now, maybe it's a sign you need to go out on a date with him. There is no better consolation for a broken heart than male companionship."

Sophea looks at her cell phone and pulls up a series of calls from Tim over the last few days. She has not returned any of his calls, but she decides that perhaps Chas Mai has a point. Maybe it's finally time for a date with the man who tried to buy her lunch. Sophea remembers their first encounter.

Chapter 8

"What are those?" asked the tall blond man dressed in a pristine blue suit. He pointed to the bottom of Sophea's drink, looking like he just stepped out of a J.Crew catalog. "Do you actually drink that stuff?"

"It's called bubble tea." Sophea played with the straw in her mouth, unaware of her flirtatious gesture. "Those are chewy tapioca balls, and they're yummy." She pulled at her long brownish-black hair, which fluttered just above the small of her back. *Oh my gosh, this is the most gorgeous man I have ever seen in my life! This must be what they mean by love at first sight. Get a grip on yourself!*

He stared at her high cheekbones and big, friendly eyes. "Hi, my name is Tim." The stranger extended his hand for a shake. "You have a gorgeous smile. Where are you from, if I may ask? Do you speak Spanish?"

"Thank you. No, I'm Cambodian," Sophea responded, breathless. *Stay calm. This is just another forgettable encounter at the sandwich shop. Buy your sandwich, then walk away.*

"Cambodia—sure, I know where that is," he said with mock authority. "I did an eighth-grade report on Angkor Wat—the eighth wonder of the world."

"Yes," Sophea said. "A famous actress adopted her son from there." *He knows about Cambodia?! No one ever knows anything about Cambodia. He must be really smart. Oh, those eyes. I am falling in love. He's so hot. I want him. Stop it. Stop it!*

"Sorry, I don't keep up much with pop culture." Tim tilted his head upward and Sophea noticed a pronounced dimple in his chin. "But I did ace the report."

"Good for you." Sophea turned to order a sandwich. "I'll have a pork liver pâté sandwich, please." She watched as a Vietnamese woman in her sixties sliced open a baguette, spread a generous amount of pâté on the bread, then added fresh cucumber slices, cilantro, pickled carrots and daikons, and some spicy chili sauce. "For here or to go?" the woman snapped at her. Sophea was caught up in her own romantic thoughts and did not reply.

"She'll eat her sandwich here." Tim pulled out a handcrafted leather wallet bearing his initials. "Can you please also add a barbecue chicken sandwich and a Coke with that order?" He glanced at Sophea. "Do you have a few minutes to have lunch with me today?"

"Actually, I can pay for my own meal." Sophea gave the woman a ten-dollar bill. "And it's 'to go' please." *Forget it. He can't possibly be interested in you. This man was the high school quarterback, the All-American boy next door. Don't get your hopes up. These type of men do not fall for your kind. Just pay and walk away.*

"Whoa, sorry if I offended you," Tim said. "I'm just trying to be a gentleman."

"I have a deadline today and need to get back to work." Sophea didn't look him in the eye as she placed some napkins into a brown paper bag. *If he looks me in the eye, I will just die right now. No, our relationship is over. I will not allow myself to fall for an overconfident stud who will only hurt me in the end. Keep your eyes down!*

"Well, how about tonight or tomorrow night for dinner?" Tim put his hands together in a prayer-like gesture toward Sophea. He wondered why she kept avoiding eye contact.

"Are you pauning me?" Sophea laughed out loud. "That's not really needed here." *Okay, I am officially in love. Bringing home Tim will impress the heck out of Mom and Chas Mai. I feel so weak and insecure right now. Ravy would not approve.*

"Please go out with me," Tim continued. "We can even go Dutch if it makes you happy." He flashed a smile worthy of a toothpaste commercial.

"You can try me, but I'm usually busy." She handed him a business card and ran out the door, turning around one more time to remember his handsome face. *Am I so shallow that I can fall this deeply for someone because of his looks? It might be lust, but I will call it chemistry for now. If anything, do not call or think about him anymore. Make him work for it if he really wants to go out with you. Don't you dare look back again.*

Tim stared at the card, which read, SOPHEA LIM. ASSOCIATE PRODUCER.

WNR-TV. *She's obviously playing hard to get. Nothing a man loves more than a good chase.*

⊰৩৵⊱

"Is anyone in there?" Cookie waves her arms in front of Sophea. "Are you daydreaming? We have been talking to you for the last ten minutes!"

"Sorry, Mom," Sophea answers. "I was just thinking about work." She slurps up the last few drops of her now-lukewarm soup and heads out to work.

As she walks toward the bus stop, she can hear Chas Mai and Cookie yelling, "Make it a good day! Work hard! Be proud of your heritage!"

Sophea nods in response to her elders, but her mind wanders again toward Tim. She dials his number and leaves him a message. "Hi, Tim! This is Sophea, the *Bánh mì* girl from the Vietnamese sandwich shop. Thanks for all your sweet messages. I'm free this weekend if you want to meet up. Please call me."

Chapter 9

It is Thursday morning, the day Sophea usually brings in a couple dozen bagels for the staff. But today she stomps past the stack of "everything" bagels that beckons to her from the bakery window and enters the newsroom empty-handed. *This will show them that I'm no pushover,* she muses to herself. The newsroom staff scurry from task to task, and Don is calling for an earlier editorial meeting than usual. In fact, everyone is too busy this morning to think about eating breakfast, and Sophea's minor rebellion goes unnoticed.

Sophea checks the newswires. She discovers that the Atlantic Electricity Company (AEC) is experiencing random blackouts this morning, causing unexpected delays and confusion at multiple stoplights throughout the city. AEC is trying to determine the source of the problem and has sent out a press advisory asking media outlets to let commuters know of the unexpected delays. The problem is aggravated by the fact that today is the annual "Bikers Unite Ride" and thousands of bike riders are expected to convene at the National Mall to protest for safer bike lanes in their states. The weather bureau is also sending out warnings for a tornado watch this weekend.

Don calls everyone into his office and starts assigning reporters and producers to different parts of town for as much geographical coverage as possible. Janine, enjoying her new executive producer position, sits next to Don, taking meticulous notes and interjecting her instructions on how best to handle the various live shots that will be coming in all morning.

Not the least bit interested in concentrating on the news "crises" at hand, Sophea pouts and rearranges her paper clips. As Janine addresses the staff, Sophea fidgets with her hair. She attempts to signal Don with her stares, hoping that he will register her pleas to be taken off the AEC story.

Instead, he says to Sophea, "Can you stay in the newsroom and act as a backup if the assignment desk gets out of hand? It's going to get crazy trying to keep up with all of the roving reporters, satellite trucks, and swarms of people. We need you as a primary point person if the shit hits the fan. I also want you available as an in-house segment producer for the different reporters who may need help pulling their stories together."

"Can't I go out in the field with one of the reporters or camera crews instead?" Sophea asks. "You always put me on the assignment desk when a big news story breaks. Everyone else gets the glory of the story while I remain behind-the-scenes dealing with logistical nightmares."

"You're calm and organized," Don replies. "That's important when hell breaks loose in here. I need you in the newsroom today."

"Staying in the newsroom and helping others is not helping my career," Sophea argues back. "You told me I need to speak up more for myself, so I am asking for a chance to prove myself out in the field."

"Sophea, this isn't the time or place for you to voice your complaints right now," Don shoots back. "You're working the assignment desk today and helping Janine with any last-minute production needs. We're not discussing this any further."

Sophea seethes under her breath. "Fine, I'll do it one more day. But I'm going crazy here." She wipes the sweat off her brow, runs to the bathroom, and hurls into the toilet. Sophea splashes some cold water on her face and returns to the newsroom. *Don's going to fire you if you don't shut up,* she reprimands herself.

Sophea returns to a chaotic newsroom. Phones are ringing, producers are screaming, reporters are running back and forth, and interns and pages are experiencing their first major news blitz. *Get it together, Sophea. This is what you live for.* Sophea gives herself a pep talk and dives into the empty chair at the assignment desk. "I'm ready," Sophea says to her colleagues. "Tell me what you need. I'm on it."

At one point during the afternoon, Sophea looks over at Janine—the newsroom rock star. She is barking orders at stressed-out editors, reporters, and the camera crew, while typing out the opening dialogue for the show's anchors. She is seated on a high stool that gives her a bird's-eye view of the entire newsroom and what everyone is doing.

Today, Janine is encased in a tight blood-red sweater, a short leather mini-skirt, and peep-toe stilettos that show off her newly pedicured toenails. The overhead fluorescent lights somehow hit her blond, wavy hair at an angle that accentuates the shine of her newly washed follicles. While everyone else looks like a disheveled mess, Janine resembles a supermodel on journalism steroids— *a perfect candidate for the Miss Planet pageant,* Sophea fumes silently. The scene seems surreal, and Sophea catches herself snarling at the newsroom goddess once again.

Sophea allows herself one minute of media diva envy, then turns her attention back to her own work. Bikers and auto commuters have begun arguing in the streets, many frustrated by the city's delayed response to the traffic congestion that is literally halting the nation's capital. The mayor and the CEO of AEC are expected to hold a press conference in front of City Hall in fifteen minutes. There is no more time to spend shooting jealous vibes toward Janine. It is Sophea's turn to play the hero by hustling to find an available news crew to get the best footage.

Chapter 10

It's Friday night and Sophea is thrilled that Tim called her back so quickly after she left her message. Sophea stares at her reflection in the mirror and wrinkles her medium-sized, high "European" nose. It's been over six months since she has been on a "real" date. Her eyes narrow onto two brown age spots the size of raisins resting on her right cheek. Puckering her lips, she also notices a few dark hairs populating the corners of her mouth. "Mom's right," she whimpers into the mirror. "Why can't I just have wavy blond hair and blue eyes? That would make life so much easier."

"It is not good to be so unappreciative of nature's gifts," Chas Mai whispers through her closed bedroom door. "You are beautiful like a Hawaiian princess."

The silver doorknob turns and Chas Mai enters the bedroom cradling a large ceramic bowl of *kuyteav*—chicken noodle soup. "I thought you might be hungry," she says as she makes room for the steaming broth on Sophea's nightstand.

"Chas Mai, you were eavesdropping," Sophea responds. "Can't I even have one minute of peace to myself?" She picks up the bowl and places it on her lap. The heat of the broth warms her thighs.

"Why are you so hard on yourself?" Chas Mai says. "Have confidence in yourself. You are a beautiful woman inside and out."

"Did I hear someone say 'beautiful woman'?" Cookie joins in the conversation, adding French to the mix of dialogue. "This is a topic very near and dear to my heart." She tousles her shoulder-length, ebony hair and purses her raspberry-red lips. At fifty-five, Cookie can still turn heads, though her former girlish figure now holds twenty-five extra pounds.

"Want some soup, Mom?" Sophea points to the cooling broth. "This is my first date with Tim, and my jeans are already feeling a bit snug. I don't want him to think I'm overweight. Do I look fat?"

"You look perfectly plump and happy, so perhaps it's best to eat now." Chas Mai hands the bowl to Sophea. "A man should never see your real appetite, no matter how hungry you are. A little food right now will stave off your appetite later."

"Even at a restaurant?" Sophea holds the soup spoon to her lips.

"Especially at a restaurant—you will need to show restraint," Chas Mai responds. "Anyway, this soup's delicious. I put in an extra splash of *Sriracha* hot sauce. I know you love that."

"That's ridiculous advice," Cookies chimes in. "Eat the soup, then eat as much tonight as that man is willing to pay for. There is only one first date, and the way he handles the dinner bill will show you how he will treat you in the future. *Do not* offer to pay the tip. A hearty appetite shows a man you have a passion and a hunger for life. And, above all, do not eat any salads or greens— they will simply land in your teeth."

"Thank you both for your great dating wisdom." Sophea slurps up half her soup, then hands the bowl back to Chas Mai. "Staring at me won't make me finish the entire bowl. I'm full and I will definitely not be able to fit in my jeans now. Can I please have some privacy to finish getting ready?" She motions for both older women to leave her room.

"I don't understand why you young people insist on wearing such tight jeans. It can't be good for your circulation," Chas Mai says. "Women should wear dresses if they want to make a good first impression." She takes the soup bowl and makes her way out of the bedroom.

"Your breasts are at their peak right now—may I suggest showing a little cleavage?" Cookie adds. "If you continue dressing like a nun, you'll never get a husband." She kisses Sophea on the head and points to her own healthy bosom. "These were the jewels of the royal court." She lifts up both breasts and then drops them like two guillotined heads. They jiggle for several seconds until they're still.

"Where's Ravy when I could use some backup?" Sophea asks.

"She is helping out with an art gallery opening today," Cookie says. "I told her to come back so we can all watch a King Sihanouk movie together, but I think she also has a date tonight. With all these male suitors, you girls definitely take after me."

"Mom, you're obsessed with King Sihanouk films," Sophea teases. "He is like a Cambodian Elvis!"

Cookie perks up and shakes her head. "Not exactly. I think King Sihanouk saw himself more as a crooner type—more like the Frank Sinatra of Cambodia."

King Sihanouk had been an ever-present figure in Sophea and Ravy's childhood, and they knew his story by heart. The son of King Norodom Suramarit and Queen Sisowath Kossamak, King Sihanouk was appointed the king of Cambodia during the country's period of French colonization (1941–1955). When the French left, he remained Cambodia's effective ruler until 1970 when he was overthrown in a coup by General Lon Nol and the National Assembly. Aligning himself with the Khmer Rouge in order to regain power, King Sihanouk returned to Cambodia as king, but only as a puppet ruler. Then, in the years following the fall of that regime, his title and role in government changed many times.

To their delight, Sophea and Ravy had once found King Sihanouk's name in the *Guinness Book of World Records* as the politician who had served the world's greatest number of political offices, including two terms as king, two as sovereign prince, one as president, two as prime minister, and numerous other positions as the leader of various exiled governments.

But to Cookie's girls, the most fascinating thing about King Sihanouk was his penchant for appearing in Cambodia's popular culture, and how their mother and grandmother still loved to watch his old movies and listen to his songs. From an early age, King Sihanouk had a passion for the arts, including the cinema, music, and dancing. He was a composer and a singer who played the piano, saxophone, clarinet, and accordion. As king, he would often recruit family members, friends, and even political colleagues and cabinet members to act in his films, which he wrote, directed, and starred in himself. His wife, Queen Norodom Monineath, was a frequent costar.

Cookie and Chas Mai never let the girls forget they descended from Cambodian royalty. They knew King Sihanouk personally, and his role as "movie star" only added to his glamour.

Chapter 11

Sophea is putting the finishing touch on her makeup when her cell phone rings. "Hey, Tim here. I was wondering if I could swing by to pick you up tonight instead of meeting at the restaurant."

Despite all the cautionary articles she's read about the wisdom of meeting your first date in a public setting, Sophea says, "Sure."

Earlier that week, Sophea had called in a favor with a high school friend who worked in the DC Police Department. He completed a security check on Tim and left her a message that made her heart skip. "As far as I can tell, he's neither a sex offender nor a serial killer. Have fun on your date."

"The address is 441 Bungalow Drive in Arlington," Sophea continues. "We're the small white townhouse on the right with the yellow shutters. I should give you a heads-up that I have two older roommates. See you in about thirty minutes." She hangs up the phone and immediately regrets her decision.

"Who was that on the phone?" her mom asks from the living room. "Are we expecting a visitor this evening? I'll need to reapply my lipstick."

"It's just Tim." Sophea pokes her head into the entryway. "He's coming to pick me up tonight."

At that moment, she hears her grandmother shuffling across the living room floor toward her room. "Why did you tell him to come here? You don't know this man or his family. You've put us in grave danger. I'm going to call the Neighborhood Watch."

"Please calm down." Sophea rolls her eyes. "He's a financial analyst. He has a job. He owns a car. There's nothing to worry about. Anyway, you two can meet him and tell Ravy all about it. I know you're curious."

"Does he make good money?" Cookie applies a frosty pink lipstick. "In the olden days, the young man was expected to come to the woman's home and meet her family first. I'm more than happy to act as a chaperone tonight."

"Mom, he's only going to be here for a few minutes. We have dinner reservations, so there won't be time to chat." Sophea sprays some rose-scented perfume on her neck and wrists.

At that moment, the doorbell rings and Cookie yells, "I'll get it!" She is dazzled for a moment by the appearance of the handsome young man at the door. "My goodness, you look like James Dean."

"Good evening! I'm Tim." He grasps Cookie's petite hand between his two palms. "So nice to meet you. You must be Sophea's sister." Tim hands her a small bouquet of tulips, and Cookie feels like she is the one about to go on a date.

"Thank you! They are so beautiful." Cookies sniffs the petals. "Tulips are my second favorite flower, after the orchid. I'm actually Sophea's mother. You can call me Cookie."

Chas Mai grimaces at the scene before her and puts her right hand to her nose. She mumbles in Cambodian to Sophea, "You can't trust a man who smells like air freshener. I'm having trouble breathing. And he's making me sick flirting with your mother." Sophea scurries back to her bedroom to get her purse.

Tim looks over to see a thin, older woman with curly white hair standing in the corner of the kitchen holding a napkin to her nose. She stands about four-foot-five and looks angry. She is whispering to herself in Cambodian, so he does what feels most comfortable to him. He pauns hers and says, "With all due respect, you must be Sophea's grandmother. Thank you for allowing me to take her to dinner tonight. I promise I will have her home at a decent hour." He bows his head and hopes the gesture will win him some points with the elderly woman. And it does.

"Please, come and sit down in the living room." Cookie waves for him to enter. "Sophea should be ready any minute. In the meantime, can I get you a cold beer and some shrimp chips?" She hands him a bottle of Singha Thai beer and a bowl of crunchy, fishy-smelling snacks.

Before Tim even settles in the chair, Cookie pummels him with questions. "Where did you go to school? Was it an Ivy League school? What kind of car do you drive? How much money do you make? How many children do you want?"

Sophea enters just in time to witness the interrogation. Her mother is perched on the sofa, smiling delicately through the series of questions. She nibbles on salty shrimp chips in between each question. Cookie looks like she is holding court, nodding her head up and down with approval, closing her eyelids as she listens. There is a quiet elegance to her cross-examination. Chas Mai is huddled in her favorite corner by the kitchen doorway, watching over the scene like Mata Hari. The only clue that she is paying close attention to the conversation is an occasional *humph* of doubt and disapproval.

Sitting on the edge of the love seat, Tim wipes the large pearls of perspiration sliding down his cheek. His coiffed hair now sags like a wet mop. Two sweat stains seep from under his arms. Tim holds a full Singha beer bottle in his hands and two uneaten shrimp chips in between his fingers. There is not much left of his earlier preparation for the date except the slight hint of Old Spice lingering in the air.

"Mom, we need to go," Sophea interrupts.

Tim looks up to see a radiant young woman wearing a sleeveless yellow sundress. As his eyes lock on to her abundant cleavage, Tim mutters, "Wow—you can really fill out a dress. *Both* of you."

"But we're just starting to get to know each other," Cookie whispers. "Don't leave yet."

Tim wipes his forehead with a napkin and stands up to say good-bye. He leans forward and kisses the top of Cookie's hand. He pauns Chas Mai and follows Sophea to the front door. "My lady, your chariot awaits."

"Now, that is how a prince should talk," Cookie says with approval.

"I don't trust him," Chas Mai whispers back in *Khmer*. "His hands are soft and manicured like a woman's. Sophea needs a working man, not a sycophant."

Chapter 12

The next morning, Ravy demands a play-by-play of Sophea's first date with Tim. "I took Mom's advice and showed some boob. It was a disaster. I betrayed my feminist side." *But it was somewhat empowering to know that Tim couldn't take his eyes off my cleavage all night.*

"Did he take you to a Shakespeare festival?" Ravy asks. "Mom said he called you 'my lady.'" *Here we go again with another crazy man. She'd better have her head on straight this time.*

"He's not some freaky thespian," Sophea says. "I think he just has a weird sense of humor." *Hmmm, I don't remember now. Did we talk? Was he funny? He smelled good.*

"Do you like him?" Ravy holds her nose. "Chas Mai said he smelled funny. And you know how she feels about men who use too many hair products. Do you think he used too much cologne? You know Chas Mai's got an acute sense of smell."

"We had a delicious dinner at Washington Harbor overlooking the water." Sophea sighs. "Then we grabbed some coffee and dessert on M Street. It was magical. I think I might be falling in love—"

"Stop, that's not possible," Ravy interrupts. "I need to meet Tim before you start throwing the *L* word around. You're a smart woman on every front except when it comes to choosing the right man. Is there any way you can control your emotions for just a little longer? Love at first sight and 'falling head over heels' are cheap marketing tools used by movie executives trying to sell romantic comedies. They don't exist in real life. This man needs to be vetted."

"You'll get a chance soon enough." Sophea blows warm air into her cold hands. "I invited him to our family party at the end of the month. Both of our schedules are pretty packed in the next couple of weeks, but he's free that day."

"He's going to meet the family already?" Ravy says. "That's pretty serious. You don't even know him. Are you sure that's a good move?"

"This is the first man I've liked in a long time, so he might as well know from the beginning that family means a lot to me." Sophea tucks her hands into her armpits for warmth. "Anyway, why haven't you found yourself a nice Cambodian boy to marry yet?"

The two women laugh, then dig into their shared breakfast picnic: Croque Monsieur sandwiches and fresh fruit salads in the middle of DuPont Circle park. It's an abnormally cool September morning, and Sophea shivers in her thin silk tank top. Ravy wraps a light scarf around her sister's neck. They giggle and bicker like an old married couple until their "sister date" is over.

"Do you want to come over this afternoon? A couple of the aunts are swinging by to make stir-fry and play cards." Sophea attempts to stuff her empty plastic salad container into a recycling bin, but it's too big.

"Thanks, but I'm going to Eastern Market to do some antique shopping, then maybe hit this new hot yoga class," Ravy says. She kisses her sister on the cheek and walks toward the bus stop. "Don't tell Chas Mai, though! She thinks I could die of heatstroke if I'm not careful."

Chapter 13

"This is unacceptable!" Chas Mai cries from across the kitchen. "Moisten the rice paper before you wrap the meat filling. Then swaddle it like a newborn in a fitted blanket."

"Chas Mai, I've been making spring rolls for almost twenty-five years," Sophea replies in *Khmer*.

"You are still too impatient and careless when you roll," she scolds. "Our guests are almost here. Start the curry. Ravy can help me finish the spring rolls."

Sophea throws her sister a teasing glance. "She's always talking trash about my spring rolls."

"What can I say? Chas Mai obviously prefers the way I roll." Ravy winks and reminds her, "At this point in our lives, I need more brownie points than you."

In a large pot, Sophea combines a generous dash of vegetable oil, a plate of uncooked chicken, a couple of tablespoons of curry powder, onion, garlic, chicken bouillon powder, fish sauce, and a little salt and pepper to taste. Once the chicken is browned, she pours in a can of coconut milk and lets the concoction simmer on low heat.

Sophea's shoulders relax as she dices some potatoes and places the lid on the pot. The spicy aroma of the curry fills the air. Sophea looks up only to see another disapproving look. "What now?"

"Are you putting sweet peas in the curry?" Chas Mai asks. "Everyone loves my curry because I never forget to put in the peas. Cambodians love peas in their curry."

"Yes, they do," Ravy says as she slathers some water on the dry rice paper.

Sophea rolls her eyes and hears her mother, Cookie, yelling from the living room, "Listen to your grandmother. She is the queen of curry. Her parents paid for an Indian chef to teach her how to make curry when she was thirteen. And don't roll your eyes. Your eyeballs will get stuck in that position."

Cookie is watching the Asian News Channel, where a British correspondent is giving a live update about the recent United Nations–backed Cambodian genocide tribunal. Another judge assigned to the case has just resigned, frustrated with the continuing interference by government officials. *Twenty-five years have passed since the Khmer Rouge slaughtered their fellow Cambodians, including my husband and father,* thinks Cookie, *and we still can't get a fair trial to put them in jail. All of them will be dead soon if we don't hurry up. I can't stand to watch this anymore.*

Cookie throws her arms up in disgust, channel-surfs, and lands on a new episode of *Cracked: When Family Members Lose It.*

✧❦✧

Sophea surveys the three-bedroom townhouse where she grew up. The interior displays an eclectic mix of mismatched, secondhand furniture—a red-and green-striped sofa dominates a living room bordered by six folding chairs and a brown leather easy chair. The walls have remained bare except for an oversized watercolor painting of Angkor Wat at sunset.

The bookshelves bulge with French romance novels, Asian cookbooks, and Cambodian silver elephant and snake figurines. On the very top shelf, a black-and-white photo of her father and grandfather stands guard over the scene.

Sophie has tried to replace the old furniture several times, but each time Chas Mai protested, "Material goods come and go. We don't need new furniture. Invest in the family instead."

As barren as the house sometimes looked, it was literally a gift to these women. How they got the house was a real-life fairy tale. The first day Sophea and her family arrived in the United States in 1976, their family was greeted by a mysterious older man who identified himself as "Mr. Johnson, a good friend of King Sihanouk's."

His face was nondescript except for a dark scar on the upper right side of his face, just above his eyebrows. Mr. Johnson immediately pauned Chas Mai and Cookie as they exited the international arrival gate at Dulles International Airport. Though the actual flight from Bangkok to Washington, DC, took just over twenty hours, the two women wore the fatigue of their two-year journey since leaving Phnom Penh. They had lived with two of Chas Mai's other children (and their families) in a crowded one-bedroom apartment in Bangkok, biding time until they received permission to travel to the United States. The approval finally came when Mr. Johnson offered to "sponsor" their refugee family, including two very tired young children—Sophea, now seven, and Ravy, age two.

"Your Highnesses, it is an honor." Mr. Johnson grabbed Chas Mai and Cookie's modest suitcases. "I have a car waiting for you outside if you can please follow me." The exchange took place in French, since neither Cookie nor Chas Mai spoke the language of their new country. Mr. Johnson had perfected his French while working as a diplomatic advisor in Senegal early in his career.

Dulles Airport is on the outskirts of Washington, DC, and the drive to Arlington, Virginia, seemed to take forever. When they drove up to the house, Mr. Johnson escorted the women and children to the door and handed them two sets of keys. Looking at Chas Mai, he said, "I was instructed by King Sihanouk and your husband to purchase a comfortable home for you to live in once you arrived in the States. This is not grand, but I hope it suffices." He pushed open the door to their new home.

"We don't understand," Cookie said. "We have nothing, only ourselves and the few pieces of clothing in our bags. Everything else was left in Cambodia. How can we ever pay you back for this?"

"Your father was quite a savvy businessman, and he gave me money to invest for your family many years ago," Mr. Johnson explained. "Even when Phnom Penh was thriving in the sixties, he always imagined that one day his family might live in America. It was like he knew war would come to his homeland. The king introduced me to him during a dinner party one evening when I visited Cambodia. I was in charge of some of the king's international investment dealings, and your father asked me to do the same for him with his money. He asked me to create an emergency nest egg for you and your mother, which I now call the Princess Trust. You will probably still need to work to earn a living in America, but this is your father's final wish and legacy. With this trust, you and your mother will never be homeless or penniless." With that statement, Chas Mai had fallen down on her knees and thanked the Buddha.

"I had nothing but the utmost respect for your father," Mr. Johnson said to Cookie. "We tried so hard on that April day when Phnom Penh fell to the Khmer Rouge to help our Cambodian friends leave the city. We knew the United States was sending military helicopters to rescue us from the American Embassy, and I begged your father to come with us, but he wouldn't leave his officers. I still feel guilt that we American expats were able to escape on that horrific day. We left so many of our Cambodian friends and associates helpless at the hands of the Khmer Rouge." He wiped tears from his eyes before continuing. "Can you please ever forgive me? I struggle every day with these demons in my head. Whatever I can do to help your family now will still never be enough to silence them. The Cambodians trusted us, and we deserted them."

Cookie was all too familiar with demons. She asked Chas Mai to take the children, then whispered to Mr. Johnson, "Do you have any information about my husband or my father? We know nothing. I pray every night that they are safe and will join us here in America. That is what keeps me going—the hope that the children can be reunited soon with their father and grandfather."

"Your Highness, please don't make me be the bearer of bad news to you," Mr. Johnson replied. "At this time, there is no official evidence or record of anything or anyone. But what we hear is that the Khmer Rouge pounced onto Phnom Penh with an agenda to execute anyone associated with the government or leadership. Your father was a prince from the royal family and the chief of police, and I cannot believe that he was not a target. As for your husband, I do not know any more than you do. The truth is that he is an American-educated man who is married to a Norodom. I don't know how he will be able to hide those facts. But I promise to let you know if I find out anything more."

"Thank you for any information you can give us," said Cookie. "My mother and I cannot sleep at night. Our hearts burn with pain and guilt for having left our husbands behind."

Cookie continued, "I have my own demons, Mr. Johnson. Every night, I have the same recurring nightmare. In it, we are all back on the tarmac at Phnom Penh Airport. I am crying, pleading for my husband to come on the plane with us. He takes a few steps toward the plane, but then there is always the sound of bombs in the background and he turns to look at them. In that brief moment, I am transported onto the plane, screaming and clawing at the window as we fly over the images of my husband and father waving at us from the ground. I sometimes scream for so long in my dreams, I wake up hoarse. My mother and children are so accustomed to my sobs in the darkness, they are no longer affected by them. And so every night I dread falling asleep because I cannot bear to face another dream in which I am forced to abandon my husband. How can I survive the agony of not having done enough to save the one I loved the most? I should have never left my husband. I will blame myself if he dies." Cookie was solemn but she did not shed a tear.

"That's a heartbreaking story, my dear princess," Mr. Johnson said, "and one I'm afraid we share. What's the purpose of surviving, when every day you are haunted by the ones you left behind. Please don't blame yourself. None of us could have predicted it would go so wrong in Cambodia. I am sorry for everything and will do my part to ensure you are all taken care of in the future." With that, Mr. Johnson left their lives as quickly as he had entered them. He never appeared again, except in the form of a substantial check on the first day of each month.

The first check appeared in their mailbox the next day with a note that read, "I can't bring them back, but I hope this house will bring you all some comfort in the years to come." Nestled in a quiet community across from Georgetown and the Potomac River, the house was exactly what Cookie and Chas Mai needed to start a new life in America with two little girls. The women tried to reach out to Mr. Johnson after they had settled into their new home, but they were informed two months later that he had died of a heart attack while backpacking in Nepal.

From that day forward, Chas Mai lit a votive candle by the picture of her husband and son-in-law to represent their kind and generous benefactor. This nightly vigil brought her a sense of peace and strength, though hope for her husband and son-in-law's survival dwindled with every melting candle.

As for Cookie, she never spoke of her husband as she had that day with Mr. Johnson. It was as if she had finally accepted that Vaing was gone from her life.

One night, her nightmares stopped. She searched for and found comfort in the form of television and food, making a silent vow never to feel her pain again.

Remembering her last conversation with Vaing at the airport, Cookie reflected, *I, too, am from the Land of Smiles. How effective we Cambodians are at covering our pain and suffering. There is nothing worse than a self-pitying and forlorn refugee princess. No one truly wants to hear about death and loss, about what could have been. I will swallow all my hurt and fear and focus on my children. From this day on, they will only see my smile.*

Chapter 14

Sophea sets the table with plates, utensils, glasses, napkins, and disposable chopsticks from a local Chinese restaurant. She weaves through stacks of boxes and newspapers just to make it around the table. "Mom, there are hundreds of old magazines stashed in the dining room," she says. "You are the first official princess hoarder. I know a local nonprofit art group that would love some donated magazines. Or we could recycle them."

"You don't just 'recycle' good literature or give it away to strangers. Only rich Americans can afford to recycle," Cookie snaps back. "In Cambodia, not everyone is fortunate enough to have books and magazines to read. I am not a hoarder. I am a treasure collector." She walks over and caresses the stack of periodicals.

"Stop arguing, you two, or Sophea will forget to put out the Maggi and hot sauce." Chas Mai holds up two familiar colorful bottles in her hands. In the Lim household, Maggi serves as the secret Cambodian seasoning that enhances the flavor of everything—rice, bread, vegetables, soups, and more. Sophea blames her addiction to Maggi—a liquid alternate to salt—on her grandmother, who religiously dashes splashes of the salty elixir on everything that touches their lips.

Sophea fluffs up the pillows on the couches, sprays some air freshener through the rooms, and heads back to check on her curry. The aroma of garlic and cumin permeates the kitchen, thickening the air. "Yum, there is nothing like being bathed in a sauna of Indian spices." Sophea inhales her creation. "The smell of Chas Mai's curry bubbling in the pot is what I will always associate with our home and family."

Cookie walks into the kitchen and scoops up a mouthful of the curry with a piece of French baguette. "Delicious, darling. But it still needs more fish sauce."

The moment dissolves as the doorbell chimes. "Go greet your aunts and uncles." Chas Mai waves Sophea out of the kitchen. "I will finish up the spring rolls. The mob outside sounds famished."

Seconds later, throngs of reveling relatives charge through the door all at once. Sophea is mobbed by her family, and she greets each person in both the Cambodian and French manner. She clasps her palms together in a prayer-like gesture and bows her forehead to meet the tips of her fingers, pauning each relative. She then proceeds to kiss as many aunts, uncles, and cousins as she can on their cheeks. The family had just gotten together two nights before at her uncle's house, but everyone acts like they have not seen each other in years.

"Hello! Hello!" chorus a bevy of excited aunts and uncles, carrying armfuls of food, drinks, and an oversized vat of steaming white rice. "Such a nice day outside. It smells so good in here. What are you cooking? You look so pretty! Is anyone in the bathroom?" While the family finishes up their greetings, Sophea's two favorite uncles, Pou Do and Pou Bien, grab seats at the end of the dining room table and pull out some playing cards. "Who wants to play *Khatea*?"

The uncles remind Sophea of the famous comedic duo Laurel and Hardy. Pou Do stands five-feet-seven and weighs barely 130 pounds. His skeletal frame is accentuated by his sunken oblong face with large, crooked yellow teeth. He still has a full head of thick black hair, and he walks with a heavy limp on his right side from having had polio as a child. Pou Do is not handsome, but he engages people with cheerful eyes and an easy, hearty laugh.

Pou Bien stands about five-eleven (towering for a Cambodian man), and he weighs almost two hundred pounds. His cherubic face resembles a moon pie. There is a dimple in his chin, and he sports a small mustache. Well-read and serious, Pou Bien is a master of both conversation and Ping-Pong.

Best friends before they became brothers-in-law, Pou Do and Pou Bien have acted as surrogate fathers to Sophea and Ravy since the girls lost their own father in the war. Bang Vaing, as they called him, had been their close friend starting in grade school. The boys were dubbed the "Three Musketeers" after their teacher found them crouched in a dusty corner of the schoolroom one morning, reading Alexandre Dumas's classic aloud to one another.

It was Vaing who suggested that they all study abroad for college, then return to Cambodia to make their way in the "big city." Raised in a poor, small village on the outskirts of Phnom Penh, they promised each other they would become educated, worldly men despite their rural upbringing. After receiving their engineering degrees in America, Japan, and France, the three graduates returned to Cambodia to make a name for themselves.

Bang Vaing was the first of the three to find a job as a manager at an alcohol distillery. He promptly hired his two friends to work at the same company. Pou Do and Pou Bien were just adjusting to their newfound full-time positions and salaries when Bang Vaing led the way once again to their next goal—finding wives.

Acquiring a degree from abroad was like a badge of honor for these young men. They had their pick of brides from the multitudes of young, pretty, and ambitious women vying for a husband. What the three did not anticipate was that one of them would meet a real princess from the Norodom family who also had two sisters who needed to get married. The three childhood friends would eventually become brothers-in-law, all marrying into the Cambodian royal family.

During many conversations over the years since arriving in the United States, Pou Do and Pou Bien struggled with the loss of their dear childhood friend. Why did Vaing not make it out of the country in time, when all the other family members had been given the same warning by their father-in-law, General Norodom? Being the head of police in Phnom Penh, the general was privy to highly confidential military information that showed that Cambodia was in a state of turmoil. He also read American and European periodicals that validated his suspicions about the conflicts and battles brewing in Southeast Asia, specifically between the United States and Vietnam.

Putting all these pieces together, the general warned his four children and their husbands to start leaving the country one by one. Because of his high-level position, he was able to attain passports for his children and their families more easily than other Cambodian citizens. One by one, each of Cookie's sisters and their families followed their father's counsel and quietly exited Cambodia without much notice from government authorities. The process for the entire family to leave the country took over three years, but almost everyone managed to escape before the Khmer Rouge took over.

Pou Do and Pou Bien begged Vaing to leave with them in 1973, but he was stubborn. He had just been promoted to the head of the country's largest alcohol distillery, and Vaing felt he was finally in a position to provide for his family. "They are just rumors right now," he would say to his brothers-in-law. "Cambodia has always been in some sort of upheaval or battle with our neighboring countries or amongst ourselves. What proof is there that anything more can happen in the future? My entire family is back in the village, and they are counting on me for financial support. Without the support of my parents, I would have never studied in America and gotten this job. I have an obligation to take care of my family. You two are in the same positions with your families. I respect your decision to leave, so please respect my decision to stay."

"How can you be so unwilling to hear about the possibility of war, my dear brother?" Pou Do asked. "*Sdach Ta* says that ever since Lon Nol overthrew King Sihanouk in 1970 and imprisoned some of the members of the royal family, it is no longer safe for us to be here. We must all leave as soon as we can."

"If nothing else, you must think of your wife and daughter," Pou Do continued. "They are now your immediate family, and you have an obligation to them. If there is any truth in what our father-in-law is saying, you must do everything in your power to help them escape the country. They will neither leave without you nor survive without your blessings."

After a few moments of silence, Vaing replied, "I cannot promise that I will leave Cambodia right away, but I will make sure my Chanthavy and Sophea are safe. It will break my heart to tear our family apart, but what other choice do I have? We three friends are closer than even some brothers related by blood. Should anything happen to me, please promise that you will look out for my children as if they are your own. I promise to do the same for you." He clutched both of his friends' hands in his.

"Of course, we are your brothers for life, and we promise to take care of your wife and children if something should happen to you," Pou Bien said. Tragically, Pou Bien and Pou Do had to keep their promise.

In 1969, the United States began a secret bombing campaign on the Cambodian border, where North Vietnamese forces had installed bases. Thousands of Cambodians were killed. Backed by the Americans, Prime Minister Lon Nol overthrew King Sihanouk in a coup, ending his thirty-year reign, and proclaimed himself president of the newly created Khmer Republic.

King Sihanouk was exiled to China, and Lon Nol would eventually share the same fate. His five-year regime had been largely dependent on American aid that, in the end, was not backed by enough political or military resolve to help the beleaguered republic. On April 1, 1975, Lon Nol resigned and wisely fled the country. When the Khmer Rouge invaded Phnom Penh on April 17, 1975, one of their top priorities was to execute all leaders and high officials from the Khmer Republic—and Lon Nol was at the top of that list.

Always a survivor, King Sihanouk tried to make a comeback. While in exile he had aligned his interests with the Khmer Rouge, hoping they would restore him to power. But he was only a puppet in their government. In 1976 he resigned his role as head of state, giving way to Khieu Samphan. Pol Pot became the prime minister and quickly began his reign of terror.

Of course, all this was still an unknown future on that muggy July morning in 1973 when Vaing accompanied his two childhood friends to the airport. They were headed to Thailand with their families under the guise of a vacation to the seashore. The three men embraced one last time, just like they had done when they were young boys playing hide-and-seek in the schoolyard. From the sky, both men stared down at their friend, who waved from the tarmac. It would be the last time they ever saw Vaing.

Chapter 15

Sophea emerges from the crowd of kissing Cambodian relatives and catches a glimpse of Tim hovering at the front door of the house. She catches his eye and makes her way toward him. "Hi! You made it." She gives him a hug. "Are you still sure you want to come and meet my family? This is your last chance to run."

"What I know is that to date an Asian is to date her family," Tim responds. "Don't think I don't notice how you all travel in multigenerational packs and take lots of group photos. I'm so into this. Thanks for inviting me." He gives her a peck on the cheek.

Awkward. Sophea is unsure if Tim misspoke, but she excuses it as nerves. He is looking particularly handsome today in a button-down blue shirt that brings out his eyes and a pair of fitted khakis. Tim presents her with a bouquet of wildflowers. "Beautiful daisies for my daisy."

"Who's this dapper young man?" asks her aunt Ming Map. "Did you bring flowers for all of us?" She leans over to smell the daisies. Cookie is the eldest of four sisters. Ming Map is the second-oldest daughter and is a virtuoso of Cambodian double-speak. She has also mastered the art of "hmmphs"…being able to relay many different emotions without saying one word.

"This is my friend Tim," Sophea does not offer any more information than necessary. She looks over at Tim, who is pauning her aunt. Ming Map does not look impressed. She squints her eyes suspiciously and waves for the other aunts to join in the conversation.

Sophea smiles. On their first date, she had given Tim a few pointers to prepare him for meeting the family. "If you want to impress my family, you need to know a few things. First, Asians never wear shoes in the house. Shoes come off when you step inside. Next, if you want to earn extra points with my family, keep pauning them—when you greet them, when you thank them, when you say good-bye. And if they start speaking in Cambodian and you don't understand, just smile, nod your head up and down, and paun. They will love that you are showing respect to them as elders."

঩৵঩

Before Sophea can give any warning, Tim finds himself surrounded by a flock of aunts squawking at him in broken English. He looks for some assistance from Sophea, but it is too late.

A stern-looking, short-haired woman in her fifties introduces herself. "Tim, I am Sophea's aunt Ming Bonna. You met Ming Map. Here is our other sister, Ming Khana. We are pleased to meet you." She points to a younger woman in her late forties who has pretty features and smiles graciously.

Ming Bonna is the third-eldest daughter and is known as the "Laundromat Queen." She is a serious businesswoman renowned for chastising new college students and immigrants who come unprepared to her laundromat. "I have no quarters here," she has been known to say to laundromat virgins, fresh out of their parents' home. "You see machine over there? Put a dollar in and you get your quarters! No bother me here."

"Who are you, Mr. Tim?" Ming Bonna inquires. "What do you do? How did you meet Sophea? What are your intentions? Do you plan to marry her?"

"Leave the poor boy alone," Ming Khana interjects. "He just got here. Can I get you something cold to drink?" She hands Tim a glass of coconut juice with pulp. Ming Khana's husband is a wealthy exporter twenty years her senior. Pou Moni rarely attends the family get-togethers, since he is always traveling. Though a loving uncle to Sophea and Ravy, Pou Moni is not a devoted husband to Ming Khana.

"Why are you interested in Sophea? Do you plan to marry her? This house has too many women in it. It needs a man," Ming Map pushes. Tim opens his mouth to respond, but no words come out. Sophea is about to rescue him when she notices him cleverly attempting to paun his way out of the cackling mob. She hopes his cunning maneuvers will prevail.

"Do you come from a wealthy family?" Ming Bonna asks. "Sophea would make a perfect wife, but at thirty we worry that time is no longer on her side."

"Let's get something to eat." Sophea rescues Tim from her aunts' questions. "You mentioned on our date that you're allergic to garlic, so I made you some fried rice without garlic. It's in this bowl."

One of the shorter aunts, hidden in the pack, cries out, "Who's allergic to garlic?"

"Garlic and fish sauce are the backbone of our cuisine," Ming Khana explains.

"A man allergic to garlic cannot marry a Cambodian girl," Pou Do pipes in.

"Don't force an American to eat fish sauce—he will smell for days," Ravy says, moving across the room to give Tim a hug. "Hello, I'm Sophea's sister. So nice to finally meet you."

Tim looks down to see a pretty, petite Cambodian girl walking toward him. "You two don't look like sisters at all. You sure your mother didn't go home with a rickshaw driver?"

Ravy lets out an uncomfortable laugh. "Sophea didn't tell me you were so funny." She steps away from Tim. "Technically, we call them *tuk-tuks* in Cambodia."

Ming Bonna joins the group. "Todd, be careful what you say as the sole white person here. Or we'll sneak garlic into your food."

"His name is Tim," Sophea corrects her aunt and joins Tim, who has found a seat in the corner of the room.

"I'm never going to remember all their names," he says. "And it's true: All Asians do look alike. I can't tell one aunt from another."

⊷❧⊶

At that moment, Chas Mai enters the room carrying a large tray of spring rolls that look like they've come straight from a *Food & Wine* photo shoot. She stops in her tracks as her eyes register Ravy's new hairstyle.

"What did you do to your hair? Cambodian girls have straight, shiny black hair," she informs the young offender.

"They're called highlights," Ravy says.

"You look Spanish," Chas Mai says. "Dyeing your hair will poison your brain."

"I'm never going to be one of those old Asian ladies with short, permed hair and mismatched clothing," Ravy retorts. "But don't give up hope on Sophea."

She grabs her older sister and they start to dance the *Romvong*, a very popular Cambodian dance done at parties and weddings. Sophea places her hands one in front of the other in a fan motion, stepping in sync to the traditional Cambodian music jangling off a pirated CD. Chas Mai winces, but lets out a laugh. With the tension relieved, other family members eagerly jump into the circle.

"Where is Tim?" Cookie asks. "He should be out here dancing with his bride." An embarrassed-looking Tim is discovered seeking shelter behind the uncles, who are now occupying a table and washing down fried noodles with homemade Vietnamese iced coffee.

"Who knew Cambodians are so into line dancing," says Tim. "We are definitely not in Texas anymore."

Undeterred by Tim's sarcasm, Sophea continues to move to the upbeat rhythm with her sister and aunts. The house booms with music and conversation. Sophea surveys the scene, and one of her grandmother's favorite adages springs to mind: *Who needs friends when you have family?*

❦ ❧ ❦

Later that evening, Sophea pulls Tim onto the dance floor. His arms flail like broken wings. "It's hard to dance to this kind of music," Tim complains. "I can't find the beat. It's just a funky mix of sounds without any kind of melody."

Sophea stops dancing and listens to the familiar mix of wind, string, and percussion instruments playing in the background. "That is the most relaxing sound to me. I feel like we are back in Cambodia."

"This is too much." Tim looks down at his Rolex. "I didn't realize we were going to be with your family all night. Don't they ever get tired? When are they going to stop dancing?" He points to her aunts, uncles, and cousins who are now doing the Cha-Cha-Cha in the middle of the living room.

"Cambodians love to dance!" Sophea joins her family on the makeshift dance floor. "It costs nothing and makes us happy."

❧ ❧ ❧

From across the room, Ravy watches her sister trying to coerce Tim to dance. She approaches the couple and notices that Tim's lips are swollen like two banana slugs. "Yikes—what's happening?" Ravy shrieks and points his direction.

"Your mom fed me some noodles, and now my upper lip feels like it's ballooning into my nostril." Tim cups his neck with his two hands. "I can hardly breathe."

"No problem." Ming Khana hands him a bunch of parsley. "Eat some of this, and the swelling will go down." She runs into the kitchen to get some ice water.

This is a nightmare, Tim thinks to himself. "Sophea, your mom tricked me. She thinks I'm lying about my garlic allergy. Your family's crazy."

Businesswoman Ming Bonna scoffs. "Don't be disrespectful. Until you two are married, you're still an outsider."

In the background, Pou Do and Pou Bien raise a glass of whiskey to toast their lost friend. "Here's to our brother Vaing, who would have outdanced all of us tonight!" Cookie smiles and remembers what a great dancer her husband was. It was he who taught her how to do the Twist and the Mashed Potato—two popular nightclub dances he had learned while studying in America.

Chapter 16

A couple of months have passed since Janine took over as executive director, and Sophea still can't let it go. Working late one Friday evening, Sophea sees Don still at his desk. She knocks on Don's door. "Can I talk with you for a few minutes?" she asks. "We haven't talked that much since Janine got promoted. I want to make sure everything is okay between us."

"What do you want, Sophea? You did a terrific job today," Don replies. "How much more reassurance do you need?"

"I've been in the same job for three years now and have been passed over for four promotions," Sophea begins. "It's becoming clear that being nice and working hard is not a good strategy for moving up at this station. Can you please help me out here?"

"Sophea, we've been over this a hundred times," Don explains. "People would kill to have your position. You've gotten great reviews over the years and good pay raises."

"I know, but I want to be a journalist in the field, not just behind a desk," Sophea replies. "Why won't you give me that chance? I feel that you're punishing me for being so good at my job that you won't let me move on to something else. That's not fair."

"Sophea, we've both had a long day. I know you're frustrated," Don says. "Have you ever thought about going to a smaller market and becoming an on-air reporter? I have a lot of news director friends around the country. You'd be great."

"No, as much as my mother would love to imagine that I am the next Connie Chung, it would break my grandmother's heart if I moved away from here. I can't do that to her," Sophea says. "Anyway, I prefer doing the behind-the-camera work. That's more like me."

"Well, that's not normally the response I hear when I offer to help someone get an on-air job," Don replies. "But I understand. You've told me about your family situation, and I respect it."

Sophea looks at her friend and mentor, takes a deep breath, and says with all the firmness she can muster, "But I do need a change of pace, and I need it as soon as possible. I overheard that there are some problems in the consumer/investigative unit. Maybe I can help."

"You know nothing about running a consumer/investigative unit," Don argues. "Yes, Dale, the current producer, informed me today that he needs to take a one-month leave of absence for a family emergency. But I don't have any more information than that right now."

"Don, it would be a perfect break from the newsroom," Sophea begs and refuses to take his lack of enthusiasm for an answer. "I've been the ultimate shopper since I bought my first pair of sandals when I was eight. I'm a good saver. I'm always on the lookout for people who want to cheat me out of my money. I wrote the *Frugal Fangirl* column for my college newspaper. If you remember, last year I helped with the holiday shopping segments during November sweeps month."

Don looks over at Sophea, who is now trembling and fighting back tears. He shakes his head and flicks his pen back and forth. "I don't appreciate your guerrilla tactics at the end of a long news day, but you've caught me in a weakened state. Fine, you can start the job next week until we get a little more clarity on the Dale situation. But then you're back on the assignment desk."

"Wow, that's fast," Sophea responds, a bit bewildered. "I don't know if I'm ready to do that so soon."

"Look, Sophea, one minute you say you want change. The next minute you backtrack," Don says. "I'm starting to lose patience with you. This is what I've got—take it or leave it." Don demonstrates he's done with the conversation by waving her out of his office.

"Yes, I'll take it!" She rushes over to hug Don. "I promise you're making the right decision. I won't let you down."

Yay me! It's time to celebrate! Sophea rummages to the bottom of her file drawer and pulls out a bag of mini Snickers bars. She stuffs three of them into her mouth at once. The taste of chocolate, caramel, nougat, and peanuts melts into her mouth.

Sophea's love affair with Snickers bars began at the age of thirteen. While Chas Mai and Cookie worked during the day, she and her sister, Ravy, were latchkey kids after school. While other children went off to gymnastics practice or piano lessons, the two girls would scurry home to make a hearty mid-afternoon bicultural snack, such as scrambled eggs with a touch of duck sauce or leftover fried rice with ketchup.

They then plopped down in front of their ten-inch black-and-white television set, where they experienced one of their most impactful introductions to American culture—*Flicks at Four* on the local ABC station. Each week showcased a new movie theme or actor, like Frankie Avalon and Annette Funicello in *Beach Blanket Bingo*, upbeat Elvis movies, or Hitchcock thrillers.

One day, during a commercial break, Sophea rummaged through her grandmother's secret stash of chocolates hidden in her closet. Chas Mai, who had passed many days with the royal family in Cambodia, had always looked down at "American" chocolates, pastries, and food. She was fond of remarking, "In Cambodia, we only ate the finest French chocolates. We dined on *foie gras*, *pâté*, and caviar. American chocolates cannot compete with European confections. It's just a fact."

But that afternoon, Sophea found a bag of snack-sized Snickers bars in Chas Mai's closet. What was a simple American chocolate bar doing stashed away in between the Toblerones, Leonidas, and La Maison du Chocolats? The hypocrisy of it all compelled Sophea to devour the entire bag in one sitting. Snickers had been her favorite candy bar ever since.

One of the desk editors looks up and blurts, "Sophea, are you okay? You're in your own world. And by the way, you have a big piece of chocolate smeared on the right side of your mouth."

Am I okay? Sophea congratulates herself. *I'm great! I just got myself another job at this station.*

Still in a daze, Sophea calls her boyfriend, Tim. "Sweetheart, it's me! Between our two-month anniversary and my new job—yes, *my new job*—we have to celebrate! Can you come over to my house tomorrow night? I will figure out a way to get my mom and grandmother out of the house so we can have some time alone."

Chapter 17

Sophea dabs a little coconut oil on her neck and pouts into the mirror. She sucks in her stomach and winks back at her image. *Tonight's the night I will give myself to Tim. He's the one.*

Knock! Knock! Knock! Tim is banging on the front door. "Where's my girl? Let me in. I'm dying to hold you."

Don't mess this up! Say something super sexy. Sophea runs to the door and throws herself into Tim's arms. "Get over here, you big, white medallion. I mean stallion! We have the house all to ourselves tonight!" She gives him a deep kiss on the lips. "Aww, are you coming down with a cold? You have big bags under your eyes, and your breath smells a little sour. Do you want a mint?"

"Am I that offensive? How about we jump in the shower together instead?" Tim nuzzles Sophea's neck. Her skin smells like fresh coconut. He puts the mint in his mouth and starts to caress her face with his lips.

"Wait, what do you think of my good news?" Sophea squeals. "I start in the consumer unit on Monday!"

"Yeah, that's my baby! Let me give you proper congratulations." Sophea closes her eyes and feels the warmth of Tim's mouth on her lips. She is thrilled that the mint worked.

"I've never dated anyone with so many muscles before." Sophea's hand brushes across Tim's oxford shirt, still crisp from the dry-cleaners. "You're so hot, you should be a fireman."

"Would you like to see my fireman's hose?" Tim loosens his jeans to reveal some maroon skivvies. "How much longer are you going to keep me waiting and begging? I'm about to burst like a fire hydrant."

"You have been so patient with me," Sophea whispers as Tim moves on top of her and places his head on her chest. "I think tonight is the night."

"Hey, babe. I've been waiting for you to green-light this for the longest time," Tim says. "You're shaking. Don't be scared. I have a few magic tricks up my sleeve to help you relax. Just follow my lead." Tim starts to unbutton her blouse.

"I trust you," Sophea says. "I've been waiting for this day for a long time, too." She takes a deep breath and closes her eyes again.

"Your boobs are like down pillows," Tim whispers. She moans and guides his hands past her midriff. His fingers are like electric prongs sending shock waves of pleasure throughout her body. "Let me hear how good that feels." He slaps her buttocks.

"Ouch! Why did you do that?" Sophea asks. "I think I prefer a little tenderness for my first time. The spanking just reminds me of what my mother did when I acted out as a little girl." Sophea remembers her mother's affinity for whacking her with a wooden ruler each time she misbehaved. But sometimes, she just used her bare hands, which stung even more against her skin.

"That's the point," Tim says. "You relax, and I'll do all the work. I see where you're going with this. So, you want to do some role playing? I'm right with you."

"Role playing? This is our first time making love," Sophea replies. "Aren't I enough? Do you really need to play games right now?" She sits up and tries to close her shirt.

"Whew, you are one uptight virgin." Tim shakes his head. "I'm trying to help you relax and enjoy yourself. Maybe we should have started with a drink, but wait, I forgot. You don't drink. You gotta give me something here, sweetie, or 'Elroy' might lose interest soon." Tim looks down and points to his groin.

"His name is Elroy? Why are you trying to ruin this first time for me?" Sophea pleads. "I'm in love with you. I want you. Please, let's start over. Just you and me, no games, tricks, or gimmicks please." She places her hand on his lower abdomen.

"Oh, don't be a bore. I'll tell you what would really turn me on. Let's pretend you're a Thai hooker and I'm your john." He rubs his two palms together and points to Sophea. "I'll take this virtuous doll for five dollars!"

Tim grabs Sophea and starts to kiss her again. In a moment of passion, Sophea unleashes her most smoldering moan and extends both legs up into the air, wrapping them around Tim's torso. "Now that's what I'm talking about," Tim says. "I knew that good Cambodian girl was just an act. You're my dirty little whore."

Suddenly, Sophea hears Chas Mai's voice in her head. *"Child sex trafficking in Southeast Asia? Is this how you honor yourself and your family?"*

"Can we please stop? This is totally inappropriate." Sophea disentangles her right leg and kicks Tim off the couch. "I can't do this. What kind of girl do you think I am?" She sits up and pulls down her skirt.

"I thought you wanted me to talk dirty." Tim gets up from the floor. "You made some pretty convincing sounds." He stands naked, glistening with sweat.

"Well, you heard wrong," Sophea interjects, angry with herself. "I'm not for sale. No woman should ever be up for sale."

"What are you talking about?" Tim asks. "We're just role playing. This is what couples do for fun and sex. You're a tease. You older virgins are never going to give it up."

"Thai prostitutes? Is that all you've got?" Sophea says. "Know your audience. We could have played Jane and Tarzan, Stranger in the Bar, but not this scenario. It hits too close to home for me." She scrambles to find Tim's underwear and hands it to him.

"Look, this is getting out of hand," Tim says. "Don't all of a sudden act like you didn't want this as much as I did. You sent your mom and grandmother off for the evening and lured me into your love cave. Can't we call a truce and start over?" Still naked, he moves toward her.

"No, we can't. The mood is over." Sophea backs up. "Please put on your clothes. My grandmother would never approve of this." She hands Tim his jeans and shirt.

"Why are you bringing up your grandmother right now? No offense, but that old lady creeps me out," Tim says. "Every time I come over, all she does is sneer at me from the corner of the room. She, your mom, and all those loud aunts of yours huddle like a coven of witches hurling evil spells at me in a language I don't even understand. All I wanted tonight was to make love with you. Why did you have to bring up your grandmother?"

"So, an old woman gives you the stink-eye and you're traumatized?" Sophea says. "Please don't attack my family. You have no idea what they mean to me, and it makes you sound like a racist."

Tim's remarks about Chas Mai hurt Sophea deeply. Her grandmother had sacrificed everything to give Sophea and Ravy a chance at life in America, and her "sour" face masked all the hurt and hardship she had endured over the years. *Why can't Tim see that behind her "evil eye" is just a wounded spirit needing some love and assurance?*

"Your family is a bit intense," Tim says. "One of your aunts told me they can't accept me as part of the family until I propose to you. I don't even know if I'm in love with you yet, so marriage is the furthest thing on my mind. I just want to get to know you better and have some fun together."

"It's obvious you have no interest in getting to know my family at a deeper level," Sophea snaps back. "You have no idea what we've all been through. Not everyone can be a trust fund baby like you. I thought I was in love with you, and I thought we were in a committed relationship."

Tim grins for a moment and tries to relieve the tension between them. "How many generations of Asians does it take to ruin a relationship?"

"How can you be making jokes right now?" Sophea asks. "I don't think you understand that my feelings are really hurt. I feel very rejected by you."

"Lighten up, Sophea, we are a couple," Tim says. "I'm sorry if I messed up. You made me sound like some kind of sex predator, so I'm just feeling a bit defensive right now." He puts his pants back on and looks under the sofa for a missing sock.

"Pretending that I work at a Thai brothel is not a turn-on for me." Sophea bites her nails. "That's *your* sick fantasy, and I should have never played along."

"So, it's a trigger for you. I get it," Tim replies. "But you can't just throw out the word *racist* every time you're offended. You're high-maintenance."

"High-maintenance? I never ask anything from you," Sophea snaps back. "I feel like you have no respect or understanding of my culture."

"I want to have fun with you, and that's about the extent of it for me right now," Tim says. "We're still in the learning and exploration phase of our relationship, as far as I'm concerned. Don't box me in, or I'll run."

"Is that a threat?" Sophea seethes. "I'm not trying to force love on you, but this is not a game for me. I'm thirty, and I am looking for my potential husband. That should not be a surprise to you."

"It's been two months, and we've never had sex yet," Tim says. "The physical stuff helps me get closer, but you claim to still be a virgin. I don't believe it—there are no true virgins in this day and age. I think you're just using it as an excuse not to have sex with me."

Sophea throws a pillow at Tim. "Of course, I wanted to make love to you. I thought I was in love with you, but it's obvious you don't feel the same. How do you expect us to get intimate anytime soon when your heart is not even in this? This is not the evening I envisioned for us tonight."

"You're actually going to use the word *love* to blackmail me about sex?" Tim asks. "This is like a crazy movie. Imagine, a thirty-year-old virgin who still lives with her mother and grandmother. She can't have sex with her boyfriend, because her grandmother's disapproving face pops into her head whenever they're getting it on. That's just wrong."

Sophea paces back and forth, then points to the front door. "Get out or I will call the police and have you escorted out of this house!"

"You're gonna regret this decision, Sophea," says Tim. "I can get any woman I want, but I chose you. That's gotta count for something." He makes his way toward the door and leaves without saying good-bye.

Wondering whether she overreacted, Sophea feels a migraine coming on and reaches for the ibuprofen. Her grandmother's voice echoes in her head, *"Be a good Cambodian girl and save your virginity for someone who will appreciate it."* These words comfort her.

Tim stands outside of her apartment, replaying their date in his mind. One minute, Sophea was lying in his arms with her legs spread in the air. The next, she was accusing him of being a bigot. Tim shakes his head in bewilderment and wonders if he should turn around and knock on the door.

At that moment, his cell phone rings. It's Tim's friend Jack. "Hey, buddy! How was your date with the hot Asian chick? Wanna grab a burger with us right now?"

"Ahh, no thanks," Tim says. "Maybe not tonight. You guys have fun. I'll talk to you soon." He hangs up the phone and strolls down to the street. The evening air hits Tim's face like a cold slap. There's a parking ticket on his windshield. In his eagerness to see Sophea, he had forgotten to put money in the meter.

Chapter 18

On Monday morning, Sophea tries to sneak out of the house. "Where are you going so early this morning, young lady?" Cookie intercepts her plan. "Why did you hide in your room all weekend? Chas Mai and I want to know how your Friday night date went with Tim."

"I'm starting in the consumer unit this morning." Sophea looks at her watch. "It's really not a good time to talk."

"Chas Mai is convinced you were planning your wedding, so we tried to give you some privacy," Cookie says. "We are so excited for the two of you."

"Yes, that's exactly what I was doing all weekend," Sophea says. "Let's talk later. I really need to leave right now." She rushes out the door, hoping to seek refuge in her new positive work environment.

❦ ❧ ❦

"The consumer unit is our station's *Titanic*," Don explains. "The ratings there are dismal. I have a feeling their producer, Dale, is not coming back. It's just a matter of time before we may have to shut the whole department down. Remember that this is only a temporary position, so don't get too comfortable up there."

"So, in other words, I've got one month to turn this ship around?" Sophea says. "Perfect. I'm ready, boss. Just don't give up on us yet."

"No promises, but be my guest," Don says. "Show me what you can do, Sophea."

❦ ❧ ❦

The consumer unit is located two floors up from the main newsroom—tucked away behind a small door, hidden between human resources and library services, which leads to a long, narrow hallway crowded with yellowed magazines, old reels of film, and random objects ranging from a child's toy truck to rolls of unused paper towels and boxes of detergents and cleaners. The hallway feels a bit claustrophobic, and Sophea walks briskly to an open workspace at the end of the hallway.

"Who's there?" a deep, female voice yells from the corner cubicle. "I'm busy right now. Go away."

"Hi! I'm the temporary producer," Sophea replies. "Didn't Don tell you I was coming today?"

Sophea looks over to see a tall, attractive redhead staring at her from behind a huge pile of mail. "Nobody told me anything. I'm Edie. How do I know you're not one of Don's minions spying on us?"

"Wow, you're a bit defensive." Sophea looks around at the small office space surrounding them. There are papers strewn everywhere, boxes piled high on the floor and on empty desks. "I'm here to help you, not destroy you." She settles next to Edie and starts to read through some of the older press releases and periodicals.

Edie eyes Sophea with suspicion from across the room. "How did you know we needed help? Don and I just spoke on Friday about replacing Dale. Information sure moves fast in the newsroom."

"Let's just say I was ready for a change. I saw an opportunity and pounced on it," Sophea replies. "Look, I think we're both in a pickle here at the station. It might behoove us to try to make our relationship work. I need to prove to Don that I can do more than work the assignment desk downstairs. And, you, my dear, need help to keep the consumer unit alive or you'll be out of a job soon."

For the next few hours, Edie and Sophea sort through the piles of mail and papers without exchanging a word. Around noon, Sophea's stomach begins to growl and she says, "I'm going down to the cafeteria for a quick bite. Do want to join me for a tuna sandwich or something?"

"Thanks, but I'm not hungry right now," Edie says. "Anyway, I tend to bring a bag lunch since I'm a picky eater."

"Okay, I'll be down there perusing the salad bar if you change your mind." Sophea heads toward the doorway.

⋘ ❧ ⋙

After lunch, Sophea returns and finds Edie lighting an incense candle. "I cleared out this cubicle for you." She points toward a big desk. "It's not great, but the computer works and it's in the corner, so you have some privacy. I hope you like it." Sophea smiles and hands Edie a chocolate chip cookie in return.

"Dale and I promised Don that we would produce two to three segments every week," Edie explains. "The truth is, Dale was so focused on his wife's illness, things just fell apart. I got lost without a producer pushing me."

Sophea takes out a broken hair clip hanging from Edie's long strawberry curls and notices a button missing from her blazer. "Don't worry, we all need support. Um, I think you might have some lipstick smeared on the front of your teeth." She hands Edie a tissue.

"I do?" Edie pulls out a compact from her purse. "This should be embarrassing, but that's the least of my worries right now. If you can't help fix this department, I'm going to be out of a job soon."

Sophea flips through the contacts in her phone. "Let's start with a makeover, and then I know a good communications consultant who can give you some feedback on your video segments."

From the corner, she hears Edie's muffled sob. "Are you okay?" asks Sophea. "Are you crying?"

"Don't judge me," says Edie, fighting back her tears. "I was the station sweetheart in Salisbury. It's a small town, but they loved me there."

"I can relate to that more than you can imagine." Sophea remembers Don's comment about her being the newsroom sweetheart. "We'll be alright. Trust me. I'll work on a couple of segments this week that we can have 'in the can' while you take some time off to get rejuvenated, get your hair cut, and buy yourself some new clothes. Does that sound good to you?"

"You would do that for me?" Edie grins. "I could definitely use a break if you could cover for me for a couple of days. I promise to come back refreshed and camera-ready."

"It's my pleasure—don't worry." Sophea gives her the thumbs-up sign. "Don and I have a great relationship. My goal in the next few days is to fly under the radar but still get some work done. I'm excited!"

Chapter 19

"Alright, tell me again why you prefer the beef burger over the veggie burger," Sophea says. "But this time, put a little more passion into it. I'm not really feeling that you prefer beef over bulgur. Roll it!" She motions for her cameraman to start filming.

Sophea glances over at the makeshift picnic table she and Bob set up in the middle of the National Mall two hours earlier. The red plastic gingham tablecloth she purchased the night before at the Dollar Store transforms their portable fold-up table into a lively countryside stand. On it sit four covered plates. Each plate holds a different kind of burger—beef, chicken, turkey, and bean. A big jug of lukewarm lemonade looms beside them. All this for a "Fall Burger Wars" segment.

Without Edie to help, Sophea is searing burgers on the grill with one hand and cajoling harried tourists to take part in a blind taste test with the other. The top of her head feels charred on this unseasonably hot autumn afternoon, but she does not want to ruin her hair with a hat. Sophea focuses her attention on her last taste-tester.

"I dunno," says the little boy. "Cuz it tastes better?"

"Cut, cut, cut." Sophea pleads, "All I need is just one short sound bite. What does it taste like? Do you like the smell? What does it feel like in your mouth? Please, concentrate!" She waves for the cameras to roll again.

The boy pierces a toothpick into another piece of beef patty and thrusts it into his mouth. He chews slowly, then screams into the camera, "Ewwww, this meat isn't cooked! I'm eating raw beef, Mom!" He spits the piece of meat into his right palm and flings it at Sophea. It smacks her in the eyelid and splatters onto her white top.

"Ouch! That hurts!" Sophea removes a piece of warm ground beef stuck in the corner of her right eye.

The boy lets out a wail and runs to his mother. "How dare you try to poison my child?" she screams. "I'm going to report you to the Better Business Bureau!" The family scurries away toward the Smithsonian Air and Space Museum. The boy looks back at Sophea and sticks out his tongue at her while his mother continues to fuss over him.

Sophea puts a piece of the undercooked beef patty in her own mouth and spits it back out in her hand. "Let's call it a wrap for the day. I'll make do with the footage we have."

⊰৩৽⊰

"You've been in the consumer unit for less than twenty-four hours. Why am I dealing with an irate mother? She's threatening us with a lawsuit. What the heck happened at the shoot?" demands Don.

"She *begged* us to interview her son since he'd already been in a few commercials." Sophea clenches her fists. "My focus was on getting the sound bite instead of watching the barbecue grill. I'm sorry. The meat was undercooked, but the boy didn't swallow anything. He spit it back into my eye."

"Be more careful next time, Sophea." Don walks over to his desk. "I'll let this one slide since you just joined the consumer unit, but no more mistakes like this, please."

"Tell you what, Don." Sophea scribbles in her notepad. "How about if we do a huge exposé on food poisoning for tomorrow night's broadcast? The title will be, 'What's Killing You at the Salad Bar?' We'll be at the forefront of E. coli education." She jumps out of her seat and gives him a thumbs-up sign and a huge smile.

⊰৩৽⊰

Three years earlier, Don had met Sophea at a job recruiting conference for Asian American journalists. Wearing an aqua-colored power suit and a pair of hand-me-down Christian Louboutin heels she'd unexpectedly nabbed at the flea market one day, Sophea had followed Don after his participation on a panel discussion and introduced herself to him.

79

"My name is Sophea Lim. During your presentation, you mentioned that we should work on our networking skills," she mumbled. "Do you have time for a quick cup of coffee?" She pointed toward a complimentary coffee station nearby.

"I'm in a hurry," Don replied, but something about her made him stop. "How about I give you five minutes to give me your spiel?"

"I thought all you said we had to do was introduce ourselves and be friendly," Sophea confessed. "I'm great at small talk but not so much at selling myself." She took a deep breath.

"Every encounter with a news director is an opportunity to sell yourself," Don replied. "I have tons of young people knocking at my door, trying to get a job at WNR-TV. We're the best station in town. Unless you have a breaking news story to share, I really don't have much time for small talk." He looked down at his watch, but settled in a seat with his cup of coffee. "Go ahead, tell me about yourself, Sophea Lim." Don glanced at the résumé she just handed to him.

"Okay, I'll give it a try." Sophea cleared her throat. "I currently work as the lead researcher for the national desk at WABD-TV, right down the street from you. I double-majored in English and political science at Wellesley College on a full scholarship and spent my junior year abroad in France. For three straight summers, I interned at various newspapers throughout DC. My first job out of college was as a page at WABD's national desk. When the researcher job opened, they promoted me and I've been there ever since. A friend told me about WNR-TV's push for a more diverse workforce, so yes, I would love to have the opportunity to work for you should anything open up." Sophea felt the dampness of her shirt collar against her neck and grabbed a drink of water.

"That's all good stuff," Don challenged Sophea. "Now tell me something unforgettable about you."

"My family and I escaped Cambodia just a few months before Pol Pot and the Khmer Rouge invaded Phnom Penh." Sophea steadied her voice. "It was just me, my mother, who was then pregnant with my sister, Ravy, and my grandmother. We lost everything in the war, including my father and grandfather, and had to rebuild a new life here in America. My mother says my sister and I were born as 'war babies,' so that means we work hard and never give up."

Don noticed Sophea's right leg shaking up and down. "Alright, now that's interesting information." He glanced at his watch and put her résumé in his folder. "I'll give you a call in a few days, and we'll see if you can't come by the station to meet some of the other folks in the newsroom. I think we might have an opening in the news department if you're interested." Two weeks later, Sophea started her new job as an editor at WNR-TV.

❦ ❦ ❦

Getting a last-minute interview with an E. coli expert from the Centers for Disease Control and Prevention turns out to be a more difficult task than Sophea had anticipated, but she is able to lay down her final voice track and finish the editing by 7:00 p.m.

Sophea is cleaning her desk when the phone rings. It's her grandmother, Chas Mai. "Where are you? When are you coming home? It's getting dark soon, and your mom and I are waiting for you. This new job is bad for your health." She speaks to Sophea in *Khmer*. Twenty-five years of reading books from the local library has made her quite proficient in English, but Chas Mai prefers to pretend she neither understands nor speaks English. It forces her granddaughters to reply in *Khmer* and is an effective tool for when she is eavesdropping on conversations that do not concern her.

"I'm still at work," Sophea responds back in *Khmer*. "Don't worry, I'll be home soon. Please eat dinner without me." *I'm thirty, and I still have to report home for dinner. Can't they see I just started a new job and need to prove myself in this position? A few missed meals is not going to kill anybody—especially me.* She grabs hold of her love handles.

Chapter 20

After working late every night in the consumer unit her first week, Sophea attempts to make it home on time for Friday night dinner with Cookie and her grandmother.

"You're late!" says Chas Mai as Sophea opens the front door. "I was just about to ask your mom to call the police and file a missing person's report."

"I told you I had a pre-holiday networking event at the National Press Club this evening," Sophea says.

"What do you do at these events?" Cookie perks up. "Do the men wear suits?"

"People meet each other, grab a drink or something to eat, and get to know each other," Sophea explains. "It's how you build a career."

"It sounds like a party to me," Cookie says. "I want to go!"

"If these networking events help you so much," Chas Mai asks, "then why are you always complaining about work?"

"You just don't understand." Sophea reaches for her purse. "It's an American thing. You have to put yourself 'out there' if you want to be in the know. Here, look at my business card." She takes out two cards and gives them to the women.

"You hand out all this personal information to strangers you meet at a party?" Cookie reads the card carefully. "We never did that in our day."

"That's inviting danger into your life." Chas Mai's face is crimson. "There must be better ways to meet men than to throw yourself at them at work."

"What Sophea is saying is that these people are more important than us." Cookie looks unimpressed. "That's why she's late for dinner."

"You two and Ravy are the most important people in my life," Sophea says. "Speaking of Ravy, where is she tonight?"

"She's working late again," Chas Mai says. "I'm worried about her. She's getting too thin."

"Only in America is obesity considered a problem." Cookie walks over to the bookshelf. "While people around the world are starving, all you girls want to do is lose weight. I will never understand." Cookie recalls an incident in her childhood when she was eating a big bowl of steaming hot white rice with two delicious barbequed ribs on the outdoor steps of her parents' home. It was monsoon season, and the rainfall made the food taste even more delicious and satisfying. Cookie had placed her bowl on the steps for just a few minutes to go grab a glass of water.

When she returned, a maid had taken her bowl back to the kitchen to be washed. "I thought the princess had finished her meal," the maid explained. "There were only a couple of kernels of rice left in the bowl. I am so very sorry." Cookie recalls how she begged for more food, only to hear her mother say, "You have had more than your share. A princess must always show restraint when it comes to eating. You do not want to look like a glutton." Chas Mai's lesson had an unintended consequence on her daughter. From that day on, Cookie always felt hungry no matter how much food she ate.

"It's called healthy living, Mom. Why don't we start taking a thirty-minute walk together in the morning to get your blood pumping?" Sophea marches in place and swings her arms from side to side.

Cookie pulls out a book on the jewels of England's royal families. "If I want to get my blood pumping, I can read up on what's happening with the royal court back home. You know they have a website now."

"Mom, you're obsessed with the royal family," Sophea says. "Don't you know nobody cares about that here in the States?"

"You are part of that royal family, too," Cookie reminds her daughter. "Why deny your blue blood?"

"It might have mattered back in the day," Sophea says. "But in America, royalty doesn't mean much. Especially when you come from a third-world country and don't have any money."

"It's not our fault we lost everything in the war," Cookie says. "You should be proud of your family instead of always trying to hide from it. Your grandfather was raised in the same palace as King Sihanouk. He was like a brother to the king—"

"Let's not argue right now, when we should be celebrating," Chas Mai interrupts. "Come into the kitchen, Sophea. We have something for you!"

Sophea relents and follows her grandmother into the kitchen. It smells like Chas Mai's massaman beef curry with peanuts. "Yum, I love this curry," she says, putting her head over the pot and taking in a deep breath. "I wonder if they have ever tested curry powder as a form of aromatherapy." She takes a piece of French bread and scoops up a mouthful.

"I put in extra garlic and fish sauce tonight," Chas Mai explains. "Are you planning to see Tim? Americans can't stand two smells—fish sauce and durian." Sophea visualizes the spiky Southeast Asian fruit that some say stinks of old gym socks.

Cookie glides into the kitchen and places a small, silver box in the center of the kitchen table. "This is for you, from me and Chas Mai. It has been in our family for many years. We hope you will like it." She walks over to Chas Mai, who is stirring the curry; the two women beam.

Sophea opens the silver box and pulls out a huge ruby, jade, and diamond ring that resembles an art deco building in New York City. She slides the ring onto her right middle finger and it sits like a giant skyscraper of colorful gems on her slim, tan hand. "Wow—this is a mega-ring," Sophea says politely.

"I have been waiting more than twenty years to give this to you," Cookie says. "You're a woman now. It's time men know how much you are worth. Consider this an early Christmas gift!"

Does everything have to be related to men? Sophea extends her hand, then brings it back closer to her face, "It's so big, it's like IMAX in 3-D."

"We couldn't smuggle much out when we left Cambodia," Cookie says. "But I wore this ring right past the military police at the airport. This ring made me unstoppable."

"Your mom thinks the ring helped us escape the war," Chas Mai says. "Since it has been a few months now that you and Tim have been together, we hope this ring will bear great blessings for you and Tim."

"Is this what this is all about—a man?" Sophea is exasperated. "I just met him!" She wonders whether she should explain to Chas Mai and Cookie that she and Tim have not spoken since their fight. She wants to tell them the truth, but having a reprieve from their constant pressure on her to find a mate has been *heaven*. Sophea chooses to keep the façade of a strong relationship between her and Tim going in exchange for some peace of mind.

"When it comes to men, size matters," Cookie says. "Tim needs to know you will not settle for anything but the finest luxuries in this world."

Chas Mai strokes Sophea's hair. "One day you will get married to a nice, young man who loves you. This ring will help make that happen faster. Trust its power."

The Sorceresses of Phnom Penh, Sophea thinks. She gives both her mother and her grandmother a grateful hug. "I want an awesome career. Getting married is the last thing on my mind," she says. "Anyway, you can't make a man love me. He needs to do that on his own."

"A man sometimes needs some nudging." Chas Mai elbows Cookie.

"I wish I was sixteen again and back in Cambodia with hundreds of suitors lining up at our front door," Cookie responds with a frown. "A little competition keeps a man on his toes. The bigger the ring, the more he loves you."

Instead of arguing the virtues of feminism with her mother, Sophea leans over and kisses her on the cheek. "Thanks to both of you for always thinking of me. This is the biggest, most magnificent ring I've ever seen in my whole life!" The three women sit around the kitchen table and pass around the bowls of steaming rice and curry. Cookie and Chas Mai bask in the glory of their gift.

Chapter 21

Gifting Sophea with the ring brings back a flood of memories for Cookie, many of them joyous, others filled with pain. Looking at the cherished heirloom makes Cookie long to be back in the arms of her beloved husband. She wants once again to be the star of her own romance, being seduced by her knight in shining armor who was, after all, just a poor farm boy from an obscure Cambodian village. On their first encounter, Vaing had given her a gift and won her heart. It was love at first sight.

In 1966, Cookie was twenty-two years old and indisputably the most desired princess in Cambodia. After her presentation during the visit from Charles de Gaulle, suitors lined up to have a chance at the princess who spoke fluent French and had gained the admiration of the great foreign statesman. For upper-class Cambodians, speaking French was the sign of a privileged and reputable upbringing. Only the most cultured and educated Cambodians in the small, elite community of royals and wealthy families had access to French nannies and tutors.

Several princes from the royal family courted Cookie with promises of wealth and a grandiose life filled with beautiful jewels, exotic cars, and abiding servants who would honor her role as the princess of the household. Cookie relished the idea of being treated like a true royal, since both her parents always seemed to downplay that factor in their lives. *What is the point of being born with blue blood if you are told to act like a commoner?*

"Do not think that you will end up with one of those royal suitors," her father scolded. "They are quick to feed your ego and fill your head with visions of a life that once was, but we are on the verge of a major class war. Marrying princes who have been schooled in nothing practical except bragging about their ancestry and commanding servants will do you no good in this modern day. What you need is a simple, honest man who is willing to work hard and love you for who you are as a person. If the monarchy collapses—which it has done before—the title of princess will mean little to anyone but you."

"Listen to your father, dear child," Chas Mai said. "Should anything happen to Cambodia in the future, you will need an educated, resilient man who is not afraid of change and can help you rebuild a life—wherever that may be. Your father and I believe an engineer or a doctor is the best kind of husband for our daughters, since there will always be a need for them in this world. And they make the most money." She smiled at her husband.

"Are you saying you want me and my sisters to marry commoners?" cried a confused Cookie. "I thought it was important that we carry on the Norodom name and continue the royal bloodline! Marrying a prince is a guarantee that I will be part of the grandeur that you and Mother have been a part of for all these years."

From the moment Prince Sihanouk was crowned king of Cambodia in 1941, Sophea's parents had always been a part of His Highness's "inner circle." They were invited to the palace every day for dinners and dancing. Only the most prestigious Cambodians were included in these decadent gatherings that reminded Cookie of what Henry VIII's court must have been like. Watching her parents get ready to go to the palace since she was a little girl, Cookie knew she wanted that same fate. *I want to be a part of the royal court. It is my destiny.*

"My job as a father is to protect my children from unexpected harm," Cookie's father continued. "The best way I know how to do that right now is to ensure you marry a man with proven skills and abilities that are valued in the real world. Your mother and I agree that the best husband for you in this day and age will be a common man who has the tenacity to succeed in life on his own two feet. He will be a perfect complement to the royal princess that you are. Together, you will be the best of both worlds. Please trust us."

One evening, the general called his daughter to the living room, where her mother was seated on their formal sofa, her hands crossed on her lap. Next to her was an older couple and a young man about ten years older than Cookie. He was taller than most Cambodian men—about five-foot-ten—and he wore a custom-fitted black suit with a thin blue tie. His mannerism was traditional, but he carried himself differently than any other man she had ever met.

"Chanthavy, we would like for you to meet Vaing Lim and his parents." Her father waved at her to paun at this kind, but modest-looking family. "Vaing has just finished getting his master's in engineering from the University of Georgia in America. He is fluent in French and English. He is filled with many stories from his life as a student in America."

Vaing stared at Chanthavy from behind his black-rimmed glasses. Chanthavy could not help but think that this strange man looked like some kind of movie actor. She was immediately starstruck. His dark brown eyes took her breath away. She smiled graciously and peered down at her bare feet.

"It is my greatest pleasure to finally meet you," Vaing said. "Even in America, we who went to study abroad heard about the princess who rendered Charles de Gaulle speechless." He smiled and looked directly at the general.

"Tell me, Vaing," challenged the general. "As a poor boy from Kampong Cham, why do you think you are good enough to marry our daughter? She is a beautiful and sought-after princess. You are a commoner." He took a swig of whiskey.

"All my life, I have known that my fate would be larger than the life I was born into," Vaing explained. "My parents may be poor and humble, but they are as pure and solid as the ground that we stand on. They taught me from the moment that I was born that I am responsible for my future. I never saw limitations in my surroundings or my lack of wealth. Every day was an opportunity to work hard and give back to the land. Early on, I had a knack for numbers and figuring out problems. I knew that if anything, I had been blessed with the ability to think and never settle. I do not live life with fear of what I cannot do, I think of the possibilities that are in front of me, including attaining your daughter as my wife. I know that I would be a devoted husband to her. I could provide for her and our children. If she can look past the fact that I am a commoner only by name, I will love your daughter with every ounce of my soul, as well as honor your great family name. I promise to take care of Princess Chanthavy as the royal jewel that she is—that will never get lost on me."

The general looked at his daughter with a sparkle in his eye. "Well, that sounds very convincing to me. I admire a young man with gumption and ambition." Turning back to Vaing, he said, "Now, I will leave it up to my daughter to decide for herself whether you are worthy of her. Her mother and I have raised her to think for herself. If you can win over my daughter's heart, then you will have our blessing."

Vaing pulled a record album from under his legs and said to Chanthavy, "I hear you like music and dancing. Here is the latest album from a band that I think you will enjoy very much. They are called The Beatles. I play the guitar and am trying to learn how to play their songs. Perhaps I can play them for you one day." He handed her the gift and captured Chanthavy's heart. *I see nothing "common" in Vaing*, she thought. *He is more regal and chivalrous than any prince I could ever marry.*

It took only two more meetings before the princess agreed to marry the poor farm boy from Kampong Cham. Once Chanthavy made her decision to love Vaing, she never looked back. No one else had managed to steal her heart and keep her wanting more every day. Vaing adored Chanthavy and promised that he would love her and keep her safe forever.

But Vaing hadn't kept his promise. He had kept her safe, but not himself. The old familiar pain crept into her heart before she could shut it off. Wiping away a tear, Cookie composed herself and walked to the kitchen to see what Chas Mai had to eat.

Chapter 22

Inspired by Cookie's and Chas Mai's ring antics, Sophea decides to call Tim, and he picks up the phone this time. "Hi, honey. It's me, Sophea. It's been over a week since our fight, and I haven't heard from you once. I'm really sorry that we argued. Can we please talk?"

"Listen, I can't talk right now," Tim responds. "My secretary is calling me right now. I gotta run." She hears a woman's voice in the background.

"Sweetheart, we need to talk and smooth things over." Sophea looks down at her ring. "Anyway, I want to show you something. Can you come over Saturday night?" *That's strange. He doesn't usually work this late.*

"This has been a really hard week, and I'm exhausted," Tim says. "Can we talk next week instead? I think I still need some time apart."

"No, please come over Saturday," Sophea says. "I'll be waiting for you. I can't wait to see you. Please don't stand me up." She hangs up the phone. *This man does not love you. He even said it to your face. How much more humiliation and rejection will you endure in the name of love? You are weak and pathetic. Yes, I am. For him.*

Saturday evening comes, and Cookie is waiting at the front door when Tim arrives at the house. "It's been a while since we've seen you," she says with a sly grin. "Do you have something special up your sleeve tonight for our little Sophea? She's all dressed up for you."

Tim throws a confused glance over at Cookie, does not greet her with a paun, and says to Sophea, "Let's get going." He does not return his girlfriend's warm embrace.

The couple heads out the door, and it is drizzling outside. The streets are busy with Friday night partygoers and holiday shoppers. Sophea pushes her head back and catches a droplet of rain on her tongue. The rain feels good on her face, but she worries that it might also ruin her makeup. Sophea grabs Tim's hand. *Maybe this will help him relax.*

They stroll hand in hand on Wilson Boulevard toward their favorite restaurant, Little Saigon. Sophea is overdressed, but she plans to take Tim to the top of the Key Bridge Marriott overlooking the Potomac and Georgetown later tonight, which she thinks will be romantic and sweet.

"Are you okay? You're so quiet tonight," Sophea says to Tim. "I know you're still upset with me. I hope we can make things right between us again." She clings to his arm.

Tim pulls her into the entrance of the Rosslyn Metro Station, which provides them with some shelter from the pounding rain. "Sophea, I can't do this anymore. I don't want to have dinner with you and act like everything's okay, because it's not. You're an emotional wreck, and I think you have a codependency issue with your family. It's not normal."

Sophea looks around at the rush-hour frenzy taking place around them. Serious faces, stiff bodies sporting black and tan raincoats. Everyone is in a suit. This is Washington, DC—ambitious, fast, educated, and worldly college grads, all probably working for senators, public relations firms, or government agencies. She sees Tim's mouth moving in slow motion and thinks to herself, *Is this jerk breaking up with me in a public transit station during rush hour?*

"Where is all this coming from?" Sophea pleads. "I know we got into a fight, but it doesn't have to be the end of our relationship."

"This past week gave me some time to realize that we don't belong together," Tim explains. "You're right, I must be a racist because there are some fundamental differences in our cultures that I can't get over."

Sophea interrupts. "I misspoke—you're not a racist. You just need a little diversity training. It's challenging to date someone with a different background than what you're used to. We can work through this."

"Listen, I don't want to be with a woman who still lives with her mother and grandmother," Tim says. "This multigenerational thing doesn't work for me."

"If we get married, of course I would move out of my family's house to be with you," Sophea argues back.

"My family's quiet and reserved. We see each other on holidays and special occasions. That's more than enough for me," Tim says. "Your family is loud, late, and everyone has to be together all the time. It's like a roving pack of Asians everywhere we go."

"Are you ashamed to be with me?" Sophea asks. "My family can't be the only reason you want to break up."

"I've wanted to tell you this for a while, but we never have any privacy at your house. Your mom and grandmother are always watching us, hovering around the doorways and stairwells. It's like a prison state in your home, but that doesn't seem to bother you."

"How long have you been thinking about this?" Sophea spits out her words. "Why didn't you say something sooner? I thought we were just in a fight. I was hoping that you would call me and try to fix it, but you didn't. Can't we talk through this? I know we can make this right again. I love you. Please don't break up with me!" Chas Mai's voice rings in her head. "*Never, ever let a man hear you beg. He must come running after you, or he will never fully value your worth.*"

"Let's get something straight. You never loved me. And we were never in love," Tim clarifies. "I've met someone else. Her name is Angela. I told her about our fight, when you accused me of being a bigot and a sex offender. Those are violent words and she helped me get through the emotional pain and anguish of being compared to a monster. Angela saved me from years and thousands of dollars' worth of therapy."

"Who's Angela? It hasn't been that long since our fight, so I don't quite understand what you're saying." Sophea puts her hand to her heart to squelch the pain. "Are you cheating on me?"

"You ordered me out of your house and threatened to call the police if I didn't leave," Tim counters. "You're the one that broke us up. Anyway, it's not like we were that serious. You never loved me; you love your work."

"Stop lying, we never broke up. We just got into a bad fight." Sophea's heart is breaking into a million little pieces. "You still haven't answered my question about Angela. How did she get involved with us?"

Tim reaches out a hand to console her. "When you threw me out and you didn't call me the next day like you normally do after we fight, I thought we were over. Angela comforted me when I needed support. The magical thing is, I think I'm falling in love with her. It's not something I can control."

"You're lying to me," Sophea sputters. "Have you two already slept with each other? Is this your way of punishing me?"

"Don't blame Angela when this is about you and me," Tim says. "The truth is that Angela and I have a very deep emotional and physical connection that you and I never had. Can't you be happy for us?"

"Oh my gosh, you are so cold." Sophea is sobbing deliriously. "All I know is my heart is burning right now and you get to move on to someone new while I'm left all alone. That's not fair. You made the move on me first, and now you're ditching me?"

Sophea takes one final, deep breath and then slaps her hand across his cheek, leaving a red mark. Before he can react, she flees the scene, leaving Tim alone and relieved on the rainy street.

Chapter 23

Sophea is now in her own romantic comedy gone awry. With mascara running down her face, she eerily resembles Bette Davis's character in the 1960s cult classic *What Ever Happened to Baby Jane?* Sophea's "lucky" Louboutins are beginning to cause blisters, and she questions whether dry-cleaning can fix her soaking dress. *I hate him. I hate him. I hate him. May he and Angela drown slowly in a fiery pot of curry*, becomes her mantra as she runs barefoot in the rain across the Key Bridge.

No man will break my heart, Sophea empowers herself. *I won't allow it. If Chas Mai and Mom could survive losing their husbands in the war, I can get over a cheating scoundrel!* She cowers at the sound of thunder in the sky above her. There is bumper-to-bumper traffic on the bridge. A black Honda Civic pulls past her, and a group of guys yells, "Need a ride, pretty lady?"

Sophea shivers as cold rain pellets hit her bare arms. *I want to go home.* Still seething, Sophea aims her middle finger at the carload of men. "I'm your mother, sister, or girlfriend. Leave me alone!" She hails a taxi home.

⋘ ❧ ⋙

Sophea tiptoes past Chas Mai and Cookie, who have fallen asleep in front of the television set. On the screen, Sam is singing "As Time Goes By" from *Casablanca*. Sophea scampers into her bedroom and turns the lock. She throws her wet dress onto the bathroom floor and jumps into a hot shower. *Why? Why does this have to hurt so bad?* Sophea lets the warm water defrost her frozen hands.

Sophea puts on her favorite adult onesie and reaches under the bed for her "comfort" basket filled with Snickers bars, caramel popcorn, and peanut M&M's. She turns on the television and catches the end of a French cult favorite, *Betty Blue*, and then settles in to watch as *One Flew Over the Cuckoo's Nest* comes on.

"*I love him. I love him. I love him. We're perfect for each other. I can't live without him. Why me???!!*" she mumbles out loud between bites of stale popcorn.

Suddenly, she notices a text message from Tim on her phone that reads, "*Stay strong.*" Sophea dials his number and it goes directly into voice mail: "Hi, this is Tim. Leave me a message or stock tip. See ya!" "I hate you" is all Sophea can muster up in between sobs.

Sophea, unable to stop herself, proceeds to war-dial Tim into the wee hours of the morning. Part of her knows she's being ridiculous, but part of her also wants Tim to acknowledge the pain he's caused. "Where are you?" she asks into the phone, aware of her own desperation. "I've called you nine times and each time I got your voice mail. Do not play games with me. You're a coldhearted snake for teasing me with a text, then turning off the phone." She puts a few more Snickers in her mouth.

Fifteen minutes later, Sophea leaves one final message. "I want to clarify one last thing, Tim. You didn't dump me. I threw you out of my house, and I'm glad I did it. Tonight, I will cry my eyes out for you because my ego's hurt. But tomorrow, you will be yesterday's news to me. Good-bye." Somewhere between the last bites of chocolate peanut clusters, Sophea's body falls into a deep food coma.

That night, Sophea dreams that she is traveling the world in search of something she's lost. She travels to China and walks the entire length of the Great Wall but can't find the object she is seeking. She takes a plane to Paris and climbs the Eiffel Tower, but nothing appears. She swims across the ocean to Hawaii and searches for it in the sea, but she ends up empty-handed. Her final destination is a small village in Tibet, where Sophea chases a faceless man down a mountain path but she can't seem to catch up to him. She runs into an old lady on the road who says to her, "Why are you trying to chase that man down, when you gave it to him so freely?"

"I don't understand," Sophea replies. "Why won't that man give me what is mine?"

"Foolish girl, you gave him your power," the old lady responds. "In your blind pursuit of love and companionship, you relinquished your true self to someone who did not deserve it. You must learn to love and stay in your power. That is the only way for true love to flourish. No man will respect you if you are weak and give yourself away."

⁂

Later that evening, Chas Mai and Cookie sneak open Sophea's bedroom door and see her stretched diagonally across the bed, surrounded by a sea of candy wrappers and tissues.

"Why does she make so much noise when she sleeps?" Cookie asks. "Do you think she has sleep apnea?"

"Busy night, these young people." Chas Mai pulls the covers over Sophea's bare feet. "No, I think she's congested from a cold. I told her to cover up from the rain and of course, she didn't listen. We'll ask her what happened tomorrow."

Chapter 24

"So, let me get this straight, he cheated on you with another woman and you left him almost a dozen voice mails begging him to take you back?" Ravy tries to steady her voice. "That is like stalker territory. Why are you being so pathetic? You should have called me instead!"

"I'm heartbroken and have fallen into a well of utter despair," Sophea says. "Please go easy on me while I'm hurting." Her head collapses onto the table, and she starts to cry. They are at their favorite French café on Wisconsin Avenue.

"Honestly, I don't know what you ever saw in that man," Ravy says. "He was arrogant, offensive, and all-around insensitive at times. Why do you put up with that kind of behavior?"

"Call me shallow, but I thought he was drop-dead gorgeous," Sophea responds. "We were so physically attracted to each other, and I let that chemistry get the best of me. I promise I will never let myself fall so fast for a man ever again. I feel like such a fool." She drops her head back onto the table.

"Oh, sis." Ravy leans over to kiss her head. "I know it hurts. I hate seeing you like this. But even for you, this is a bit overdramatic. You weren't together that long, and I don't think it was true love. Your ego's bruised, that's all."

"He wasn't supposed to break up with *me*. I want him even more, now that he rejected me. I am a weak, weak woman," Sophea surmises. "Where's the waiter? Give me my salad Niçoise or I will go crazy." She summons the waiter, who takes their lunch order.

"Good riddance. He was a jerk anyway," Ravy continues. "He never respected our family. You deserve better."

"He was very resentful of my relationship with mom and Chas Mai," Sophea says. "He doesn't understand why we all have to live together." She takes a gulp of mineral water.

"Well, he's got a good point there," Ravy says. "Living at home can't possibly help your dating situation. I think it's time for you to put on your big girl panties and move out on your own."

Ravy shows Sophea an article she found, titled "The 20-Day Plan." "The theory is that it takes twenty days to change a habit. Instead of wasting your time thinking about Tim, start a new exercise plan, write that book you've always wanted to write, or start planning your move. The goal is to forget about him."

"I appreciate your 'to do' list, but can't you see I'm still suffering?" Sophea responds. "Not all of us were born with hearts of steel. I need more time to heal."

"Arrghh, stop being so weak," Ravy retorts. "Why must you always act the victim? You're my older sister, but I feel like I have to take care of you all the time. It's exhausting. We're always dealing with your drama. When was the last time you asked me about my life?"

"I'm your biggest fan in every way!" Sophea insists. "I have never missed one of your art shows, and I am always defending you when the hens attack. Chas Mai is always saying that you date too many people. You know that a good Cambodian girl does not do that."

"I won't apologize for being picky," Ravy explains. "As a matter of fact, this new online dating thing is perfect for me. It almost *encourages* serial dating when you have so many choices at your fingertips. You should try it."

"Okay, so can I go home with you after this?" Sophea pleads. "I haven't said anything to Chas Mai or Mom about me and Tim. I don't want them to know yet."

"You're going to have to tell them the truth sooner or later." Ravy takes a bite of her quiche. "They are going to hit the roof, but you can't run and hide like a six year old."

"So, does that mean I can go hide at your house today?" Sophea says. "I need some time to figure out how to deliver this information without giving Chas Mai a heart attack."

"You can come over, but you have to stay really quiet," Ravy says. "I have a phone date with a Moroccan man I met online. You can't act grossed out if we start talking dirty."

"Ewww, that's not possible," Sophea says. "I think I'll go check out a matinee instead. Maybe Chas Mai is right about your dating habits."

"You're turning into Little Chas Mai," Ravy says. "You shouldn't let her old-fashioned values interfere with your modern love life. Take a risk sometimes."

"I had the strangest dream last night where I traveled the world searching for something I couldn't identify," Sophea explains. "In the end, I was in Tibet chasing a faceless man who had what I wanted. A little old lady told me I had given all my power away to him in the name of love and he was never going to give it back to me. I think the takeaway is that I really need to be more confident in relationships and feel my own worth. Maybe I need to take some time to focus on me and what I want in life. I'm going on a man hiatus until I find my power again."

"Hallelujah! I've been trying to tell you that all these years, and it takes an old Tibetan lady in your dreams for you to get it?" Ravy exclaims. "Whatever works. Are you sure it wasn't just heartburn?"

As the sisters exit the restaurant, Ravy grabs Sophea's hand. "I know I'm tough on you. You've got a bigger heart than me, and I just don't want to see you get hurt all the time. I love you. I wish you had more confidence in yourself. My cup runneth over. Please take some of mine anytime." She laughs and heads toward the Metro station.

Chapter 25

After another busy day at the office, Sophea stumbles to the living room sofa and turns on the television. She rubs her swollen ankles with some tiger balm and clicks through the channel listings. Her breakup mantra repeats itself in her head like a broken record: *Do not call Tim. Do not call Tim.*

Sophea is just placing the bucket of fried chicken she picked up for dinner on her lap when Chas Mai and Cookie corner her. "You have been avoiding us. What's going on?"

Nightmare, Sophea thinks. Out loud, she says, "Please, I'm exhausted. Can we talk another time?" *I hope Mom's not hungry. There's not enough chicken to feed all of us.*

"No, we are talking right now." Chas Mai raises her voice. "Where is Tim? Why have we not seen him in a while?"

Sophea licks the salty crumbs off her face and responds, "He broke up with me. He doesn't want to get married. He has a girlfriend. There's nothing else to report right now." She keeps chewing.

"I knew it," Cookie blurts out. "I knew you couldn't keep him long enough to get married." *That child is so stubborn. How will she ever get married if she cannot compromise?*

"This is not possible," cries Chas Mai. "Do you know how many hours I have prayed to Buddha that you two would get married? This is a huge betrayal."

"What are you talking about?" asks Sophea with dismay. "This is between me and him. It's *my* relationship with *my* boyfriend. You two really have no say. If anything, you should be supporting me and comforting me right now."

"This is an embarrassment for our family," Cookie says firmly. "We told everyone you are engaged. We already started planning the wedding. The monk has been reserved, and a tailor has been hired to help you with your wedding costumes. I even paid extra money to hold the best Cambodian caterer in town. She has already started rolling and freezing the spring rolls for your wedding!"

"How could you do that without my consent?" Sophea blurts out. "Being dumped at the Metro stop is humiliating enough. I'm still trying to understand what happened between us. He blindsided me on Friday."

"You do not think of us or the family," Cookie continues. "You have dishonored us by not doing what it takes to keep him. How will we ever show ourselves at the pagoda again? Cambodians do not break engagements. This is just not how it is done. Have you no shame?"

"But we were *never* engaged," Sophea says, exasperated. "And he cheated on me!" *Mom has totally lost it. How dare she make up lies about me to bolster her public image?*

"You two misled the family by being a couple and acting like you were heading toward marriage when you were with us," Cookie says. "Men cheat. Women deal with it. There are more important things to worry about, like where he was educated, what he does for a living, and whether he can provide for you and the family! Men may stray, but they don't leave if you can turn a blind eye."

"I cannot believe my ears right now," Sophea says. "This is not how you raised me and Ravy. What are you saying? You can't possibly be condoning cheating?"

"Men need a lot of attention and care. Did you spend as much time tending to Tim's needs as you do your job?" Chas Mai asks. "Don't be angry—that is a fair question." Sophea responds with an eye roll and a sigh.

A long time ago, Chas Mai accepted that in exchange for being married to a prince who gave her prestige and wealth beyond what she could imagine in her life, she would have to accept his love of other women. The first time she encountered her husband in bed with one of the young housekeepers, he simply responded, "My commitment and devotion are with you, but with all your obligations to the children and keeping up the household, you are in no position to satisfy me as a man in the way that I need to be satisfied. I will not fault you for your lack of amorous affection if you do not fault me for pursuing what you cannot give to me."

❧ ❧ ❧

Chas Mai and Cookie are near tears and comforting each other. "How can she be almost forty and not married? What did we do wrong? What will we tell the family? What will we tell the caterer and seamstress?"

Cookie reaches into the bucket and chomps one of Sophea's chicken wings. Sophea has cried too many of her own tears over the last few days; she picks up a chicken wing from the bucket. "Wait, I just turned thirty, and *I'm* the one who went through the breakup—not the two of you," Sophea says. "Stop scolding me and making me feel bad. Please leave, my show is about to start." *I knew Mom was going to eat my food!*

"How dare you speak to me and Chas Mai that way!" Cookie screams. "We raised you! Did you forget that? We are still here when Tim is gone. This is how you treat us? You dishonor me, and you dishonor Chas Mai!" The whole time she is yelling, sauce from the chicken wing is dangling from her lower lip.

"I don't owe you an explanation!" Sophea is crying now. "How is *my* failed relationship an insult to *you*?" She excuses herself and runs into her room.

The two women huddle in the kitchen. Chas Mai says, "Buddha will punish Tim for breaking our Sophea's heart. How can you trust a man who doesn't eat garlic?"

Cookie is still enraged. *How dare Sophea yell at me like I'm just nobody in her life? Daughters do not raise their voices toward their mothers. This would never happen in Cambodia.* Cookie remembers a treacherous July day when she was twelve years old. The heat of monsoon season made her irritable, and she gave her father an attitude when he asked her to get him a glass of water. Cookie's father promptly sent her out to stand under the burning morning sun like a human scarecrow in the middle of the rice paddies with both of her arms lifted in the air. After two hours, Cookie's arms burned so badly from the pain of having to keep them elevated that she was convinced her limbs would fall right off. She longed for rain to cool down on her aching body, but the rains would not begin until later in the afternoon.

Her father warned from a lounge chair under the banana tree that if she dared drop her arms, he would add another hour to the punishment. Cookie cried so hard that morning that her salty tears burned a small indentation on her cheek that followed her to adulthood. However, her father's cruel but creative punishment worked wonders. Cookie never dared raise her voice at her father or mother ever again. From that day forward, a couple of her sisters gave her the nickname "Her Royal Scarecrow."

Chapter 26

"Chas Mai and Cookie hate me." Sophea blows her nose into a shredded tissue. "I feel really bad about this. It just eats me up that I'm causing them grief." She frowns at Ravy, who has joined her at their favorite local bar in Georgetown.

"What has happened now?" Ravy waves for the bartender to take their order. "Why do you let Mom and Chas Mai treat you like a child? You're feeding in to the centuries-old Asian teaching that the young must always respect their elders—even when the elders are misbehaving. That's not realistic."

As the handsome bartender serves Sophea her Diet Coke, Ravy throws back her shot glass and says, "You're gorgeous, and I'd like another if that's alright." He returns with another glass. "This one's on me, sweetie."

Sophea stares at Ravy with admiration and envy. "Ever since you were little, Chas Mai and Mom gave you a pass to do whatever you wanted. Remember when you dyed your hair green and red one Christmas, or when you refused to go to piano lessons and took up skateboarding instead?"

"Yeah, Chas Mai was not too thrilled about that." Ravy smiles. "Mom was also livid when I decided to go to our community college instead of a traditional four-year college. I think she actually went to the pagoda to seek counsel from the monk that day."

"Well, if it makes you feel any better, Chas Mai was afraid I would turn into a lesbian when I went to an all-women's college." Sophea laughs. "Now, she can't stop telling everyone Hillary Clinton went to Wellesley College, too!"

"Listen, they weren't as easy on me as you think. I just fought back a little harder than you did," Ravy explains. "When they screamed at me, I yelled back. When they threatened to cut my hair, I shaved it all off. When they threatened to send me to the pagoda for a week of 'discipline and cleansing,' I moved out. We had some rough times between us."

"Wow, I had no idea all that happened," Sophea replies. "I never dared talk back to Mom because she scares me. One wrong word and that princess temperament of hers would flare. It was just too stressful for me."

"Ha! I loved it," Ravy says. "We're both the Year of the Dog, so bring on the dogfight." She motions for the cute bartender to bring them a menu.

"Sophea, does it bother you that every Friday night you have 'movie night' with Chas Mai and Mom?" Ravy asks. "It's cute to see you three 'hens' laughing it up and munching on fried rice and Doritos. However, I think your senior discount card is not arriving for another thirty years."

"Can you please not lecture me today?" Sophea responds. "What I need right now is nonjudgmental, unconditional love from my only sister in the world." She takes a bite of her Caesar salad.

"Remember your first date with Tim? This new guy comes to pick you up at the house and has to enjoy happy hour with two old Asian ladies. They entice him with a cold bottle of Singha beer, then grill him about his intentions. What's up with that?" Ravy is indignant.

"They were all just trying to be nice with one another," Sophea explains. "Anyway, I think Tim appreciated the free drinks, now that I think about how cheap he was sometimes."

"You're going to grow old and wrinkled alongside Chas Mai and Cookie if you don't make a stand for your own life soon. The difference is, they both had a chance at their own lives, with their own husbands and households. It's not cool that they're not letting you have yours. Enough with the martyrdom, Sophea."

Sophea changes the subject and asks Ravy about her work. "So, tell me about that grant you just got from the East Asian Foundation. That is too exciting!"

"I'm going to present a high-tech art exhibit titled *Apsara and Beyond: The Dancing Goddesses of Angkor Wat*." Ravy's voice gets fast. "In addition to my artwork, I'm trying to get the Royal Cambodian Ballet Troupe to come to America and perform their famous Apsara dance. They've never been to the States before, so we can also use this event as a fundraiser!"

"Oh my goodness, you are brilliant!" Sophea exclaims. "I love Apsara! She is the quintessential Cambodian female deity. Almost like an Asian Aphrodite. Your event is going to sell out. Maybe I can get Edie to emcee the event if you want a local celebrity. I'm sure the station can send over a camera crew to tape the event."

"You would do that for me?" Ravy lets out a high-pitched scream. "I just have to find a location for the event and some kind of backdrop of the Angkor Wat temples to set the mood. That's the one thing the ballet director requested." Ravy looks down at her watch and waves for the check. "Speaking of which, I gotta get back to the studio to meet with a set designer," she says. "Don't waste any more time thinking about Tim. Channel that energy and think about moving out. My landlord has an apartment opening up just a couple of floors below mine that would be perfect for you."

"Do you really want me living that close to you?" Sophea asks with a smile. "Is there at least room for a couple of extra cots if Chas Mai and Mom want to spend the night? You're asking me to go cold turkey here on my living arrangement."

"I have faith in you and an extra night-light if you're afraid of the dark." Ravy laughs, kissing Sophea on the cheek. "I'm going to start charging you for these lunchtime therapy sessions."

Chapter 27

"Nail salon fumes—should you be concerned for your health? We ask local experts about how to protect yourself and your cuticles the next time you get your nails professionally done." Edie waves a couple of bottles of nail polish in front of the camera. "Join me, Edie Brown, tonight at six for WNR's investigative report on the dangers of nail salons."

"Cut! That's excellent, Edie," Sophea exclaims. "Three more teasers and we're done." She walks across the studio floor to give additional instructions to the camerawoman.

Since her big fight with Chas Mai and Cookie, work has been a refuge for Sophea. May Sweeps Month is just a few weeks away, and she is writing as many consumer stories as Edie is capable of delivering on camera. "Smoothies: Fat or Fab?" "Technology Tip of the Week," "Debunking Salmonella and Other Food Scares," and "Credit Score 101" are just a few of the many scripts she has in the can.

"It's great to do fun feature stories like 'Summer's Hottest Toys' or 'An Organic Taste Test,'" Sophea tells Edie. "But to make a real impression in May, we need a harder-hitting, investigative story that'll catch our viewers' attention. Maybe something on identity theft or Internet scamming, which can cause people to lose a lot of money. What do you think?" She continues to flip through Dale's old Rolodex of contacts.

"Honestly, I'm a little bored myself," Edie responds. "Let's brainstorm some more ideas later this afternoon. I need to make an important call right now." She takes off her microphone and snatches a manila folder off the anchor desk.

"Wait for me. I'm going back upstairs, too," Sophea says. "You seem distracted all of a sudden. Are you okay?"

Edie pushes the door into the stairwell and pauses for a minute. "Am I okay? No, I'm not," she blurts out. "I'm mad and frustrated with management. They treat our consumer unit like the ugly redheaded stepchild. I want to go back to my old station." She pulls back her auburn hair into a ponytail.

"Don't you dare leave me," Sophea says. "We're just starting to hit our groove. I promise it will get better. This all just takes some time. Please be patient, Grasshopper."

"With all due respect, Sophea, you're here for a while and then you're going to leave," Edie says. "Where will that leave me then? Here, alone, trying to restart with another producer? It gets old after a while. Work is no longer fun for me."

"That's not true. I want to stay here for the long-term," Sophea replies. "I promise I won't desert you. It's been a few months and Don hasn't closed us down yet."

"Sophea, you and I are newsroom throwaways," Edie says with a solemn face. "No one really cares about us here. We've been shunned into the grungiest, darkest office way in the back of the station. If we died, no one would even know."

"Okay, now you're being ridiculous," Sophea says. "The stench of our decaying bodies would eventually make its way downstairs to the newsroom. Trust me—they would not be able to ignore us."

"You can joke all you want, but I have a call with my old news director in a few minutes," Edie says. "I'm just exploring opportunities, but I would like a bit of privacy right now, if you don't mind." With that, she waves good-bye and closes the door to her tiny office.

Sophea stares at the closed door for a minute, then makes a call to the Washington, DC, Bureau of Consumer Affairs. "Hello, this is Sophea Lim with WNR-TV's Consumer and Investigative Unit. May I please speak with your director?" The receptionist fumbles for a minute, then forwards her call to another number.

"Hello, this is Adam Zellner. Can I help you?" a deep, masculine voice asks.

"Hello, my name is Sophea Lim and I'm the new producer of WNR's Consumer Unit," Sophea replies. "We've got a whole investigative team ready to tackle some heavier news opportunities. Might you have any leads you would be willing to share with us at this time?"

"No offense, but I've left your office almost ten messages over the last few months and no one's ever returned my phone calls," Adam says. "You all lost out on some great stories."

"Look, Adam, I'm new here and trying to do the best I can," Sophea says. "I'm sorry no one returned your phone calls, but I'm calling you now. We want to help you bring criminals to justice and highlight the important work your office is doing for consumers and constituents. I'm sure your boss, the mayor, would like that. How about we meet tomorrow and try to make peace? If you share your great story ideas with us, I'll promise you some coverage."

"Alright, now you've got my attention," Adam says. "We're working on a number of cases, including a major sweep of car lots, beauty salons, and barbershops in this city that are operating without licenses. We've got an Internet payday loan scam that targeted military personnel. And, of course, we've always got complaints going against back-alley auto repair shops and fraudulent towing companies."

"Excellent! Could I swing by your office tomorrow around ten a.m.?" Sophea asks. "I hope parking won't be a problem."

When Sophea hangs up the phone, Edie is standing at the doorway looking at her with a mischievous smile. "Who was that on the phone? Did I detect a slight flirtation in your voice?"

"Very funny, the last thing I'm thinking about is starting a new relationship." Sophea rolls her eyes. "If you must know, I was recently dumped by my boyfriend and am still recovering from a bruised heart."

"Sorry to hear that, but I heard that in this industry we're going to be married to our work anyway." Edie smiles. "Hey, how about if we go grab a quick bite to eat downstairs?"

"I actually have a date with an editor in about five minutes to work on that package about car leasing versus buying. You'll have to lunch alone." Sophea reaches for her purse. "Would you mind grabbing me a tuna sandwich?"

"Do you also want your king-sized Snickers bar?" Edie asks with a smile. "I don't know how you can take in five hundred calories of chocolate every day and still maintain your size. Aren't Asians known for their delicate bones and tiny appetites?"

"Ha! I guess it's all about perspective." Sophea laughs. "I'm gargantuan among Cambodians. My shoulder width alone exceeds that of most of my male cousins and uncles."

She runs downstairs into one of the editing bays and thinks about a possible next story: "Regular or Super Size: Today's Food Dilemma."

Chapter 28

The DC Consumer Affairs Office is located in the southwest portion of the city, near the waterfront. As Sophea enters the building, a heavy-set secretary with cat's-eye glasses greets her at the receptionist desk. "Welcome! You must be Ms. Lim," she says. "Don't mind the dreary gray walls. They grow on you after a while."

Sophea looks around and notices some of the paint peeling from the walls. "That's a nice picture of the Washington Monument there." She points to an old painting hanging behind the desk.

At that moment, a very handsome and boyish-looking man in his forties extends his hand to her. His nails are freshly manicured. He is wearing a Hugo Boss suit with expensive Italian leather shoes. His teeth are white—almost blindingly so. "Hello! I'm Adam. Welcome to our humble abode."

He leads her to his corner office, which has a huge glass window on one side. "Look at that gorgeous view you have of the Potomac River. You can even see the planes flying from the airport. Do my tax dollars help pay for this view?" Sophea teases. "Listen, I know we both have very busy schedules, so I promise not to take too much of your time."

"Can I offer you something to drink at least?" Adam motions for the receptionist to bring them water. "So, you are the great wizard behind the WNR consumer curtain."

"Hmm, I've never been called that before," Sophea says. "But I hear you are the greatest spin doctor this side of the Potomac. I've been warned of your ability to finagle stories from unsuspecting journalists."

Adam looks over with a wide grin. "Should I be flattered or offended?"

Sophea blushes and finds herself thinking about the time in fifth grade when she tried to impress her class crush. She wanted to let him know that she liked the story he had just read in front of the class, but she ended up punching him instead. For some reason, Sophea wants to punch Adam. *Stay cool. Keep the banter light. Remember that you are a professional woman.*

"Sorry, I was expecting someone a little more Washingtonian—less fashion-plate," she continues. "I did some research and learned that your department has been involved in helping the mayor clean up the seedy businesses in the U Street Corridor. It seems like a natural fit for us to work together, since you're trying to get rid of bad business owners and we're trying to help consumers avoid scams and predatory local establishments. It's a no-brainer, really." Sophea takes a sip of her water.

"Why don't you call me in a few days, and I'll see what we have in our files." He hands her his business card. "I'd like for us to get to know each other a little more before I start making any promises for stories."

"We are the number-one station in the market," Sophea reminds him. "I think you want our help. Otherwise, why did you call us ten times in the last couple of months?"

"Touché!" Adam snickers. "It's not a given that we'll give you *all* our best stories. That's all I'm saying. There are three other stations in this market, so we do have the luxury of not jumping when a media person snaps their finger at us."

"Please don't play hardball with us. You're not in a position to win," says Sophea. Adam chuckles and notices her big brown fiery eyes and full angry lips. Sophea lets out an indignant sigh and storms out of Adam's office.

What a jerk that guy is! Sophea rips up Adam's business card and tosses it into a nearby garbage can.

Chapter 29

"It's the Cambodian New Year, can we all try to make nice today?" Sophea pleads to Chas Mai and Cookie. "I know you both are still mad at me, but how much longer do you want to give me the silent treatment?"

"Alright, this is the Year of the Dragon, so it is an extra-special year," Cookie replies. "But understand that it's going to be a little stressful today for us at the pagoda. We are going to have to explain to everyone why the wedding was cancelled."

"Remember, there was *no* wedding planned. It was all in your minds. How many people did you tell? My love life is not for public consumption." Sophea cringes. "Let's just have a good day. I don't want to talk about this anymore."

"We just told a few close friends." Cookie walks toward her bedroom. "You have nothing to worry about, dear."

It's 7:00 a.m. when the three women head to the Buddhist pagoda located in Silver Spring, Maryland, to help prepare food for the monks. As the car pulls onto the small dirt road, Sophea looks up at the towering gold temple before them. "I will never get over how beautiful this building is. It's actually glistening in the sunlight," she says. "I feel like I'm in Oz right now."

The pagoda had always been a special place for Sophea and her family; it was a refuge in a foreign land, a gathering place where they could meet fellow refugees, and a place to seek Buddha's help with life's many miseries. But it was also a reminder of what they had overcome. The Khmer Rouge had banned all religion when they took over Cambodia, leaving destroyed temples and statues of Buddha in their wake. They had forced people to leave their homes, relocating them around the country. City dwellers were forced to become farmers. People lost their homes and their cars, and almost all personal possessions were banned. *Year Zero*, it was called. Pol Pot, leader of the Khmer Rouge, said it exemplified the new way of living. He even changed the name of the country to Kampuchea.

This new way of living also meant torturing and executing hundreds of thousands of educated middle-class people. They were put in special holding centers and prisons, including the infamous Tuol Sleng Prison. A million others died of starvation, disease, or exhaustion. In all, almost two million Cambodians were killed during the Khmer Rouge's reign of terror. But despite all their efforts to rewrite Cambodian history and to change the Cambodian way of life, the Khmer Rouge had failed.

This pagoda, and this gathering of people, was proof of that. They may have been transplanted to a new land, but they had kept their culture and their beliefs alive. "*What is rotten must be removed*," had been a popular Khmer Rouge slogan. Sophea couldn't help but wonder at the irony. They had tried to remove everything that was wonderful about Cambodia, but it had survived in spite of them.

Cookie spoke, breaking Sophea out of her revelry. "As you know, we Cambodians have centuries of experience building temples and pagodas. Do you notice the miniature gold-plated carvings on the deck? It may not be Versailles, but there's a lot of tradition and craftsmanship behind all this beauty."

Next to the primary temple sits an ordinary-looking ranch house where the monks and nuns reside. The three women make their way toward the house and notice a small group of men smoking near the entrance. A mom watches her young son play ball on the outside lawn. "Do we have to stay here all day?" he whines. "I want to go home!"

"Don't forget to paun everyone you meet today," Chas Mai reminds Sophea. "And I suggest you hide your shoes someplace where you can find them later. Hundreds of people are coming soon." She points to a small pile of shoes forming near the front door and places her sandals behind a flower pot in the corner.

Inside, a group of gray-haired women and nuns huddles around a kitchen table cutting up vegetables and meat. The nuns are mostly in their seventies and eighties and very thin. They wear white and tan cotton robes and sport very short haircuts, similar to those of marines. Several of them have very wrinkled, sunken faces that reveal lives of hardship and restraint. Though this is a day for celebration, these nuns look serious and contemplative. They whisper in *Khmer*, but the conversation is clearly not idle chatter.

Yum. Everything smells delicious. Sophea surveys the wide array of dishes laid out for the monks' midmorning feast: salted eggs, rice noodles, stir-fried vegetables, fish soup, and a big bowl of apples, oranges, cherries, bananas, longans, and lychee. She is tempted to steal a taste from the large plate of sliced-up baguettes and crunchy Chinese sausages.

"Sophea, you know the monks only eat once a day, so they need all the food and nutrition they can get," Chas Mai whispers from behind her. "Right now, it's time to prepare their meal. You can eat later." She swats Sophea's hand away from the tray of food.

At the other end of the kitchen, two women in their twenties are scooping up hot rice from a big metal vat into small, intricately decorated silver bowls. They talk fast in English, every so often injecting a Cambodian word or phrase for emphasis. The women have dark shoulder-length hair, and they wear beautiful silk *sampots*, or sarongs, with fitted tops.

A half-dozen women hover around the stovetop, cooking up food like professional chefs and laughing at each other's stories. "I heard through the grapevine that someone is destined to be the next nun at this pagoda if she does not make up with her American fiancé," one older woman with a red scarf whispers to Sophea. "What happened? We all thought we were going to your wedding this year."

"I thought you said you only told a 'few close friends,'" says Sophea to Cookie. "This is nobody else's business." She throws her mom an angry look.

"Now, now, don't get mad at your poor mother," the woman continues. "The seamstress mentioned that your mother cancelled the wedding costumes. News travels fast at the pagoda, you know."

"We're all sad about it." Chas Mai smooths Sophea's hair. "But I have a good feeling today. There is a suitable bachelor with traditional Cambodian values awaiting my princess. Perhaps we can all pray that Sophea finds a husband this year."

"Can we talk about something else?" Sophea pleads. "When is the children's dance troupe performing this afternoon? I love to see them do all those traditional folk dances in their cute outfits."

In addition to the traditional Khmer ballet that is often performed at the New Year's celebration, the folk dances represent daily activities in the villages, such as men courting women, farmers harvesting rice in the fields, and fishermen gathering fish from the Tonlé Sap River. Sophea loves the upbeat tempos and rhythms in the simple dances that use coconut shells, bamboo sticks, and straw fishing baskets to bring a common Khmer village to life.

"We could use an old-fashioned courting dance for you right now, Sophea." Cookie laughs. "Perhaps if we all pray very hard in unison, we can get my daughter a husband today." The women roar with laughter as they carry food to the monks who await their first meal in a nearby room.

Sophea walks back toward the table where the two younger women are still chatting. One of them, a very pretty girl with an unforgettable black mole right above her left lip, says, "Don't worry, Sophea, I just got engaged. If I could get away with it, I'd go to Vegas and elope."

"If you don't mind me asking, how old are you?" Sophea inquires. "You can't be more than eighteen. You know you can have your own life and career before committing to a husband at such a young age. This isn't Cambodia. We have more choices here."

"I don't want to wait until I'm your age," she answers. "You're a legend here at the pagoda. Very few of us can wear singlehood with such dignity and grace. I admire you. You don't look nearly as old as they say you are."

"Thank you for those uplifting words," Sophea says. "Perhaps I should pioneer a spinster program here at the pagoda. The wool-spinning eats at my social life sometimes, but overall, I'm pretty happy." To change the subject, she motions for the two other women to help her prepare more food for the monks.

Chapter 30

As the morning service begins with the familiar Sanskrit prayer that Chas Mai taught her, Sophea closes her eyes and chants along with the monks. She resists falling asleep as the sound of the monks' droning voices soothe her in the same way as her CD of Gregorian chants. Then Sophea feels someone's bare toes touch hers and she squirms. *This room is too crowded and hot. I can't concentrate on praying when everyone is breathing down my neck.* Sophea moves a little to the left, only to hit another person on the arm. The older woman beside her smiles, showing a mouthful of black teeth rotted by a lifetime of chewing tobacco. Sophea is intrigued and smiles back at the gentle woman.

Sophea tries to concentrate on her prayers again. Deep in thought, she winces as her right buttock begins to cramp. She is sitting with both of her legs folded in one direction when the familiar feeling of prickly numbness enters her bare feet. She unfolds her legs and places them in the other direction. *I need to stretch my legs or I will pass out.*

"Keep still, Sophea. You are worse than a five year old," Chas Mai reprimands. "The service is going to continue all day, but you can get up to stretch your legs. Why don't you make your way to the front of the room to light an incense candle for Buddha and donate some money to the pagoda? Don't forget to bow three times to the floor at the end of your prayer."

Sophea obliges, then returns to her seat near Chas Mai just as her favorite part of the prayer ceremony takes place. The lead monk submerges a homemade straw brush into a black bowl and sprinkles holy water onto the cheeks and foreheads of those assembled before him. Sophea pushes her face forward and welcomes the feel of the cold water against her brow. She can smell the scent of the rose petals that the nuns tossed into the water that morning. *This is what I've been waiting for.* Sophea lets out a sigh of relief.

It is almost noon, and the spicy aromas from the monk's lavish spread spark Sophea's appetite. She rubs her growling stomach and makes her way out of the temple to meet Ravy for some lunch. About fifty food vendors are lined up along the dirt road, selling a wide variety of Asian delicacies including Siem Reap noodles; fried rice with Chinese sausages; *prahok* (a fermented fish paste often served with steamed white rice and fresh vegetables); barbecued meat skewers, rice, and pickled vegetables; fresh vegetable rolls made of white noodles, shrimp, carrots, lettuce, and bean sprouts—all wrapped in a thin white rice paper; deep-fried pork and shrimp spring rolls; and bananas and sticky rice packed in banana leaves—the succulent rewards of contemplative prayer.

Outside, Ravy lounges on a lawn chair, eating a bowl of *amok*, a classic Khmer salmon dish steamed in a banana leaf. She looks pretty in her black leggings and silk blouse embroidered with Asian designs. "That curry smell is killing me," Sophea says. "I'm starving! Want to walk with me?"

The sisters head toward a skinny woman wearing a large straw hat. She is preparing a plate of stir-fried beef on a bed of cabbage, tomatoes, carrots, red onions, fish sauce, lime juice, mint leaves, and a dash of peanuts. "Yum, I want some of that." Sophea begins to devour her food.

Finding a seat on the grass, Ravy notices a tall American man playing *Bos Angkunh,* a Cambodian children's street game in which players try to knock each other's stones out of the way. She stops to watch the kids play and catches the man's eye. "Hello! Would you ladies like to join the game?" he hollers.

Sophea refocuses her eyes and marches up to the interloper. "I had you figured as more of a champagne and opera guy. What are you doing here, crashing our Buddhist temple? This is one of the only places we Cambodian refugees have here in the states to be with our own people and culture. Our religious temple is not a place for you to play tourist."

"Don't mind my sister, she's just been through a lot lately," Ravy interjects. "We welcome anyone who wants to pray and celebrate with us, especially on this day filled with so many cultural festivities. It's the best day to join us!"

"Hi, I'm Adam. I already had the pleasure of meeting your lovely sister a few days ago." He glances over at Sophea.

"Please don't slap any of the vendors with a food safety violation," Sophea responds. "It's a religious holiday for all of us today. We are here to get Buddha's blessings and to celebrate the New Year of the Dragon. I hope you don't do anything to ruin that for any of us." *Why am I being so mean? I shouldn't take it out on all men just because Tim hurt me.*

"I'm here to celebrate Cambodian New Year, too," he explains. "I was a Peace Corps volunteer in Thailand right out of college. It gave me the chance to travel extensively in Laos and Cambodia. That's where I learned to appreciate spicy foods and the Asian way of life. Today, it's just me with no official hat. I didn't know I had to pass such personal inspection to spend the day at the local pagoda." He smiles at Ravy.

"Would you like some special medal for your accomplishments as a Peace Corps volunteer? You sound like an insecure expat when you have to brag about your 'extensive' travels in Southeast Asia." Sophea's peaceful day at the pagoda has been shattered. "Volunteering to help a third-world country does not make you Asian. Next you're going to tell us how you converted to Buddhism." Sophea glances over at Ravy who shoots back a disapproving look and mouths, "Stop it."

"Nope, I'm Jewish, but I think our cultures have a lot in common," Adam replies. "Want to debate whether Buddhism is a religion or a philosophy? Looks like you're rarin' for a fight!" He gives her a big smile.

"I don't think you should rile my sister up any more," Ravy says. "She's a little on edge until we get more food in her. I, on the other hand, would love to hear more about your journeys to Southeast Asia. It sounds interesting." She winks at Sophea.

Sophea rolls her eyes and walks to a nearby booth to buy a plate of her favorite Cambodian dessert, *nom kruob kanau* (sweet mung bean rolls). Adam and Ravy follow behind, lost in conversation. Sophea bites into the soft, sticky dessert and savors the chewy sweetness in her mouth. Ravy was correct—eating does soothe her nerves.

◈ ❧ ◈

"Sorry about Sophea. I'm not sure why she's so irritated by you." Ravy laughs. "She's usually really sweet. I'm the one with the mouth."

"She's probably still mad at me from the other day," Adam says. "Sophea asked me to get her some story ideas, and I pushed back a little. Come to think of it, I wasn't actually the nicest person, either." He tightens a blue and white *kroma* scarf around his neck. "A little boy gave this to me when I was digging wells for one of the local villages near Siem Reap."

"That's sweet, but I wouldn't share that with Sophea right now." Ravy laughs again. "This new job is really important to her. Can you please help her out? It would mean a lot to both of us."

"Sure. I'll look through my files and see what we can do for her." He waves at Sophea, who is making her way toward them.

"Are you ready to go, Ravy?" Sophea pulls her sister away from Adam. "I hope I'm not interrupting any tales of your great world travels."

"No, we were just talking about work," Adam teases. "I was sharing stories about challenging colleagues in the workplace."

"You know, Adam, we hardly know each other, but you talk with a level of familiarity that actually makes my skin crawl," Sophea replies. "Is it possible for you to show even a modicum of professionalism when we are together?"

Adam sits cross-legged on the grass and closes his eyes. "Shhh, I'm trying to meditate on that."

Sophea yanks Ravy's arm so hard she nearly falls. "This is our cue to leave!"

"So nice to meet you, Adam," Ravy says. "I hope we'll run into you again soon."

"You know where to find me," he responds with a smirk. "I'll probably be hovering around the food booths or under some banyan tree. You two have a good afternoon."

"He's so offensive," Sophea mutters under her breath.

"I think you have a crush on him," Ravy blurts out when they are alone. "You get really rude and defensive when you like someone. It's so obvious. There's some definite chemistry between the two of you."

Off in the distance, Adam befriends a little boy with a head full of ebony black hair and chocolate drop eyes. "Will you play soccer with me, mister?" He kicks a ball toward Adam. "My sister doesn't want to play with me." He points to a tall, svelte girl about fifteen years old playing with her hair on the pagoda steps. Adam obliges and returns the ball with his right foot.

Chas Mai and Cookie huddle and gossip with a group of women on the front porch of the side house. They watch as throngs of visitors walk through the pagoda grounds for the New Year festivities. "Doesn't it feel good to be with so many other Cambodians?" Chas Mai says to her daughter.

Cookie nods her head in agreement and takes a long sip of her Vietnamese iced coffee. "Life is good today."

Chapter 31

"She used to be such a good girl," Cookie whispers. "I don't know what's happening with her anymore."

"A good Cambodian girl—is that too much to ask for, Buddha?" Chas Mai pauns and looks up to the ceiling. "We have made years of sacrifices to give her an incredible life in this new country, and she pays us back with her defiance and disrespect."

"I thought for a minute I was dreaming, but this is a nightmare," Sophea exclaims. "You two are hovering over me like two coroners over a corpse. What are you doing?"

"It is ten in the morning, and we need to get on the road soon," Cookie says. "I'm very hungry."

As part of their Cambodian New Year tradition, the Lim women always eat out at a buffet the day after the pagoda festivities. When they first arrived in their new land many years ago, Cookie struggled to figure out what the "American Dream" looked like. She searched for it at work, in schools, in shopping malls, and even at playgrounds. Then, one day, she stumbled onto *her* American dream—abundance in all its glory and offerings. Cookie became a buffet aficionado.

No matter where Cookie traveled in America, she could find a buffet restaurant. The idea of an "all you can eat," "go back as many times as you want," "no one will judge you" culinary experience reminded her of the days back at the royal palace in Cambodia when food was plentiful.

Cookie despised the idea of a normal sit-down restaurant with just one plate of food. She felt deprived and stifled by an à la carte menu. Instead, Cookie dragged her two daughters to buffets for breakfast, lunch, and dinner throughout their childhood. From the Home Town Buffet to the China Buffet, from the Filling Station to every Mother's Day buffet brunch at the local hotels—Cookie saw herself as the Scarlett O'Hara of all-you-can-eat buffets. "I'll never go hungry again!" she would say.

And Chas Mai would respond lovingly, "My dear, you have never gone hungry in your life." She would then look over at her two young granddaughters and say, "We Asians always appreciate a good feast."

As a first-generation immigrant in America, Cookie's wish list was simple: hit at least one buffet each day. She did not ask for a big house, a new car, or even jewelry. She just wanted a full belly with others who shared her passion for boundless quantities of food served on silver plates.

Though she loved Asian food, Cookie grew to love American and Italian food, as well. She would heap potato salad, ambrosia, fettuccini Alfredo, pounds of salami and olives, ladles of seafood salad, and bread pudding onto a single plate.

She would then carefully cover the dubious delectables with blue cheese dressing in hopes of disguising this miniature mountain as a mere salad. Cookie's creativity at the buffet table made her legendary among the buffet vultures in her neighborhood.

Both Sophea and Ravy grew up learning two essential buffet strategies: get dessert first if you want the biggest and prettiest-looking cakes and pastries, and pile vertically. As Cookie explained to her daughters, "A woman can eat as much as she wants. But no one has to know exactly *how* much." She would then give a slight wink, discreetly wipe her mouth off with a handkerchief, and then walk gracefully toward the dessert table for a third serving of cheesecake.

⊰≳⊷⊰

"I know how important this buffet tradition is to you, Mom." Sophea hesitates. "But I don't feel very well this morning. Would you mind if I skipped it this year?"

"Absolutely not. You are coming with us! By noon, the food will be gone. We go now, or we all stay home and suffer together," Cookie replies, exasperated by her daughter's suggestion. "Why are you being so difficult? Ravy will be waiting for us. Get dressed immediately."

"My head is killing me," Sophea protests. "Last night, Ravy and I went to the New Year party sponsored by the Washington, DC, Cambodian Association. It was fun, but we stayed out too late and I think I'm paying the price now." She grabs her ibuprofen that is sitting nearby on the nightstand.

"No, you two partied and now *we* have to pay for your selfishness," Cookie snaps. "I ask for one thing every New Year's, and you can't even give that to me."

"Let's all relax for a moment and let Sophea get ready," Chas Mai says. "Ravy's waiting for us at the all-you-can-eat Chinese restaurant. I think a little food will make all of us feel better." She takes Cookie's hand and leads her to the living room.

My mother is such a spoiled princess. She always has to get her way. Sophea slips on a baggy dress, another buffet tip she has learned from her mother over the years.

❧❧❧

Ravy is already sitting at the table closest to the buffet when the other three women arrive at the restaurant. "Sorry we are late, but your sister said you two were out late last night," Cookie says with frustration. "Glad to see you here without any complaints. It's eleven a.m.—let's eat before the lunch crowd arrives!"

"You look like death warmed over," Ravy whispers to Sophea. "What happened? The three of you look like you've been to a funeral."

Sophea makes her way to the buffet and puts a small spoonful of rice, some Chinese greens, and a little fresh fruit on her plate. "I'm not going to pay ten dollars to watch you eat like a bird," Cookie reprimands. "Children are starving in Cambodia. Eat when there is abundance offered to you, and be grateful you have food to eat."

"I think she is on a diet." Chas Mai takes some soup. "Only in America do people pay other people to help them lose weight. Have you ever heard of such nonsense? In Cambodia, people are poor and want to eat. There is no one to pay unless you want favors from the government."

"I know this is hard for the two of you to believe, but I'm just not hungry," Sophea replies. "I also want to go for a run after lunch, so I don't want to eat too much right now."

"Why do you want to punish your body with strenuous activity when you are working yourself to death at that television station?" Chas Mai admonishes. "I read somewhere about a woman who was eaten up by a Stair-Master machine. She was walking and it literally ate her feet, then the rest of her body. Exercise can kill you."

Chas Mai is persistent. "Back when I was young, I used to row boats on the Tonlé Sap River in Phnom Penh. My grandmother was afraid I would drown, so I stopped and took up needlepoint instead."

"But you know how to swim," Ravy chimes in. "So you gave up something you loved just to make your grandmother happy?"

"Yes." Chas Mai smiles and walks back to their table.

Cookie is on her second serving of food. She looks at Sophea's plate with contempt. "Is this what you call 'portion control'? Cambodian New Year is about celebrating and feasting. Is this all you're going to eat today?"

"Mom, can you please leave Sophea alone?" Ravy interjects. "I'm going for my third plate of food. I will even take two extra desserts for the team. She just isn't hungry today. Why is that so hard to understand?"

"Do whatever you want, Sophea," Cookie responds. "Just know that I'm watching how little you are consuming right now. If I'd known you were going to ruin our meal, I would have made you stay home. You've taken the joy out of eating."

Sophea gives in to her mother's bullying, marches toward the buffet table, and heaps up a plateful of rice, meats, fried appetizers, and veggies drowning in brown gravy. "Are you happy now, Mom?" she asks.

"That's more like it," Cookie says. "Now we can concentrate on more interesting topics, such as the status of your love lives. Chas Mai and I are very concerned that both of you are still single. We both prayed at the pagoda yesterday that good men will enter and stay in your lives this year. It has been heartbreaking for both of us to watch you two turn into old maids." She looks over at Ravy, who is picking at her food with her chopsticks.

"Sophea, who was that man at the pagoda yesterday?" Chas Mai says. "He had beady eyes. I don't trust him."

"It's just someone I work with," Sophea says. "It was a surprise to see him."

"Is it wise to date your boss?" Chas Mai asks.

"Adam is not my boss. He's just a colleague, and we don't even work at the same company," says Sophea. "Anyway, I'm not interested in dating him." Ravy clears her throat.

"We were not born yesterday," Chas Mai continues. "That man has eyes for you. Be careful of his intentions, Sophea. Men don't talk with women because they want to be friends. Keep your guard up."

"It's hard to find a good man you can trust," Cookie chimes in. "Most white men are respectable, but beware of those with an Asian fetish. First they join the Peace Corps and teach English for a few years. Then they start using chopsticks, watch Kung Fu movies, and think they're Asian. Before you know it, you're the Oriental ornament dangling from their arm."

Sophea starts to laugh and shakes her head with disbelief. "Yeah, Mom. All white men want a mail-order bride."

"I'm confused," Ravy says. "So, you two want us to find husbands, but you don't trust men. What I'm hearing is that Sophea and I should stay single. And that white men are bad news." She laughs to herself. "Why do you bash men if you want us to marry them?"

"Your mother is only trying to protect you," Chas Mai adds. "Listen to her."

Ravy senses the two older women are on a warpath and excuses herself to get more food. "Not so fast," Cookie says. "We hear you had a date with an Arab you met on the Internet. You can't trust Arabs or gypsies—they steal your money."

"First of all, he's very rich." Ravy tightens her lip in anger. "His name is Karim, he speaks beautiful French, and he makes a decadent couscous. I will definitely make a trip to Morocco one day because of him. Now, please excuse me, I need dessert."

"Are you making enough money as an artist?" Chas Mai asks. "We can give you money if you need it. Your mom tells me you are selling yourself on the Web. I know nothing about these fancy boxes that you call computers. But remember that even the smartest creatures can get trapped in a black widow's web. We worry about your safety."

"It's called online dating, and the Web has nothing to do with spiders." Ravy regrets that she mentioned her date to her mom in a moment of weakness. "And just to be clear, I'm not prostituting myself. I'm a graphic artist." Chas Mai shakes her head in disapproval.

"Want to take another trip to the buffet with me?" Sophea says to her sister. "I think my appetite is coming back." Ravy obliges.

"Well, this is fun," she continues. "Are you okay? Their comments make me cringe, too. They should know better. Cambodia is not exactly the most diverse place on the planet. They're just trying to protect us."

"It's embarrassing to hear their blatant racism sometimes," Ravy says. "But I know they can't change who they are." She puts a handful of grapes and some mango slices on her plate.

An hour later, their lunch comes to an end and Cookie insists on paying the bill, as she does every weekend. When Cookie is not looking, Sophea slides a fifty-dollar bill into her mother's purse. It is the "I will take care of the check" dance that they have been doing for years.

The four women are walking out of the restaurant when they hear the sound of a plastic tumbler cracking against the tile floor. "Chas Mai, did you steal this from the table?" Sophea points to the cup. "You already took extra soy sauce packets for the house."

At that moment, an Asian waiter in his fifties wearing a white shirt and black bow tie joins the conversation. "Ladies, is there a problem?" Ravy hands him the cup. "I'll take that, thank you!" He walks away and mutters in Mandarin.

"Don't judge me!" Chas Mai fires back at both girls. "We paid for it." She takes a cup off of another table with her right hand and exits the restaurant.

Sophea, Ravy, and Cookie chuckle and follow Chas Mai out to the car.

Chapter 32

The phone rings and Sophea answers in her most upbeat voice, "Consumer Unit—this is Sophea! Can I help you?"

"What, may I ask, got into your cup of coffee this morning?" the deep voice asks. "Is this the angry, sullen television producer with a chip on her shoulder?"

"Hmm, let me guess who this is," Sophea says. "Our annoying pagoda crasher?"

"Ouch, is that any way to talk to someone who has an awesome story for you?" Adam asks. "Do you have time for a quick meeting today?"

Sophea perks up. "Yes, but can you come over here? I'm in editing all morning and can't leave the station."

"I'm actually in your neighborhood right now," Adam says. "Can you meet me out front in a few minutes?"

"Sure, I'll be right down," Sophea searches for her compact and puts on lipstick. Her stomach churns as Chas Mai's voice plays in her head, *That man has eyes for you. Be careful of his intentions.*

When she arrives downstairs, Adam is already waiting by the receptionist desk. "Thanks for meeting me on such short notice," Adam begins. "So, here's the scoop. We found a guy named Russ McGraw who's charging illegal immigrants big money with the promise that he can help them get their U.S. citizenship in a week. They pay him a fee up front to submit paperwork to the proper government agencies, but the truth is, once he has their money, he claims their request for citizenship was denied. Most of his victims don't dare file complaints against him for fear of being deported. This is a huge scam targeting poor people who already have nothing."

Sophea leads Adam to a nearby sofa. "This is huge, I can't believe he's getting away with this. Do we know how many people have been affected by this?

Would anyone be willing to talk on camera about their experience?" She jots down some notes.

"Russ has actually been doing this for years in other states like California, Florida, and Texas," Adam says. "We just found out that he started a fake business here in Washington a couple of months ago, so let me see who we can find for you. Again, I don't think they would want their faces to appear on camera, so this is a sticky situation."

"If you can get me a victim who's willing to talk, we'll blur out their face and even disguise their voice," Sophea says.

"We've been working closely with the local police here on a sting operation to catch this guy," Adam says. "We've got an undercover agent posing as an immigrant from El Salvador who's supposed to meet with Russ this afternoon. That's when they plan to arrest him. Do you think you can send a camera crew to cover it?"

"Done! Maybe we also can get a sound bite from you and the police chief," Sophea says. "What time will all this happen?"

Adam hands Sophea a small piece of white paper. "Here's the address of Russ's house. Be there by two p.m."

As Adam starts to exit the building, Sophea yells out, "Hey, Adam! Thank you! I owe you one." She runs upstairs to the newsroom to gather Edie and a news crew.

Chapter 33

The next day, Sophea is reviewing the video footage from the sting. "We nailed this story! I love this shot of the police taking Russ away in handcuffs. He actually yelled a few choice words right at our camera."

"Yeah, it was my first real crime scene investigation," Edie rejoices. "I was terrified and excited at the same time."

"The first time you're in the middle of a police shootout is like losing your journalism virginity," Sophea says, then wrinkles her nose. "Truth be told, it was my first time, too."

Both women beam as they watch a video of Edie running after the alleged criminal. "Sir," she shouted, "is it true that you're running a fraudulent immigration business and scamming innocent people out of thousands of dollars?"

Russ pushes the mike away and screams, "Get the camera out of my face!"

There is a scuffle between Russ and the two policemen escorting him to the car.

"Keep the camera rolling no matter what!" screams Sophea in the background.

After two more hours in the editing room, Sophea and Edie are ready to present their piece to Don. "This is the kind of journalism we should be doing all the time," Edie says. "I'm so proud of us."

"I love this story, as well as all the other stuff we've been doing for the viewers," Sophea says. "We make a pretty great team." She puts her arm around Edie's shoulder as they leave for their planning meeting with Don.

Later that afternoon, Sophea decides to call Adam. "Thanks again so much for your help yesterday. You gave us a gem of a story. Edie and I are still pinching ourselves." Sophea feels the familiar butterflies in her stomach again.

"That's great. For a moment, when we were all waiting there, I was afraid that the sting would be a bust," Adam says. "Glad it all worked out. I'm happy to do some filing this afternoon after all that action yesterday."

"Well, the story's going to air on the six p.m. show," Sophea says. "You can record it, or I'd be happy to make a copy for you."

"Listen, would you be interested in grabbing a drink or maybe even dinner tonight after work?" Adam asks. "Feels like maybe this is a good opportunity for us to reboot our relationship. I think we got off to a rough start. There's a nice Greek place in Adams Morgan if you're interested."

"I think my grandmother was planning to make me dinner tonight, but I know that place," Sophea says. "They have the freshest Mediterranean food."

"I don't want to interrupt plans with your family, but I'd love to see you tonight. Would seven p.m. work?" Adam pushes.

Edie overhears the conversation and jumps up and down, motioning for Sophea to accept Adam's invitation.

"Sure, that would be nice," Sophea responds with hesitation. "See you this evening."

"Are you and Adam going out on a date tonight?" Edie probes. "I had a feeling he liked you. Yesterday, I caught him looking over at you a few more times than was needed." She winks and lets out a loud laugh.

Sophea ignores Edie's comments and calls Chas Mai. "I know you were planning to make us dinner, but is it alright if I go out instead?"

"Yes, I was just going to reheat some leftover fried rice for us," Chas Mai says. "Are you sure he is not a serial killer?"

"I'm not sure," Sophea jokes. "If I'm not back home by eleven p.m., you have my permission to call the police. Don't worry." She hangs up the phone and reads through some press releases that have been piling up on her desk.

≈ ✤ ≈

"Right over here, miss," the restaurant hostess says. "Your date requested the corner table by the window." She walks Sophea to the back of the restaurant where Adam is waiting with a bouquet of sunflowers.

"These are for you," Adam says. "I ordered us some appetizers. Hope you're hungry."

Sophea nods her head. "These are beautiful. Thank you."

"Edie says you're the reason the consumer unit still exists at WNR-TV," he says. "She says that for the first time since she arrived at the station, viewers are stopping her in the street and asking for her autograph."

"She underplays her role in all of this—we work as a team. You know, I could give Edie a call and see if she wants to join us tonight. I think she's still at the station." Sophea bites into a dolmade. "Yum, I love these stuffed grape leaves. Good choice."

"Thanks, I aim to please," he says. "Why don't we invite Edie another time? I was hoping to spend this evening just with you. I know we got off on a rough start," Adam continues, "but I'd really like to get to know you better. You are intriguing, Sophea."

Intriguing? No one has ever called me intriguing before. Sophea bites her bottom lip and drums her fingers on the table. "Thank you again for the story tip. We got some great footage." She stirs the straw in her Diet Coke.

Adam blushes and says, "You're really good at your job. I think you're great." He picks at a piece of fried calamari.

Sophea tries to break the ice. "How about we play a little get-to-know-you game? Do you prefer to use a fork or chopsticks when you eat?" She holds her breath for his answer.

"Fork," he says. Sophea exhales.

"What kind of action movies do you watch? Do you prefer, let's say, Indiana Jones or Bruce Lee?"

"Neither, really. I like comedies," he replies.

"You spent two years in Thailand surrounded by Asians," she says. "After a while, did you begin to feel like you were one of them?"

"Huh? What are you talking about?" he responds.

"Nothing. Forget it. This gyro is delicious." Sophea bites into her lamb and pita sandwich.

"That's a peculiar set of questions," Adam notes. "Is this what it's like to date a journalist?"

"I didn't know we were on a date," Sophea responds. "I hope a few personal questions don't scare you."

"No, not at all," Adam says. "The interrogation feels great. I'm more than happy to get past the superficial chitchat so we can get to know each other better."

"I agree." Sophea takes a drink. "How about if I stop asking so many questions, and you tell me something about yourself that I don't know."

"Alright. As you know, I'm Jewish. You're Cambodian." Adam hesitates. "I'm sure you're aware, but our people share a profound, traumatic human experience. We lost six million Jews in the Holocaust, and the Khmer Rouge killed almost two million Cambodians. My grandfather lost his parents and two siblings during the Holocaust. He came to America alone and had to rebuild a life here. Perhaps that's part of the reason I'm so interested in you and your country. We share a genocide that took place in this lifetime."

Sophea clears her throat. *There is no way I am going to tell him about my father. We don't know each other well enough. It's just too personal.*

"Sorry, I guess that came across a little too strong." Adam straightens in his chair. "It's just that I spent a few years in Cambodia and came to love the country and its people. Everyone was so kind and friendly. They had nothing, and yet they gave me everything. Walking among the crowds of people in Phnom Penh, it was easy to forget that many of them were survivors from the Pol Pot regime. These people had suffered so much, and yet everyone was still smiling. Prime Minister Hun Sen has been ruling the country since 1985, and it doesn't look like he's about to give up his reign anytime soon."

"You know more than I do about my own country," Sophea says. "I haven't been back since we left in 1974. I'd love to go back one day soon." She tears up thinking about her father.

"Oh boy, look what I did," Adam says. "I made you cry on our first date! That's it, no more talking about genocides. How about we go back to your get-to-know-me game. My turn to ask the questions."

"Please don't be weirded out. One day I will tell you why I'm crying." Sophea grabs a napkin and wipes her eyes. "Shoot—I'm ready for your questions."

"Excellent. I think you're fantastic." Adam hesitates, then proceeds. "Israel—pro or con?"

"Pro—for sure," Sophea says. "People want to take their land away from them. They have a right to defend themselves."

"What do you think about Friday night Shabbat dinners at my parents' house?" Adam snickers.

"That would be wonderful." Sophea bats her eyes. "I love *challah* bread with my meal, but I'm not a huge fan of gefilte fish."

"Hanukkah or Christmas?" Adam blurts out.

"Christmas, of course," Sophea says. "I need my blinged-out tree and presents. But lighting the menorah is a glorious experience. I love listening to the traditional songs and chants. They're so beautiful and full of joy."

Adam asks one last question. "Do Asians have the market cornered on sushi?"

Sophea winks at Adam and says, "Absolutely not. The Jews love their lox. Isn't it called 'Jewish sushi'?"

"I really like you, Sophea," Adam says. "But you know a little too much about my people. Are you sure you're not trying to be Jewish? That makes me very uncomfortable." He squirms in his seat.

"Oh my gosh, are you actually trying to use my own game against me?" Sophea laughs. "Truth be told, we have neighbors who are Jewish. Over the years, we've all become super close and they invite us to all their holiday gatherings and potlucks. In return, Chas Mai makes them spring rolls."

"Phew, you scared me for a minute there." Adam stares at Sophea. "Listen, I don't know what happened to you before meeting me, but I get the impression you are on the defensive with me. I have a pretty tough skin, so if you want to call me a white man with an Asian fetish, I'll take all your jokes and pestering. But I just ask that you give me a chance. I'm a nice guy, and I think you're pretty amazing. I'm interested in you, but I will win over your friendship first if that's important to you. I'll do whatever you want, because I'm putty in your hands." He grins sheepishly.

"Aren't we officially on a date? Because we have definitely veered off the professional track." Sophea blushes. "If so, that means you can't expense this dinner."

"Listen, Sophea, I would love for this to be our first date. I also want to protect the professional integrity between us," Adam says.

"Ha! I think it's a bit late for that." Sophea smiles. "I am having fun with you tonight, but I still can't figure you out."

"Good, I like making you laugh," Adam says. "You know, I saw you rip up my business card and throw it into the trash that day you came to visit my office. That was my first clue that you were really into me."

"Oh my gosh, I'm so embarrassed!" Sophea exclaims. "I just thought you were full of yourself. And that you were playing hard to get with all your stories. That just made me mad."

"Good to know that it doesn't take much to offend you," Adam replies. "Listen, I am interested in seeing you more after tonight. If you feel the same, let's keep talking and getting to know each other. No pressure. And I promise to keep our professional side separate."

"Is this a dream?" Sophea asks with a girlish giggle. "I imagine lots of women throw themselves at you. My grandmother thinks you're a player—"

"Yes, I play with women's hearts," Adam interrupts. "I especially like to prey on young, attractive Cambodian women during religious holidays while their elders watch from afar. It makes me feel like a true holy man."

"You lived in Asia for a while, so none of my grandmother's paranoia should be foreign to you." Sophea smiles. "And as someone once told me, to date me is to date my family, too."

The two finish their dinner and prepare to leave. "I'm going to do everything I can to make your grandmother fall in love with me." Adam pays the bill. "Just watch!"

Laughing, Sophea suggests they walk down to her favorite French bistro on Wisconsin Avenue for dessert and coffee. Adam takes her hand and leads them out of the restaurant. Sophea relishes the warmth of his other hand moving down the small of her back as he opens the door for her. For the first time in weeks, Sophea is not thinking about Tim.

Chapter 34

The next evening, Sophea dashes home with a bag of Mexican take-out. After a hard day at work, she is eager to get into her pajamas and call Ravy to tell her about last night's date with Adam.

As Sophea enters the kitchen, she notices that Chas Mai and Cookie are dressed in colorful sarongs, pretty lace and silk shirts, and big jewelry. "You both look dressed up tonight. What's the occasion?"

"The last few weeks, you've been hiding out in your room after work." Chas Mai gives her a prolonged hug. "We miss you and hope you can join us for dinner tonight? We invited some special guests, and I am making your favorite salmon *amok* with spiced red curry, bell peppers, and spinach."

Sophea looks at her bag of Mexican take-out and says, "I'm not feeling too social today. Can I just go into my room and eat these tamales instead?"

"You are a selfish little girl," Cookie reprimands her daughter. "Can you not see that Chas Mai has spent hours in the kitchen making this special meal? Your tamales can wait."

"I'm sorry. The *amok* does smell delicious," Sophea whispers to her grandmother. "I do appreciate you cooking. It was just a rough day at work. I am not the best conversationalist this evening."

"Ridiculous excuse!" Cookie blurts out. "Does the president cancel a state dinner because he 'doesn't feel good'? Does Queen Elizabeth back out of a charity dinner because she is 'not in the mood'? We did not raise you to be a wallflower who is socially inept. Go get pretty and then help me get ready for our dinner party." She shoos a reluctant Sophea toward her bedroom to change clothes.

"You'll be pleased to know that your uncle, Pou Chan, and his family are visiting here from Cambodia." Cookie flips through some of their old French and Cambodian record albums. "They are not only bringing fresh news about King Norodom Sihanouk, but he has been asked to accompany Prince Chakra, a direct descendant of the Sisowath side of the royal family, on his visit to America. We have some very high-ranking guests with us tonight, so the answer is no, you must eat at the table with the rest of us."

"Nobody told me we were going to have guests for dinner tonight," Sophea says. "Can you please remind me who Pou Chan is? Everyone is either an aunt or an uncle, even if they're not blood-related. I can't keep track of all our relatives."

"Pou Chan is a dear friend of the Cambodian royal family," Cookie explains. "He's got strong political influence in Cambodia right now and supports the monarchy. We need people like him who still believe in our family." She looks ravishing tonight in a fitted rose sampot skirt and white lace shirt.

Chas Mai looks tired from cooking, but she adds in her two cents: "Your mom is right. We are a family. You live with us, but you act like you don't owe us your company. It is selfish and hurtful. Please get dressed, as our guests are arriving soon."

Once again, Sophea feels like a child in her own home. She lets out a heavy sigh and heads to her room to put on a *sampot* for dinner. She loves both her mother and grandmother very much, but she feels irritated and smothered by their constant demands. *Eat this, not that. Do this, not that. Sleep here, not there. Wear this, not that.* Chas Mai and Cookie never seem pleased with any decision she makes for herself. She's in awe, even after all these years, by her mother's and grandmother's ability to criticize her even under the guise of supporting her.

"What are you so afraid of? They are just two little Asian women," Sophea says to her reflection in the mirror. But she knows what she's afraid of. She is afraid to hurt them, anger them, disappoint them, desert them.

Ravy's voice plays in Sophea's ear. *This is centuries of Asian daughter guilt being handed down from one generation to another. In America, we call it passive-aggressive behavior. Chas Mai and Cookie had no choice but to do what their parents asked. We, on the other hand, have a choice.*

Sophea feels a headache coming on. She rubs some tiger balm on her forehead and under her nostrils, then takes a deep breath. She pauns the small ivory Buddha figure sitting on her nightstand and prays, "Please give me the strength to stand up against Cambodian pressure tonight. I just want to enjoy Chas Mai's *amok.*"

Chapter 35

ophea enters the living room and notices a group of three serious-looking Cambodians sitting in polite silence on the couch. As Chas Mai finishes preparing the meal in the kitchen, Cookie fumbles through her record collection and puts on Frank Sinatra. She sways back and forth to the music and introduces Sophea to the group. "Pou Chan, my dear and loyal friend; Ming Davy, Pou Chan's beautiful wife; and His Royal Highness Prince Chakra Sisowath, I present to you my honorable daughter, Sophea. Can she get you anything?"

"Good evening, Pou Chan and Ming Davy. It is a pleasure to finally make your acquaintance." Sophea pauns and addresses them in proper *Khmer*. "It is my honor to meet you, Prince Chakra. I hope you are enjoying the States so far."

"You are more beautiful and charming than the pictures your mother has sent me over the years," Pou Chan replies. He is a handsome man in his sixties with a full head of hair, an easy smile, and high cheekbones; Sophea imagines that he has wooed many women in his lifetime in addition to his pretty young wife.

Chas Mai joins the group and sets down a tray of appetizers. Sophea is uncomfortable with the stilted conversation. She politely smiles and grabs two fried wontons. "I envy the way American women eat with so much passion and abandon," Ming Davy says with genuine admiration.

"Thank you, I suppose. I just got off work and am a little hungry," Sophea replies with a slight grin, reaching for a shrimp vegetable roll and dipping it into her favorite peanut sauce.

"So, what brings you all to America?" Cookie attempts to move this embarrassing conversation in another direction. "It has been almost two decades since we last met in King Sihanouk's hotel suite in New York City. Do you remember?

I can still taste the fragrant wine and delicious French pastries he and Queen Monique offered us that special day."

"Of course I do. You are as radiant today as you were twenty years ago," Pou Chan responds. "This time, we are on official business to introduce His Highness to some of the country's proudest and best Cambodian families. Prince Chakra studied at the Sorbonne and just received his master's degree from the London School of Economics and Political Science. He is now interested in coming to live in the States."

Sophea is impressed by Prince Chakra's academic background, but she wonders if he is capable of speaking on his own behalf. The prince has a slight build and stands about five feet tall. His skin is pale for a Cambodian, and his face is long and thin. He wears a silk black suit with a bright pink bow tie, and his shoes are shiny leather. Sophea notices the diamond-encrusted Rolex on his skinny left wrist. Prince Chakra has the presence of someone who has been catered to most of his life—a silent swagger, perhaps. He is neither the most handsome nor the most interesting man she's ever met, but Sophea imagines that many Cambodian women would aspire to have him as their husband.

"I have had the honor of meeting the most genetically blessed Cambodian women who come from families endowed with riches and influence beyond what I could acquire in my humble life." Prince Chakra directs the conversation to Chas Mai and Cookie. "But your Sophea is a glorious female conundrum. As a Western-educated man, I am not intimidated by a strong woman with a healthy appetite."

"Our Sophea went to Wellesley, and she works at a television station," Cookie says. "We hope you can look past her age and see her pedigree. Lest I need remind you, she, too, is of royal descent from the Norodom side of the family."

Sophea stays silent, but wonders what her mother is up to. *Why is she talking about her age and her pedigree? And why does Prince Chakra keep staring at her?*

"We have traveled to China, France, Canada, and California to find a woman suitable for His Honorable Chakra," Pou Chan says. "Your Sophea is sophisticated, educated, and blue-blooded. We cannot ask for a better combination of traits. I will let the king know immediately of this good news. It is always nice to keep marriages within the family."

Sophea almost chokes on her shrimp chip. Everyone raises their wineglasses to her and says, "To Sophea, glorious Sophea." The four of them clap and cheer in unison. "Tonight we celebrate the union of two very special people," Pou Chan continues. "I cannot wait to send a telegraph to the king about this very happy news. He will be so pleased."

Sophea looks with horror at Chas Mai and Cookie and says, "What's happening here? Why would you set me up like this? I thought we were just having dinner."

"You will sit down and behave like the young lady we have raised you to be," Cookie charges back. "This is no way to show appreciation for Prince Chakra's kindness and affection toward you. Becoming a good wife requires that you immediately start respecting your future husband."

"What country are we living in?" Sophea snaps. "I am not going to take part in this ancient matchmaking ritual. It feels like some kind of virgin sacrifice, and I'm the helpless victim!"

Chas Mai nods to the three visitors whose mouths are now agape. "Yes, we can confirm that Sophea's virtue is still intact."

In the corner, Cookie fumes. *How fast will the news of my daughter's disrespectful and undignified behavior travel back to the palace? And who would refuse the prince's attentions? The rumor mill might even put the word out that Sophea is mentally unstable, as well. Oh, it is too much!*

Thinking fast on her feet, Cookie attempts to salvage the evening and the situation. She smiles graciously at her three guests, as though nothing unbecoming has occurred, and says, "Please excuse Sophea and me for a few minutes. This is the perfect time for us to serve some aperitifs. We will be right back. Feel free to look through our music collection and put on whatever you would like to listen to." She hands Pou Chan a compilation of Andy Williams's greatest hits to place on the record player.

Once behind the kitchen door, Cookie takes Sophea by the arm and drags her to the back bedroom. Chas Mai follows them with heavy breathing and a heavy heart. Sophea can feel her mother's nails piercing her skin.

Chapter 36

"How dare you raise your voice and act like such a spoiled child in front of our royal guests!" Cookie points her index finger at her daughter's face. "You disrespect me, so I disrespect you! You have gone too far this time!" There are daggers in her tone and in her eyes.

Sophea looks at her mother's tortured, angry face. She wonders how it is possible for such a gentle and loving face to become a mask of hatred within seconds.

"Mom, do you have any idea what kind of position you have put me in?" Sophea asks. "You were basically promising me to a man whom I don't even know without my permission. How far did you think this plan could go on without letting me in on it?"

"You think you are better than the rest of us. I see right through you, my dear daughter," Cookie continues. "Do you think we do not notice how you glare at us with contempt? Your silence the last few weeks speaks volumes, and I have had enough. You have no respect or appreciation for the Cambodian culture or way of life."

"I am tired of you and Chas Mai treating me like a child. You have no faith that I can ever make the right decision for myself," Sophea exclaims, with tears welling in her eyes. "I can't even get dressed or eat what I want without you two saying something negative. It's suffocating and exhausting to come home after a full workday and hear your constant criticism."

Chas Mai, who has been quietly observing the altercation, speaks up. "Do not raise your voice to your mother. We have done everything for you all your life. All we do is think about you. How can you say such cruel and hurtful words to us? We have devoted our lives to you and Ravy. We have made sacrifices beyond what you can imagine."

She thinks about the family's hasty exit from Phnom Penh twenty-five years ago. On the plane that day, Chas Mai and Cookie made a pact. From that day on they would do everything for the survival of the two children. Chas Mai encouraged Cookie to put her own dreams aside and prepare for a life where the children's needs would surpass their own desires and disappointments. *That is what good mothers do. They give up on their individual hopes and dreams so their children can have a better life.*

"That is not fair. You put too much pressure on us—on me," Sophea sobs. "I never asked you to give up your lives for me. That was your choice. I have always encouraged the two of you to do what you want, to live the life that you want."

"Our fate was determined when we left Cambodia and had to raise two small children in a foreign country where we knew no one and did not speak the language," Cookie says in a seething whisper. "We have devoted thirty years of our lives to you. We had no choice back then. Now you owe us something in return. It is your turn for once in your life to think about us and take care of us. You are a selfish and thoughtless girl."

The three women stand in silence for a few minutes. Then Sophea falls on her knees and buries her face into the palms of her hands, sobbing hysterically. "I feel so misunderstood! You are not hearing me." *Nothing I do will ever be enough to satiate the void and hurt in their hearts. I cannot replace what they lost in the war. Their personal sacrifice is a burden on me and Ravy. We never asked them to give up on their own hopes and dreams.*

Cookie hovers over her daughter and clenches her fists. She wants to strike her daughter but restrains herself. Back in Cambodia, hitting a child was not considered anything more than a needed form of discipline. But here in the States, if you look at your child wrong they can call 911 and report you for child abuse. Cookie feels helpless in her anger.

Chas Mai watches the exchange with pain that starts in her expression, then like a snake, slithers itself through the rest of her body. She rests on the edge of the bed and rubs the left side of her chest with her right hand. Her eyes scour the room for the small container of tiger balm that usually brings her swift relief.

"I will not marry Prince Chakra or any other man you choose for me unless you speak to me first," Sophea whimpers. "I *am* a good and kind girl. All I do is think about you two. I live in fear that I will hurt or disrespect you. I try to make you happy. But you cannot see anything beyond your own harsh judgment of me. Nothing I do is ever good enough. I am sorry, but I can't do this anymore."

Twenty-five years of contained resentment boils over in Cookie and manifests itself in a fit of anguish. In Cambodia, she would have been the model of a modern princess: educated, independent, confident, and wealthy. Cookie had envisioned creating an all-girl's French school that would be populated by the poorest but brightest girls she could find in the Khmer villages. She recognized the privileged life that she led, and she was determined to use her status and prestige to help girls who were less fortunate than her and her sisters. At one point, Cookie had even started talking with the *Voice of America* to become a radio correspondent for them. All those dreams ended when the war started. Now all she had was her identity as a mother, and Sophea's insolence made her feel useless and worthless.

Cookie's round face is now scrunched up and beet red. Her raging eyes pierce through Sophea like a knife, and forgetting her guests in the next room, Cookie loses all composure. "You dishonor me and Chas Mai. You are so busy thinking about *your* life, *your* dreams, *your* goals, *your* feelings! Have you ever taken even a moment to think about how your words and actions hurt us?" she screams into Sophea's face. "You do not have a right to speak to me in that tone. I am your mother!"

Sophea looks up at her mother's glaring eyes. "I am sorry, but I think the time has come for me to move out. This is not a good living situation for any of us right now. We are all stressed and unhappy. I love you both so much. But it is time for me to live my own life and start making my own decisions. Maybe one day in the future, we can live together again. I promise I will not desert you when you are old."

"Why are you punishing us for your unhappiness? How selfish of you to think only of yourself and your needs!" Cookie throws a pillow at her daughter. "We raised you. We have been there every moment of your life, holding you up when you were down, giving you money when you did not have any, making food and feeding you. Chas Mai even folds your laundry because you don't have time to do it yourself!"

"I never asked you for any of it. I tell Chas Mai that I will get to my laundry but she always starts folding and tells me I don't know how to fold laundry as well as she does," Sophea yells back. "You and Chas Mai chose to give up on all your dreams and raise me and Ravy. I thank you, but now you are angry and resentful toward us when we want to live out our dreams and goals. I'm not ready to be an old woman yet. Family and tradition are important to me, and I can still love and support you two from a distance. We don't all have to live in the same house forever."

Trying to restore order, Chas Mai says to both women, "We have to get back to our guests." Turning pointedly to Sophea, she adds, "Dear *koun*, if you love us or have any kind of sympathy for what we have done and gone through for you, you will reconsider your decision. We don't know who you are anymore."

"All this because I want to move out?" Sophea asks. "There's a life and world out there that I have been too afraid to face because you two are always here to shield and protect me. You're angry with me now because I want to see how it feels to live independently for once in my life. This *is* about me. Why are you so insulted because I finally want to go live my own life? Isn't this what people do with their children? They raise them, then set them free? This is not fair."

Cookie rolls her eyes. "Fair? Free? How dare you speak to us as if we are your prison wardens. Have we taught you nothing about the need to hold your tongue when you're angry? We ask nothing from you except to honor and obey us as your parents and elders. Why is that so difficult for you girls to understand? Honor and obey! Honor and obey!" That mantra repeats itself inside Cookie's head as she thinks, *Honoring and obeying your parents is as natural as breathing air. That is how I was raised by my own mother and father. When my girls fight me on this, I feel I have failed as a parent and a Cambodian.*

Chas Mai speaks calmly to Sophea. "You are Cambodian. We always put family first. Here in America, it is all about 'me.' Why can't you give the prince a chance? This is possibly our only chance to return to a place of stature and wealth. We lost everything when we came to this country. You have a chance to bring back that life for yourself and for us. Please reconsider, Sophea. We did this for you and your future."

"I can't, Chas Mai," Sophea responds. "You and Mom did not raise Ravy and me to depend on a man for our livelihood. The two of you worked hard all your lives to provide for us, even when we had money coming in from the trust. I remember when you took a job as a cleaning lady for the lawyers' office, working the midnight shift. You told us any work is admirable. This is what we saw growing up. We don't need Prince Chakra to save us. Anyway, isn't he a distant uncle of mine? Incest is illegal in America. What are you two thinking?"

"What are *you* thinking? Do you want to put us in an old person's home to rot away, watch bad game shows, and eat soft, tasteless foods?" Cookie says. "You cannot easily erase us from your lives like that. We matter."

Sophea stares at her mother and grandmother, then rushes past their three guests toward the front door. "I'm so sorry that I cannot stay for the rest of the dinner. The station needs me right now." She pauns and does not look back.

Cookie composes herself and announces to her guests, "Please accept my apologies for my daughter's hurried exit. Work calls and she must go. Shall we have dinner?" They head over to the dining room, where Chas Mai has laid out a huge feast.

Pou Chan looks over to his old friend and says, "Is everything alright?" Noticing the tension, he starts to serve everyone rice. His wife puts her hand on his shoulder, then takes over the task and motions for him to sit down. Chas Mai sits down next to him and smiles in a manner that says, *Everything is under control.*

From the other side of the table, Cookie shakes her head and directs her answer to the prince. "I might have misread my daughter. She was not too pleased to discover that we had betrothed her to you without her knowledge. If you still admire our high-spirited Sophea, then I would recommend including her in any major life decisions you make moving forward. You know these modern girls. They want to have a say in everything, even if we know better."

Prince Chakra starts to laugh and says, "Oh, *Chas Om* (grand aunt), thank you for your honesty. I did set out for America to find myself a Cambodian bride. The idea that I could simply go on a cross-country journey visiting potential wives seemed very logical in Phnom Penh, but I am realizing perhaps that is not the best approach to finding love here in the States. Poor Sophea, my intention was not to hurt or offend her. For that, I apologize to my sweet niece." He takes a bite of the *amok*.

Cookie cringes at the mention of the word *niece*. She continues. "There is no need for an apology, Your Highness. This is all a big misunderstanding. I assure you that Sophea is still on board with all of this. She just needs a bit of nudging. I hope this has not tarnished your desire for my daughter. If we want to be a bit more strategic, a little more traditional courting may be in order here." She serves the prince more wine.

Prince Chakra adjusts his bow tie. "Considering Sophea just ran crying out the door, perhaps the timing for our nuptials is not right. With all due respect, I think I need to go back and think about what I am doing here in America. I'd like to think of myself as a modern man rather than a troglodyte. It's not fair to push a marriage on an unsuspecting woman. For that, I take full responsibility."

The royal guests take their cue from their hostesses and resume eating but cease talking. It is now officially a formal dinner, with no conversation except a few exchanges of niceties about the food and décor. Even Cookie, who can normally feign interest in any conversation with anyone, does not utter a word. The fight with Sophea has taken its toll.

After finishing his meal, Prince Chakra whispers to Pou Chan, who says, "The prince is tired. Perhaps it is time for us to say our good-byes. The meal was delicious, and we thank you for a most lovely evening."

"It is we who are grateful for your presence in our humble home," Cookie says. "Just to clarify, is the prince saying that the engagement with our lovely Sophea is over? Please, have a Napoleon." She hands Pou Chan and his wife the tray of pastries.

"Delicious, thank you." Pou Chan grabs a madeleine cookie. "Yes, that is the conclusion after tonight. However, our spirits are high and our stomachs are full. Shall we make one last toast in honor of love and the great country of America?" He raises his coffee cup.

Chas Mai has been listening intently to the conversation, but her meal is untouched. As Cookie and the three honored guests raise their glasses in unison, she reaches for her heart.

Chapter 37

ophea is short of breath and flushed from the fight with Chas Mai and Cookie. The streets are empty, even for a weeknight. Sophea replays the fight in her head. A migraine looms on the horizon. *I should have just kept my mouth shut. They didn't mean any harm.*

Sweat drips from the back of Sophea's head down to her neck. Her hair is drenched, and she pulls it into a tight ponytail. Walking past the boutique shops, crowded restaurants, and rowdy bars on M Street, she makes a turn toward the harbor area. There she settles on a wooden bench and stares at the handful of boats bobbing in the water. As a Cancer, she can calm her nerves by being near the water.

Sophea is trying to catch her breath when she looks up and sees Tim strolling hand in hand with a tall, long-haired brunette who looks like Cher. Sophea focuses intently on the worn, dark brown lumber of the dock. She hopes Tim will not notice her.

"Sophea, is that you?" Tim reaches his hand out to her. "This is Angela—my fiancée. I'm so glad the two of you can finally meet."

"Tim has told me great things about you and your family." Angela flashes two adorable dimples and sparkling green eyes. "He credits you for his love of international cuisine and culture."

"How dare you cheat with my ex-boyfriend and then pretend that you want to be my friend," Sophea replies. "You broke the ultimate girl code. We don't do that to each other. Please get away from me—both of you." She rubs her temples, surprised by her new sense of strength.

"You're out of line, Sophea," Tim replies. "You owe Angela an apology. She was just trying to be nice."

"You know, Tim, you need to close your mouth when someone doesn't want to hear what you have to say," Sophea responds. "You don't have one culturally curious bone in your body. And my grandmother was right, you *do* smell like room deodorizer. He's a poser, Angela. Don't fall for his act."

"What do you mean, cheating on you?" Angela is bewildered. "Tim said you were a Filipina foreign exchange student he met in an international study class at Washington University. You were never his girlfriend, just a friend who needed help adjusting to this new country."

"So, I guess Tim's job as a stockbroker didn't quite work out and he's a fiction writer now?" Sophea responds. "By the way, just because all Asians look alike to you, Tim, having 'round eyes' doesn't mean you get to throw us into any random Asian country. I'm Cambodian and a full U.S. citizen. I don't need anybody's green card, thank you."

"Settle down, Sophea," Tim says. He whispers to Angela, "I told you she has anger management issues."

"Yes, you're right. I'm really angry," Sophea says. "And, you know what, I'm no longer willing to act from a place of fear—fear of losing you, fear of offending you, fear of saying what I truly feel. You don't get to mistreat me and make me feel like a victim. I was not perfect, but that did not give you the right to cheat on me and disrespect my family. You're a real jerk. I wish you well, but remember that karma stinks."

Tim gets ready to speak, but Sophea holds up her right hand toward him in a stopping motion. She gets up from the bench and walks the other direction. Sophea sees Tim trying to comfort a very distraught and angry Angela. But at that moment, Sophea hears Ravy's voice. "Sophea! Sophea! I thought you'd be over here by the water," she says, panting from running. "I have been trying to reach you."

"What is it? What's wrong?" Sophea asks with concern.

"It's Chas Mai. After you left the apartment, she collapsed in the kitchen," Ravy explains. "They called the ambulance and she's on the way to Lincoln Hospital right now. They think it was a heart attack. It's not your fault."

"It is my fault," Sophea cries. "I did this to her. I broke her heart." The two sisters hug and run toward Ravy's car. "I'm so stupid and selfish. I should have never told them I wanted to move out."

Chapter 38

I t is a little past eleven p.m., and Sophea and Ravy run into the main entrance of Lincoln Hospital, located in the Foggy Bottom area of the city. The night outside is quiet and still. A few cars pass on the street. Inside, the hospital emergency ward is buzzing with activity. The fluorescent lights are so bright that Sophea has to blink several times before she can see the receptionist. Ravy explains their situation, and the nurse directs them upstairs to the ICU on the fourth floor.

Throughout the lobby, other families rush in to see their loved ones. One harried husband escorts his pregnant wife and explains to the nurse that her water just broke. At this time of night, the hospital patrons all look weary and lost. Sophea is thankful for the nurses on the night shift who are accustomed to this late hour and handle each frantic new patient with calm and confidence. Their smiles act as a reassurance, even if they mean nothing more than "Hello and welcome."

Sophea's head swirls as she thinks about the idea of losing Chas Mai. *This is not possible. This is the woman who raised us. I can't live without Chas Mai.* She looks at Ravy. "Do you remember when Chas Mai used to rub Vick's Vapo-Rub on our chests and make our colds disappear overnight?"

"Of course," Ravy says. "I loved when she would rub tiger balm on my cuts and bruises. It stung, but her hands were so tender. I loved it."

"Chas Mai was the one who bathed us, fed us, and put us to sleep at night," Sophea says. "She still does all of that for me and Mom. What are we going to do if anything happens to her?"

"Learn to cook and do your own laundry," Ravy replies. "Just kidding, sis. I don't know what Mom would do without Chas Mai. Let's not think about that right now."

The girls rush off the elevator to find that a nervous group of Cambodian relatives have taken over the waiting room. Ming Bonna, the "Laundromat Queen," is barking orders at her sisters to pray. Ming Map, the "Double-Speaker," looks up at the girls with accusatory eyes and loudly says, "Is there anything you girls need to tell us about what happened tonight?" A hush falls over the room as the relatives wait for an answer.

Sophea loses her breath at the spectacle and grabs a chair for balance. She then notices Ming Khana, the kindest of the sisters, moving toward her with a wet paper towel. "Dear children, we have been waiting for you. Your mother is in the ICU with Chas Mai. Let me take you to her." She throws a stern glare at her sisters and motions for them to stay quiet. Ming Khana places the wet paper towel gently on Sophea's forehead, and they walk down the silent hallway toward Chas Mai's room.

The girls find Cookie nestled in a corner chair, reading an issue of *Today's Royalty* magazine. Her face lights up when she sees her daughters, and she motions for them to come sit by her. Cookie's face is solemn as she kisses their cheeks and foreheads.

"I am so sorry, Mommy! Can you ever forgive me?" Sophea blurts out. "I need to see Chas Mai. This is all my fault. I feel so guilty."

A nurse beckons Sophea and Ravy into the small but clean room beside where Chas Mai is being held overnight. "Your grandmother is stable and resting now," she says. "By tomorrow, we should have her in her own room. We just want to keep an eye on her the next few hours. You can go in for a while, but only one person can stay with her overnight. Perhaps you can tell your relatives they can come back in the morning to visit."

The girls enter the ICU room to see a thin and frail old woman lying still under the sheets. The rhythmic sound of the respirator pump and bells and whistles from the various machines and IVs hooked up to Chas Mai fill the air. "She looks so weak." Ravy kisses Chas Mai on the cheek and recites a prayer to Buddha. She strokes her grandmother's hair and kisses her hands, which are curled up and wrinkled, still smelling of mint leaves from the salmon amok.

Sophea observes the scene from the corner of the room and weeps. *How could I have taken Chas Mai's presence for granted all these years? She has made me into the woman that I am today.* After giving Ravy a few minutes to speak to Chas Mai, Sophea approaches her grandmother's side.

"Please forgive me, Chas Mai," Sophea sobs once more. "I never wanted to hurt you. You are the greatest love of my life. Please stay with us. I—*we*—need you. This is not your time to go yet."

The nurse re-enters the room a few minutes later and reminds the women that visiting hours are over. "Your mom looks really tired," she nudges. "Perhaps one of you should take her home soon."

"It is my fault that Chas Mai is at the hospital. Please let me stay with her tonight," Sophea insists. "I will not leave her side." Cookie and Ravy quietly agree to head home.

In the dim light of the hospital room, Sophea stares at Chas Mai's sunken but still pretty face. She clings to her grandmother's hands for dear life. She repeats a Buddhist prayer and kisses Chas Mai's hands. "I'm so sorry. I am so sorry. I love you. I love you. Please do not leave us. Please stay. Please stay. I need you, Chas Mai, please don't leave me." This Sophea recites over and over until she finally falls asleep hours later.

✤✤✤

The next morning, Sophea feels Cookie's hand on her right shoulder. "Do you want to lie down, honey?" she asks. "I have some coffee and a croissant for you. You didn't have any dinner last night."

"I am hungry, Mom, but I feel too guilty to eat," Sophea declines the pastry.

Cookie finds a seat nearby and begins to devour the croissant. "No use wasting a good pastry," she mutters.

Sophea does not let go of her grandmother's hand all morning. Inside, she prays to Buddha for strength. "Chas Mai, I never meant to hurt you," Sophea whispers. "All I wanted was a chance to go see for myself what the world has to offer. Please get better. I'm here and will never leave your side again." She rests her head on Chas Mai's arm.

A few hours pass and Chas Mai wakes up. The nurses come in to wash her face with a towel, feed her, and check her blood pressure. It is past noon and

Ravy joins them again at the hospital. The three women wait all afternoon, until Chas Mai's doctor comes to give them an update.

A very well-mannered and handsome African American doctor enters the room and flips Chas Mai's health charts. He is wearing green scrubs, which brings out his dark chocolate skin. He does a quick survey of the room with his hazel eyes and introduces himself to a drowsy Chas Mai.

"Good afternoon, Mrs. Norodom. Nice to see you awake. My name is Dr. Michael Tyler. I tended to you last night when you came into the hospital." He reaches out to shake her hand. "How are you feeling today? I see you have a lot of visitors already this morning." Chas Mai squeezes his hand but does not reply.

"Thank you, Doctor. Our grandmother seems to be feeling much better this morning," Ravy says. "We can't thank you enough for what you did last night. It was awful to think we almost lost her. She's the rock and heart of our family." Ravy stares at Chas Mai's doctor for a moment too long and blushes.

"Your grandmother suffered a heart attack last night, but it looks like she will be all right," Dr. Tyler explains. "Luckily for your grandmother, someone knew to give her an aspirin and call 911 immediately. That quick thinking saved her life."

"That was my mother. She called 911 and tended to our grandmother until the ambulance came." Ravy points to a nervous-looking Cookie, who is pacing back and forth in the hospital room.

"My mother had a heart attack and collapsed in our living room. Are you sure she is not going to die? What do we do now?" Cookie frowns and gestures for more answers. "Is there any other doctor who can help us with our questions or give us a second opinion? What if you're wrong? May I ask where you got your medical degree?"

Ravy's jaw drops in exasperation, and she attempts to cover up her mother's social blunder. But Dr. Tyler lifts his eyebrow and gives her a quick wink as if to say, *Relax, I've got this.*

"Ma'am, you have a lot of valid questions, which I will try to answer." Dr. Tyler removes a pen from behind his ear and jots down some notes. "We did several diagnostic tests to determine how much your mother's heart was damaged and to see what degree of coronary heart disease she may be facing. At this point, we expect her to make a full recovery in a couple of months. She'll just need to get plenty of rest, eat a healthy diet with less fat, salt, and sugar, exercise regularly, and take some heart medication."

"And what will happen to my mother once you release her from the hospital?" Cookie continues. "She just had a heart attack! In Cambodia, we could stay in the hospital for as long as we wanted. Can't she be moved to a temporary holding place until she feels a hundred percent again? This is just too much pressure on all of us. I am not a physician! Is there another doctor who can better explain to us what is happening here?"

Sophea remains uncharacteristically quiet, stroking her grandmother's hand and massaging her legs and feet during the tense conversation. *Ravy can do this for once*, she thinks to herself.

"Calm down, Mother," Ravy snaps. "*You're* going to have a heart attack if you continue acting like this. Can you let him finish?" She smiles at Dr. Tyler, who returns her smile.

"I plan to continue seeing your mother regularly in the next four to six weeks so we can do some more stress tests and make sure she's on track to full recovery," Dr. Tyler is speaking directly to Cookie now. "If these lifestyle changes don't work, then yes, of course, there is always the possibility of surgery. But that is not a concern right now. My immediate concern is that she gets plenty of rest. And no stress!"

"I hope you are not trying to imply that this is my fault. I'm just trying to find the best care for my sick mother." Cookie throws him an agitated look.

"We don't need another doctor," Ravy says. "Dr. Tyler has been taking amazing care of Chas Mai and fully understands her condition. I trust that he will continue to take great care of her until she is completely well." Once again, her stare lingers on the doctor.

"Let's see what Chas Mai thinks," Cookie barks back. "You're not the patient here."

"Mrs. Norodom, if you're okay with me being your doctor, I will consider it a privilege and an honor." Dr. Tyler turns to Chas Mai, who nods in agreement.

"She's on drugs. You're hijacking this answer from a half-conscious old woman," Cookie retaliates. "And you never addressed my question of your credentials. What proof do we have that you are even qualified to take care of my mother? You could still be an intern here for all we know."

"Please don't judge the rest of us by my mother's bad behavior," Ravy pleads. "Our mother does not function well under great duress."

Dr. Tyler looks up with an amused smile at Cookie as if this is not the first encounter he has had with a skeptical patient. "Of course, I totally understand your mother's concerns. It's only natural that she wants the best caretaker for her mother. I completed my premed studies at Stanford and obtained my M.D. from Yale School of Medicine. I did my residency at Johns Hopkins University. Besides a passion for tennis and my grandmother's homemade sweet potato pie, medicine is what I know and love."

"Did you say Stanford and Yale?" Cookie is still wary of this new doctor, but she softens a bit after she learns of his educational pedigree. "That is very comforting to me. Do you mind if we call you Dr. Michael? It's easier to remember."

"I promise I will do everything in my power to ensure your mother's full recovery," Dr. Michael reassures Cookie and the rest of the family. He writes on the back of his business card and offers it to Ravy. "These are my personal cell phone and pager numbers. Feel free to call me anytime with any questions you or your mother may have. We will give your grandmother the best possible care. I'll be back to visit with you later." Ravy stands up and places her hand on the back of his shoulder to show her appreciation. Cookie is still unimpressed and walks over to the windowsill.

Chas Mai motions for Sophea to come close to her face. "Sophea, my love, hospital food is very bland. Can you please ask Dr. Michael if he can find some Maggi for me?"

At that moment, Ming Bonna walks in waving a small bottle of Maggi. "I've got it! I know our mother's basic food needs."

Dr. Michael takes the bottle, looks at the sodium content, and shakes his head. "She's going to need to start watching what she eats. I would start with saying no more of this stuff." His response is met with frowns from all three generations of women.

Chapter 39

"Come in, kiddo." Don waves Sophea into his office. "How have you been? I haven't seen you as much lately. But I've seen your pieces, and they look good."

"Thanks, Don," Sophea responds. "You should come up and visit us sometime. We love visitors now that we've thrown out about a decade's worth of junk. There's even a place to sit and visit near the window—we use the sofa to brainstorm ideas and eat lunch."

"How's your grandmother doing?" Don asks. "There's a lot going on in your life right now."

"Good, she's been home for about a month now," Sophea responds. "We're taking it one day at a time, but she's a strong woman."

"Well, I've been looking at these Nielsen reports all morning. Don't know what happened, but looks like you and Edie were a big hit with our viewers during Sweeps Month," Don says. "I haven't seen numbers this high for a single reporter in a long time."

"You've got to give it to Edie. She's got so much energy and enthusiasm for life—it's contagious to the viewers, too," Sophea says, glowing. "That girl will do anything from taste-testing diet bars to trying out new workout videos or confronting bad business owners on their front steps. It gives me a lot of freedom as a producer."

"I want you to know that Dale sent me his resignation letter last week, and Human Resources will be posting the job opening tomorrow," Don says. "You told me you only wanted the consumer beat as a temporary gig—I haven't forgotten about you."

"Wait, I never said I wanted to leave," Sophea sputters. "Edie and I make a really good team. I want to stay."

"The newsroom needs you back," Don counters. "If you stay up in the consumer unit, I am going to have to open up your job down here."

"Having a consumer-investigative unit at WNR-TV differentiates us from the other stations in this market," Sophea keeps her voice slow and low, though her heart feels like a burning meteorite. "But we need a bigger budget. I would like to be the executive producer for the unit because I've proven to you what I can do. I would also like a salary that corresponds with my new title." Sophea breathes a sigh of relief, proud she has stood up for herself professionally for the first time in her life.

"Looks like Dale's extended leave of absence has boosted your confidence," Don says. "Your ratings are good, and you have proven to be an asset to the consumer unit. Are you sure you want to give up the security of your old job in the newsroom for a position in a failing division of the station? I'll be watching your ratings numbers very closely. If they don't stay up, I can't guarantee your job back down here."

"I've never been more sure of anything," Sophea replies. "I am totally up for the challenge of turning around the consumer unit. But I am also serious about being paid at the level of an executive producer. It's been two years since my last raise. I think it's time to pay me what I'm worth."

Don regards Sophea and her new attitude for a few minutes, then replies, "Fine, let me see what we can do. If you are doing the work, then I suppose we owe you a commensurate pay. I'll get back to you by tomorrow morning with an update. Now, scoot. I have a meeting in a few minutes."

Sophea strides across Don's office and embraces him with both arms. "Yay! I can't wait. You know where you can find me." She marches upstairs to the consumer unit and starts to run the numbers in her head. If Don pays her the salary of an executive producer, she will finally have the funds to live on her own. Sophea is thrilled at the prospect of having her own apartment. But clouds quickly roll in to spoil the perfect picture. How will her mother and grandmother take the news?

❧❧❧

"Are you coming home soon?" Cookie calls Sophea at the station. "Can you please swing by the grocery store and pick up a roast chicken for dinner? I've got brown rice and steamed broccoli here. Since Chas Mai had her heart attack, we've all had to eat a lot healthier. It's not as much fun."

"That sounds delicious, Mom," Sophea teases. "Thank you for cooking for us. I know princesses don't usually cook."

"Chas Mai is recovering because you are home with us every night," Cookie says. "It does her heart good to see that we are all together and happy. This is the way it's supposed to be."

"No pressure, Mom," Sophea says with sarcasm. "Do you still have some Kahlua and cream? I think I am going to need some tonight. See you in a bit."

Chapter 40

As Sophea prepares to leave the office, she calls Ravy. "Hey, I finally got you in person—why haven't you been returning any of my messages? Can you join us for a King Sihanouk film at the house?"

"Sorry, but I've got a date tonight," Ravy says. "Michael and I are going to listen to some jazz at Blues Alley. He's got the night off."

"Are you serious? Ah! That's why you've been so secretive. When did this happen? I need details pronto," Sophea announces. "Come to think of it, you two were making googly eyes at each other that day you met at the hospital."

"Really? Was it that obvious?" Ravy laughs. "Michael's cute and fun. For a doctor, he doesn't take himself too seriously. I also find him super dreamy. What can I say?"

"Wow, glad to know he's bringing out this softer side of you," Sophea teases. "Chas Mai and Mom are going to have a field day with this. A Cambodian dating a black man? I'm so happy for the two of you, but just be prepared for their wrath. This is going to be very hard for them to accept."

"Those two women don't scare me much," Ravy says. "Anyway, they said they prayed for a good man to enter our lives this year. I think their wish just came true for me. Why don't you invite Adam to join you all instead? He can act as a decoy for me in front of Chas Mai and Mom, while I navigate this new thing with Michael."

"Good idea, I'll do that," Sophea replies. "I'm sure Mom will be asking lots of questions."

"Would you like some dessert?" Michael offers the menu to Ravy. They are just finishing up their dinner at a popular Spanish tapas restaurant in downtown Washington.

Ravy skims the menu, then puts it down. "Michael, I'm having a blast with you, but I need to talk to you about something really serious." She takes a deep breath.

"Uh-oh, did I do something wrong?" Michael grins and leans back in his chair. "Go ahead, shoot."

"I told my sister about you and me today," Ravy begins. "She reminded me that my family is not going to be too keen about us dating. I personally don't care that much about what my mother and grandmother have to say about my dating life—they are never happy with my choice of men. But it's going to be quite a trip for you if we keep dating. My mother has no couth. She just says what's on her mind, even if it's very offensive and hurtful. Are you prepared for that?"

"Baby, are you serious? I grew up in the south side of Philly, raised by a single mom who worked as a waitress most of her life." Michael moves forward and shakes his head. "From the time I was five, I wanted to be a doctor. My teachers told me to give up my dream because it would be too difficult. I got accepted to Stanford after working my butt off in school, but I almost couldn't attend since we had no money. If I hadn't received a last-minute track scholarship, who knows where I would be right now. I also got another full scholarship to Yale, but let's just say I didn't quite fit in with the more privileged kids. Only about a dozen of us were black in a class of about a hundred and fifty students. If I wasn't studying, I was working to support myself financially during those years. It was hard and I never slept. It's a wonder I'm still alive and able to take you on a date tonight." He starts to laugh.

"I'm so sorry, honey." Ravy frowns. "I had no idea it was so hard for you all those years. You always make things look so easy. You never complain about anything."

"My mom raised me and my brother by herself, working two different jobs at a nursing home during the day and at a local diner until it closed at midnight," Michael explains. "We learned early on that there was no complaining in our household or you'd get your ass whooped. When I told my mom I wanted to be a doctor, she told me to stop playing and get to work. My mom worked hard all her life, and she instilled a huge work ethic in me and my brother. That's just what you have to do to get what you want in life."

"Your mom sounds like one strong woman," Ravy says. "Do you think I would pass her test?"

"One thing my mom knows for sure is that she raised two good and responsible men," Michael says. "When the day comes that I bring you home to meet her, she'll know I'm serious about you. My mom's not that different from yours. She would love to see me married one day, too."

"That's good to hear. Now, have you ever dated outside of your race before?" Ravy asks. "You're the first black man I've ever dated, though I did date a Moroccan once. But I'm not sure if that counts or not." She reaches for his hands.

"Yeah, I did date a white woman in college, but we were young and nothing really came of it," Michael explains. "Anyway, I knew I wanted to go to medical school, so my focus was on my education and career. There was no time for dating or relationships back then."

"I'm so sorry I even have to bring this up with you, but you just need to understand what you're in for if we date," Ravy says. "Asians are a whole different breed. I may be Americanized, but don't be fooled by my perfect English. Cambodians are very nice, but they can sometimes be a bit close-minded about dating outside of the community. They're just not used to it."

"Understood. I get it. I'm game if you are, though." Michael stands up and sits next to Ravy. "All I know is, I think you're sexy, sharp, and pretty wonderful. I fell for you the first time I saw you in the hospital room with your grandmother. And if you remember, your mom was not impressed with my diagnosis that day. I think she wanted another doctor." He chuckles and places his hand on Ravy's chin. "I'm falling fast and hard. That's what I know for sure."

"Well, then buckle up, Doctor Love," Ravy says. "Just know that no matter what my mom and grandmother say to you, it's not personal—they're equal-opportunity insulters. They just want to protect me and Sophea from everyone and everything. They love us, and they have no boundaries. If you can find a sense of humor in dealing with my mom, you will make it through with flying colors."

"I'm extremely attracted to you in every way—physically, mentally, emotionally. How about we just take it one day at a time?" Michael leans in and kisses Ravy on the lips. "Let's finish up here so we can go listen to some jazz across the street. You're going to love it."

Ravy mouths *"thank you"* and kisses him back. They can hardly keep their hands off of each other, but they run out to catch the concert.

Chapter 41

It's been a couple of weeks since Sophea's meeting with Don, and he finally confirms her promotion and pay raise. "Keep up the ratings and we'll both be happy," he says to her. "Congratulations. You earned this, kid."

Sophea celebrates this news with a quick jaunt to the local coffee shop with Ravy. "I am so happy! I can't believe I got everything I asked for."

"You worked hard for your promotion," Ravy says. "I'm really proud of you, big sister. Have you told Chas Mai and Mom yet?"

"No. I figure I will let them know tonight when I get home," Sophea says. "I just want to take this in for a minute and not stress about anything else right now."

"Well, now that you've got your big raise, perhaps it's time for you to consider getting your own place," Ravy says. "If you don't do this now, you will never do it."

"Why do you have to ruin this moment for me?" Sophea says. "We are all getting along well now. That will just rile them up again."

"You and Adam are getting close. I'm sure he wouldn't mind a little more privacy for the two of you," Ravy says. "You can use Chas Mai and Mom as your excuse for not moving out, but I think you're the problem. It's time to grow up."

"I'm scared of hurting Mom and Chas Mai," Sophea says. "Can you come over and support me tonight, then? I promised Chas Mai at the hospital that I would never leave them."

"I'm supposed to have dinner with Michael tonight, but let me see what I can do," Ravy says.

"Just out of curiosity, have you officially told Mom that you and Michael are an item?" Sophea asks. "Mom is starting to ask a lot of questions about the two of you. She said Chas Mai smelled your perfume on him the other day when she went in for a checkup. You know our grandmother's got a nose like a bloodhound. Specifically, Mom said it would be an 'awkward' family situation if anything were to happen between the two of you. She is starting to say some mean and disrespectful things about Michael. You need to nip this in the bud as quickly as possible."

"Nightmare—this is exactly what I've been trying to avoid," Ravy says. "I knew Mom and Chas Mai would not be thrilled that Michael and I are dating, but I thought she might take the high road for once and think about my happiness. She's always concerned about her public image and what others think. I'm not going to think about this anymore tonight. We need to get you moved out first, then I'll have that conversation with Mom."

The two sisters hug for a long time. "You'll be fine, Sophea. Chas Mai and Mom will be fine. It's time."

❧ ❧ ❧

"We've been waiting for you." Chas Mai hugs Sophea. "Your mother just brought home a big bucket of fried chicken for you and a roast chicken for me. We called Ravy to see if she wants to join us this evening. Sit down and tell us about your day."

Sophea takes a deep breath, unsure of where this conversation will lead. "I did get some good news," she says. "Don promoted me to executive producer of the consumer unit."

"That is cause for a celebration." Cookie raises her glass. "We are so proud of you. You have become a successful young woman. What man would not want you now?" She puts a heaping spoonful of coleslaw onto her plate.

"He also gave me a raise," Sophea continues. "That means that I have enough money now to move out and take that apartment right below Ravy."

"Not that conversation again, Sophea," Cookie replies. "I thought we already made a decision. You're not going anywhere. The most important thing now that you have such an important job is to come home where you can get a home-cooked meal every night and to save that extra money for retirement instead of wasting it on something like rent." She hands Sophea the bucket of chicken and motions for her to grab her favorite—wings.

"You must take care of your mother now that I am not so strong," Chas Mai adds. "This is also a very big house that needs lots of tending. We need your help."

Sophea realizes that this is going to be an unpleasant and uncomfortable conversation. "Please, I don't want to argue again, but my feelings have not changed about moving out. At the hospital, I thought I wanted to stay here with you. But now that I see Chas Mai is healing, these feelings that I need to move out are stronger than ever. Please forgive me."

"We knew this was all too good to be true." Cookie looks over to Chas Mai. "Do you want to send your grandmother to the hospital again?"

Chas Mai sits at the dinner table. "You promised me that you would never leave us. That you would always take care of us." She stares out toward the window, where a gnat is flitting against the screen, trying to find an opening to the outside.

"Yes, I promise to always take care of the two of you. That will never change," Sophea says. "But it's time for me to move out. I want to know how it feels to pay my own bills, make my own dinner every night, and come home to a place of my own. I don't expect you to understand. But what I know and feel in my heart is that I have to do this. Please don't be mad."

"Mad? You should have just left us in the killing fields to die," Cookie screams. "You are so ungrateful for what we have done for you. What will Chas Mai and I do? How can you leave us like this? We thought you were different from your sister. America did this to you. You are not Cambodian if you can leave your mother and grandmother to fend for themselves. I am ashamed of both of you girls."

Minutes later, Ravy (who has consumed a couple of glasses of wine beforehand to settle her own nerves) comes bounding through the front door. "Fried chicken, baby! Talk about a Cambodian delicacy." She is greeted by three very somber faces.

"Wow—this does not look like a fun conversation," Ravy says. "Can someone please tell me what's going on?"

Sophea says, "Mom is in the middle of telling me how ashamed she is of the two of us." Ravy sits down and sips a glass of coconut juice.

"Mom, you and Chas Mai need to take your claws out of Sophea and let her go out and live her life," Ravy says. "She's already devoted her entire twenties to the two of you. Do you want to take another decade or two from her? She's not getting any younger. You say you want her to get married, but how can she find a husband when she is married to the two of you?" Sophea nods her head in agreement.

"It's time for Sophea to be on her own," Ravy continues. "My friends ask me if there's something wrong with Sophea, if she is a wallflower, or worse, a virgin...it's embarrassing."

"This is not a joke." Cookie glares at Ravy. "You two have no respect for our values and ways. You think we are old-fashioned. Just wait until you get old and have no one to care for you. I curse you with Americanized children who will put you away in a nursing home. We Cambodians don't do that to our elders."

"You two girls are wrong." Chas Mai presses her hand to her chest. "You do what you will, but know that I will never forgive you for leaving us, Sophea. Wait until we tell the rest of the family about your willfulness. Has anyone seen my medication?"

Ravy puts her finger against her mouth to tell Sophea to stop talking. The four women eat the rest of the fried chicken in silence. In the background, Frank Sinatra sings "Strangers in the Night." Chas Mai heads into the living room after the meal. Cookie picks up her plate and slams it into the sink. Sophea and Ravy clean up the table, removing the chopsticks and Sriracha sauce.

Sophea squeezes her sister's hand. "Mom might as well have called me a Khmer Rouge. That's how angry she is with me."

"It's okay," Ravy assures her sister. "They may never forgive us, but they won't stop loving us. We're family."

In the other room, Cookie calls all of her sisters. "I am going to disown my children! They are evil, horrible, selfish girls. Wait until everyone at the pagoda hears what they have done to me and Chas Mai. I will never forgive her. Not since that day when we left Phnom Penh have I felt this alone and abandoned."

Chapter 42

"Just a few more random boxes and I think we'll be ready to go." Ravy wipes the sweat from her brow. "You sure you don't want to take anything else from the house?"

Sophea surveys her bedroom one last time. "I packed just the bare necessities, because I want it to look like someone still lives here."

"Well, the bed, dresser, and TV are already gone," Ravy says. "Maybe Chas Mai and Mom will want to do something else with this room if you move all your stuff out. Did you ever think of that?"

"Neither of them has talked to me in two weeks," Sophea says. "Mom is so mad she doesn't even invite me to watch King Sihanouk movies with her anymore. Chas Mai feels that I'm betraying her even more than you did, because at least you never made them any promises. I'm a total jerk. I feel horrible."

"It's okay, sis," Ravy says. "I know this is hard. They will get over it. I promise. It's getting late, so we should probably leave soon with this final carload of stuff."

❧

In the kitchen, Chas Mai is cooking up some chicken fried rice and green bean stir-fry. "Let me pack this up for you so you have food to eat tonight. You can always come home if you need anything."

"I love you both very much," Sophea says. "Thank you. I promise we will see each other often. I'll still come over for dinners and movie night. And one day, maybe you can even come visit me."

"For goodness' sake, the apartment is only fifteen minutes away from here," Ravy yells out from the car. "It's not like you are moving to Timbuktu! This doesn't have to be so dramatic. You can drive back here for dinner tonight if you want. Let's go!" Sophea pauns her mother and grandmother and rushes out to the car.

Ravy's red compact drives away, and Chas Mai and Cookie stand at the door until it is out of sight. Chas Mai walks back into the kitchen and wipes the countertop. Cookie wanders over to her favorite easy chair in the living room. She turns on the East Asia News channel, where a Japanese reporter is interviewing a relief worker in Cambodia. There is a spike in dengue fever among the villagers, brought on by mosquitoes during the rainy season. The social worker makes a plea for monetary donations.

"Maybe one day the president of the United States will visit Cambodia," Cookie says to Chas Mai. "Let's eat dinner in front of the television tonight. We can watch the video of King Sihanouk's coronation again. I hope that Sophea calls soon."

Chas Mai strokes the back of Cookie's head and says, "You are a good daughter to me and a good mother to Sophea and Ravy. I will pray to Buddha and he will take care of all of us."

"Sure, Maman," Cookie replies. "Don't worry, I will never leave you. It's been us two and the children all these years. It's only fair that they get to live their lives, too, I suppose." Chas Mai puts her arm around Cookie.

Chapter 43

A few months have passed since Sophea's move, and Ravy conjures up the courage to talk to Cookie about Michael. She heads over to her mother's house after work one evening, carrying a bag of Thai take-out.

"Mom, can you please turn off the television for a bit?" Ravy asks. "I need to talk to you about my relationship with Michael." She puts the food on the kitchen counter.

"Relationship? That's news to me." Cookie presses on the television remote and beckons Ravy to sit down next to her. "Is there something you need to tell me? I thought Dr. Michael was Chas Mai's doctor. I didn't realize he has been making house calls to my daughter."

"Sophea says you've been talking badly about him, is that true?" Ravy asks. "What has he done to us except take exceptional care of Chas Mai? I think we need to be grateful here."

"I'm supposed to be grateful because he is doing his job?" Cookie responds, barely containing her anger. "When did you become his biggest defender?"

"Mom, Michael and I have been exclusively dating for a couple of months," Ravy explains. "I didn't tell you because I didn't want to deal with your drama."

"My drama? You are keeping secrets from us, and I am the dramatic one?" Cookie smirks. "You have a lot of nerve, my darling Ravy."

"Well, I'm telling you now that I'm in love with him and need you to support us," Ravy says. "Can you do that for me, please?"

"You never needed my support before, so why now?" Cookie walks toward the windowsill. "You are a silly girl when it comes to love. Michael may be special today, but trust me, he is not the right person for you."

"Why would you say that? He's kind, gentle, smart, and he loves me," Ravy says. "I can see us being together for a long time."

"Call it a mother's intuition," Cookie says. "Love may feel intoxicating at first, but the world is not ready for the two of you together. Chas Mai and I are not ready for the two of you together. It goes against our Cambodian ways."

"Why don't you just tell me the truth?" Ravy demands. "You don't like Michael because he's black. It's that simple—just say it out loud!"

"Don't you dare raise your voice at me, you insolent child," Cookie screams. "Yes, it is a huge problem for us. You cannot date someone African American. It is simply unacceptable in our culture. You should know this by now!"

"I can't help who I fall in love with," Ravy says. "Michael is the best man I've ever met. I thought you and Chas Mai wanted me to be happy and in love."

"Well, we do, but not in this way," Cookie says. "Everyone will talk about you behind your back, and Chas Mai and I will be embarrassed. This has to stop."

"I'm not going to let you or even Chas Mai get away with this kind of closed-minded behavior anymore. It's time for you both to change," Ravy says. "Mom, I love you but you're being a racist!"

"Perhaps, darling, but not intentionally," Cookie explains. "Growing up in Cambodia, we never saw anyone black. We were colonized by France, so the only foreigners we came to know and accept were Europeans—the French, the Portuguese, some Spaniards. I never saw anyone black before coming to America. Even visually, it's jarring to see the two of you together. We're just not used to it."

"Do you hear what you're saying, Mom?" Ravy says, her voice rising. "It's so offensive! You didn't raise us to be like that."

"Listen, stupid child, for a Cambodian, dating a black man is like dating a Vietnamese or a *cham* (Arab)," Cookie spits out. "You know we hate the Vietnamese for all they have done to our country over the last hundreds of years. Why must they always be infringing on our borders? Why would you betray your family and country like that? It goes deeper than skin color."

"That makes no sense. What have African Americans or even Arabs done to Cambodians?" Ravy argues. "If you're going to hate people based on who has invaded our homeland, then Caucasians should be at the top of the list—including the French and Americans."

"You know nothing about the traditions and beliefs that hold a people together," Cookie says. "Show some compassion for what you have put me and Chas Mai through. We don't understand how you can date a minority when there are so many white men available here in the States. Don't you know that they will bring up your social status here? Minorities don't do as well in this country as whites. It's a fact."

"You've been in America for twenty-five years," Ravy says. "We live in the nation's capital, where there is tons of diversity. Why are you acting like you're part of a white supremacist group when you're a minority, too!"

"How dare you call me a minority!" Cookie is offended. "You might as well have called me a mere commoner when I am of royal blood!"

"Ah, so that's what this is all about," Ravy replies. "You're still clinging to the crazy idea that some people are better than others simply by their birthright, or in this matter their skin color. You know the Cambodian revolution happened because there was such a class division between the rich and poor, the haves and have-nots. Obviously, the war didn't change your mind about anything or anyone."

"I am who I am," Cookie retorts. "It's hard to change at this age."

"Do I need to remind you that Michael is one the most successful doctors at one of the biggest hospitals in Washington? He graduated with multiple degrees from the most prestigious schools in this country. And he makes more money than any of us will ever see in our lifetime. Perhaps that will resonate with you!" Ravy is defensive. "I love Michael, and he's not going away any time soon. You need to open up your heart to him or you will lose me."

"Really, you are once again threatening to leave us for someone you just met?" Cookie says. "Family means nothing to you, does it?"

"I'm asking you to change the way you think," Ravy says. "We're not in Cambodia anymore. America is a melting pot. It's made up of immigrants from around the world, including our family. Please find it in your heart to accept Michael for the person that he is. Do you want people to hate me because of the way I look or the color of my skin?"

"He's just very dark," Cookie mutters. "What will people say when you two are together? Don't you know that people will be cruel and hateful toward the two of you? I don't want you to have to face that. And how about my grandchildren? I don't want them to have people looking at them or judging them—"

"In the same way that you are looking at and judging Michael because of his skin color?" Ravy interrupts. "Mom, we're from Southeast Asia. We're dark, too! I don't care what people think, you know that. They can throw me all their hate, but I will be okay as long as I have Michael. His love will be enough."

"You are young and foolish," Cookie says. "Please reconsider how this decision will affect the rest of your life—and ours."

"If you and Chas Mai love me, then you need to support us," Ravy says. "Michael is now a big part of who I am. There is no compromise or negotiation here."

"I feel faint." Cookie grabs a magazine and fans herself. "This is going to take some time. You are putting me in a very uncomfortable situation. How will I explain this to all your aunts and uncles…the people at the pagoda… the monks?"

"Really, you don't have to say anything," Ravy says. "Just love and support us. Everyone else will follow your lead. We don't owe anyone an explanation."

Cookie sits back in her chair and ruminates. *If I could marry someone outside of the royal family in Cambodia, then why can't my daughter marry a black man? I need to trust and support her just like my parents did for me.*

As always, Chas Mai has been in the corner eavesdropping during this heated discussion. She shuffles into the living room and sits between the other two women. There are no more words to say, so the three sit together in silence on the tired couch. The forgotten Thai take-out cools on the kitchen counter.

Chapter 44

"Can you believe it's been six months since we started working together?" Sophea says to Edie. "November Sweeps is already upon us."

"No, I can't believe how fast time is flying," Edie says. "But I know people are watching us. They come up to me in the streets to give me story ideas or tell me how helpful our piece was. It feels good to be of service."

"Let's face it, you're a local celebrity." Sophea smiles. "Everyone wants a piece of you now. That's not such a bad thing as long as you enjoy the attention."

Edie pulls her long red hair back into a ponytail and smiles. "Thanks, Sophea. I don't think I tell you often enough how much I appreciate you. I'm also very excited about emceeing your sister's event tomorrow at the Cambodian Embassy. It's so sweet of you to include me. What should I wear?"

"Don't worry. Just bring your natural charisma and energy. We'll dress you up," Sophea reassures her. "You'll be the prettiest Cambodian girl there."

"So, what exactly is an Apsara?" Edie looks at the printed program. "I don't think I'm pronouncing the word correctly."

"Pronounce it like *Ap-ce-ra*, not *Ap-Sara*," Sophea explains. "Apsaras are Cambodia's version of female goddesses, just like in the Greek mythologies. She's both ethereal and beguiling; men cannot not resist her temptation. As a matter of fact, tons of Apsara carvings and statues are depicted on the walls of Angkor Wat and the other countryside temples."

She points to a picture of an Apsara on the program. "In Cambodia, an Apsara is often shown as a female dancer dressed in gold from head to toe. I think every little Cambodian girl dreams of being an Apsara dancer one day."

"Look at her intricate hand poses," Edie says. "I know I've seen that image before in some travel magazine."

"Yep, Apsara is as familiar to Cambodians as apple pie is to Americans," Sophea concludes. "Once you start learning about Cambodia, you won't ever forget Apsara. She's a part of our history and heritage. Don't worry, you'll understand it all once you see the dance tomorrow night."

"I can't wait." Edie claps. "It's my first Cambodian fundraising event."

Sophea looks at her watch. "You're running late for the five p.m. broadcast. Don't forget you're doing fall travel tips today. And don't forget to put a little extra powder on your forehead. It was shiny yesterday."

After Edie leaves, Sophea reviews her list of calls and then dials Adam. "Hey, you. What a crazy day," Adam's baritone rings. "We just had a meeting with the mayor this afternoon. He was really pleased with your coverage of the financial scams this summer. He wants to know if you guys would be interested in participating in their job fair next month."

"Sure, I'll connect them with someone in our human resources office," Sophea says. "Are you still planning to join us tomorrow at the embassy? I'm going to need you to be on your best behavior and not offend anyone. This will be a very classy crowd of rich and upper-class Cambodians who are coming to support the royal dance troupe. Ravy really wants to raise a lot of money for the children's hospital in Siem Reap."

"So, a division of the masses and classes—just like your mother prefers it," Adam teases. "Just kidding, honey! I will be there in my best Cambodian silk shirt, and a muzzle, if that makes you happy. Trust me."

≈⋑⋑≈

"The weather is perfect tonight." Sophea hugs Ravy. "Your event is going to be a huge success! Look at how beautiful the leaves look with the sunlight going through them. It's a perfect backdrop for the Apsara dance tonight."

"Thanks, sis," Ravy says. "This is many months of work coming together. I still can't believe we were able to get everyone from the royal ballet troupe on a plane from Cambodia to here. It's a small miracle. My heart feels like it's going to burst out of my chest."

"Tonight is the event of the season for the elite Cambodian community here in DC," says Sophea. "Look at all the fancy dresses and suits!" The two women take a moment to observe the wealthy patrons making their way into the embassy.

There is only a bit more standing room left in the marble foyer of the Embassy, when the formal yet very friendly Cambodian Ambassador walks up to the podium and welcomes the audience. "We are pleased to see so many of our dear friends here tonight, supporting such a good cause. With your financial assistance, we are able to offer wonderful cultural events such as tonight's unprecedented show. It is with great pleasure that I open up this evening with a toast to Cambodia and its generous benefactors. Now, it is with joy that I introduce you to our beautiful emcee for the evening—Miss Edie Jackson from WNR-TV!"

"Good evening, everyone! We are pleased to present our feature program, *Apsara & Beyond: The Dancing Goddesses of Angkor Wat.*" Edie welcomes a group of about a hundred very prestigious guests. She looks stunning in a traditional Khmer outfit, the jade silk setting off her emerald eyes.

"The Khmer Royal Ballet Troupe is making its North American debut right here with a traditional Apsara dance that captures the true beauty and essence of Cambodian culture. After the show, please join us for some hors d'oeuvres and cocktails in the foyer, followed by a sit-down Cambodian meal created by two up-and-coming chefs." The guests applaud and look toward two young Cambodian men dressed in traditional chef coats and hats. They lower their heads and paun the audience with gratitude.

"After dinner, the Angkor Band will play traditional Cambodian music and American covers, so we hope you are wearing your dancing shoes," Edie continues. "And be sure to take a look at the beautiful artwork in our silent auction, which was created especially for tonight's event by our very own rising star, Ravy Lim. All funds from the sales of the artwork will go toward the children's hospital in Siem Reap. We thank you for coming out tonight and for generously supporting Cambodia's children. Have fun, everyone!"

Sophea marvels at Ravy's artwork. "I had no idea my sister was such a talented artist," she says to Edie. "I hope everyone brought their wallets."

"I'll remind each and every single person that this is for a good cause." Edie laughs. "Let's go meet some people!" She grabs Sophea's hand.

Chapter 45

Near the bar area, Cookie is holding court. "After all these years of being our little Cambodian rebel, Ravy is now the talk of the town. Who would have known?" She stops one of the waiters in an effort to grab more crab rangoons.

At that moment, Michael walks in carrying a bouquet of beautiful orchids. Cookie runs over to him and whispers, "Do you have a minute, Doctor? I want to say thank you for all that you've done for my mother. She has her health back because of you!"

"It's been an honor to take care of Chas Mai. She's a delightful patient," Michael says.

"A little bird told me that you've taken an interest in another member of my family," Cookie says. "Is that true?" She takes a sip of her champagne.

"That is very true," Michael says. "I know it's been difficult for you to accept us as a couple, but please know that I love your daughter. She's changed my life for the better. I'm serious about my intentions—I want to spend the rest of my life with her."

"Are you asking my permission to marry Ravy?" Cookie asks between more sips of champagne, unsuccessfully trying to hide her eagerness. "Are you two already engaged, or are you asking my permission? I think I no longer have any say about my daughters' love lives. They have both made it very clear that my opinions don't matter." She wipes her brow with a napkin.

"Well, your approval and support are important to me," Michael says. "I know that Ravy and I seem unconventional in your eyes, but I hope one day you will find it in your heart to love and accept me as part of your family. I want nothing more than to make your daughter happy for the rest of her life. And that means making sure that you and Chas Mai are well taken care of—Ravy loves you both more than you will ever know."

"Yes, you have taken great care of my mother. She reminds me how very kind and gentle you are with her during her visits to the hospital," Cookie says. "May I ask what inspired you to become a doctor?"

"My grandmother used to live with us when we were younger," Michael explains. "Part of the reason my mom worked two jobs was to help pay for my grandmother's medical bills when she was diagnosed with cancer. As you can imagine, we didn't have any health insurance back then. While she worked, my older brother and I took care of my grandmother at home. I was too young to really help, but she said that just having me sit next to her did her a lot of good. I used to make up stories with my sock puppets and make her laugh. My grandmother died when I was five. I knew then that I would become a doctor and provide care and healing to those in need since this awful disease had taken away one of the greatest loves of my life. I never wanted to feel as helpless again as I did when I was five."

"I'm so sorry. I understand that kind of loss." Cookie's heart softens as she watches Michael tear up. "I can't promise that I can change a lifetime of cultural beliefs overnight, but I will try. You will be pleased to know that we recently watched the movie *Jungle Fever* directed by Spike Lee. The movie is about inter-racial relationships in New York City. Wesley Snipes is the lead actor. Dare I say he makes my heart flutter?"

Michael winces at the sound of *Jungle Fever*, but he appreciates Cookie's attempt to make peace. "Well, if you like movies, I highly recommend *Guess Who's Coming to Dinner* starring Sydney Poitier. He's one of my favorite African American actors of all time." He scribbles the title of the movie on a paper napkin and hands it to her.

"Ravy has demanded that I be more open-minded about your relationship with her," Cookie explains. "The last thing I want to do is hurt either of you. Last night, I started reading *Roots* by Alex Haley, and I've added Michael Jackson's *Thriller* to my album collection. Music also speaks to me."

Michael chuckles. "Well, I'm glad to know that we both share a love of music. That can help transcend a thousand prejudices. I don't know anyone who doesn't like Marvin Gaye."

"I love 'Sexual Healing,'" Cookie interjects excitedly. "And I've been listening to Stevie Wonder since I was a little girl." She starts to sway back and forth.

At that moment, a group of Cookie's Cambodian women friends from the pagoda meander their way toward Cookie. "Attention, everyone! It is my great pleasure to introduce you to Ravy's fiancé, Dr. Michael Tyler. He is a very important person at Lincoln Hospital. Dr. Michael has degrees from both Stanford and Yale. We were just talking about how much the African American community has in common with Asians. They also have a lot of respect for their elders." Her friends all coo like a flock of doves.

Ravy overhears the conversation and runs over to the group. "Mother, what are you talking about? We're not engaged! Please don't start any more rumors. Didn't you learn anything from the situation with Sophea and Tim? Also, can you not point out his race every time we go somewhere? It's embarrassing."

"Can't a future mother-in-law brag about her soon-to-be son-in-law?" She turns her attention to Michael and her friends. "Do you think we can get the seamstress to dress him in the most magnificent ensemble for the wedding? He will look like an African king. Please spread out your arms, Michael, so we can see your wingspan." The women coo again.

"Mom, all this wedding talk is embarrassing and a bit premature," Ravy says. "Can you please give me and Michael a minute to enjoy being a couple?"

Michael looks over to his girlfriend and spreads out his arms. "Maybe your mom's got a point. I found my Cambodian princess, and I am never letting you go."

Ravy mouths, *"I love you."*

Chapter 46

"As you watch tonight's dance, you will notice the ornate costumes and headdresses of our beautiful Apsara dancers. These hand-made headdresses have up to five golden tips at the top which replicate those of the stone Apsaras found at Angkor Wat." Edie explains to the audience. "The ballet you are about to watch was choreographed by Queen Sisowath Kossamak in the 1940s for her granddaughter and Cambodia's first prima ballerina, Her Royal Highness Princess Norodom Buppha Devi. It was inspired by the Apsara carvings and sculptures that are prevalent at Angkor Wat. Please enjoy!"

The lights dim, and the central character of the dance, the Apsara Mera, starts her solitary dance on the top of the ancient temples. The primary ballerina moves her hands in a slow and fluid gesture as a small group of traditional Khmer musicians play their string and percussion instruments. As the dance progresses, about ten other female dancers join her on the stage. They dance in unison and create a visual sea of golden goddesses swaying back and forth.

"These women are breathtaking," Adam comments to Sophea. "I'm in a trance watching their bodies move so effortlessly. This is almost better than meditation."

"If you were in a trance, you wouldn't be talking right now," Sophea says with just a slight hint of jealousy.

The performance receives a standing ovation from the crowd. At the end of the show, Edie addresses the audience. "Before we head back inside, I want to thank the Royal Ballet Troupe for joining us this evening. It is an honor and a privilege to have these beautiful and talented dancers perform for us. I'd now like to also welcome His Royal Highness, Prince Chakra Sisowath, to the stage for a few words."

Prince Chakra is elegant in a traditional royal blue silk Cambodian long-sleeved shirt and black slacks. The audience is enraptured by this petite, enigmatic, real-life prince in their presence. He speaks softly into the microphone in almost-perfect English with a slight French accent. "Thank you, everyone, for your support of our Royal Ballet Troupe this evening. We are grateful to Princess Norodom Buppha Devi for training a new generation of young dancers to perform this classical Khmer dance. As many of you know, most of Cambodia's greatest dancers were killed in the war. With this new generation of young dancers, we hope their legacy will live on."

Prince Chakra then looks at Chas Mai and Cookie sitting in chairs in the front row. "The king, queen, and princess also send their regards to Her Highness Thavary Norodom and Princess Chanthavy Norodom. You may not know this, but Her Highness Thavary was a member of the original ballet troupe before she married Prince Viviya Norodom. The king and queen look forward to your next visit to Cambodia and hope you will bring your granddaughters with you."

Chas Mai blushes and peers at the floor after Prince Chakra's acknowledgment. Cookie is in her royal glory and waves to the crowd.

"I could get used to this royalty thing." Michael wraps his arms around Ravy. "My blue-haired beauty is a real-life princess." He winks at her.

"Wait, so you're royalty?" Adam asks Sophea. "That explains why you treat me like a serf all the time! Isn't that so, your ladyship?"

"Yes, welcome to our little fiefdom," Ravy says. "Don't tease Sophea. She takes her blue blood seriously."

"Adam, don't act like you wouldn't want to be a part of royalty," Sophea jokes. "Would you consider being the court jester?"

"That would require laughing and joviality," Adam says. "I'm not convinced yet that the royal Cambodian family has a sense of humor."

"Off with your head," Sophea says. "I only laugh when something is funny."

⚜ ॐ ⚜

Sophea sees Chas Mai sitting under the big oak tree and wanders toward her. "I am so honored to be your granddaughter tonight," Sophea says. "I love that you were one of the original Apsara dancers—that's such a huge accomplishment."

"Back then everyone was invited to be a part of the ballet troupe," Chas Mai explains. "The prince was kind in his remarks. I wasn't the most committed dancer and I quit after only a few weeks. That dancing may look easy, but it takes years of training and discipline to deliver such grace." She looks away from Sophea.

"Please, Chas Mai, will you and Mom ever stop being angry with me?" Sophea pleads. "It's been almost four months, and you are both still giving me the cold shoulder. I can feel it every time we talk."

"You are my granddaughter, and I will always love you," Chas Mai responds. "But it still hurts me that you moved out. I'm old, and it takes me a long time to get over things."

"I know that we'll never agree on this," Sophea replies. "But I never meant to hurt or disrespect you. Please know that I love you more than anyone else."

Ravy sees the tension from across the room and sidles up next to her sister. "Is everything okay?" She stares at Sophea. "This is probably not the best time to have a heart-to-heart with Chas Mai. Why don't you grab a drink and try to have some fun?"

Chas Mai finally speaks. "We have lived longer than you and we know more than you, but we're afraid to say anything to either one of you. You two are so defensive."

"I don't think it's wrong for us to want to have our own lives," Ravy explains. "You always make us feel like we are intentionally trying to hurt you. That's not the case at all."

"You girls will never understand what your mom and I gave up in Cambodia to bring you here," Chas Mai continues. "We left everything that we had—our family, friends, houses, cars, jobs, jewelry—everything. But if we had not left the country, none of us would have survived the war. We had to start all over here in America with nothing but each other. Family is everything."

"We've heard this story a thousand times," Ravy says. "We were babies back then. Thank you for what you did for us. Do you want us to be indebted to you for the rest of our lives?" She waves for a waiter to bring them some wine. "The genocide card might still work on Sophea, but I can't live a life dictated by guilt. Please, can we just enjoy each other tonight?"

"In Cambodia, no child would ever dare speak back to an elder the way you two speak to us. You break my heart," Chas Mai says. "We'll stop talking about this, but rest assured, only destiny will tell what will happen in the future. You can't control fate." Sophea does not know what else to do, and she rubs her right hand on the back of Chas Mai's shoulders.

"I'll drink to that." Adam appears from behind the bushes. He's holding a tray of red wine and hands everyone a glass. "Listen to your grandmother, ladies."

"We're in the middle of a tense conversation right now." Sophea takes a sip. "This may not be the best time to ingratiate yourself into our family."

"Oh, yeah? Check this out." Adam proceeds to flap his arms up and down, imitating the Cambodian butterfly dance. "My destiny is to dance with you." He takes Sophea's hand, and they join the circle of dancers on the floor. He whispers in her ear, "I didn't mean to interrupt your conversation with your grandmother. I just thought a bit of levity would help."

"Yes, your dancing is actually making Chas Mai laugh." Sophea looks over to her grandmother. "That makes me feel a lot better." She does a fancy turn on the dance floor and moves her eyebrows up and down in an exaggerated facial movement often used by Khmer performers to show flirtation.

After their dance, Sophea's aunts charge toward Adam and start to ask questions. "Where did you learn to dance Cambodian? What are your intentions with Sophea? Why are you two not married yet?" Adam is amused and basks in the attention. Chas Mai and Cookie look on with suspicion.

"I plan to use her up and then leave her for a younger Thai woman," Adam teases the aunts. "Do you have a problem with that?"

At that moment, Edie reappears in front of the crowd for a final announcement. "I hope you are all enjoying this phenomenal evening. I know I am. As you can see, the dance floor is officially open. The silent auction will close soon, so get your final bids in before then! Ravy Lim has asked me to let you know that she will be hosting a New Year's Eve party here at the Embassy again that will raise money to remove some of the deadly landmines in Northwest Cambodia. We hope you will help us ring in the New Year for this good cause."

Chapter 47

ophea beams at Ravy. "You've blossomed into quite a sophisticated and confident woman, my renegade sister." She watches as Michael brushes a few blue strands of hair from Ravy's forehead.

"Your mom has been really nice to me all night," Michael whispers into Ravy's ear. "Please don't be mad at her anymore. She's trying. We bonded this evening, and it wasn't over food. It was over our love for you."

The band is taking a break, and a man in a blue suit steps up to deejay. He smiles at Michael and starts to play "You're All I Need to Get By," a duet by Marvin Gaye and Tammi Terrell. Michael pulls Ravy from her seat and leads her to the center of the dance floor, where they are also the center of attention.

The two are in a full embrace, swaying to the sound of the music. Michael has her in a close hold and is whispering in her ear when Ravy's eyes begin to tear up. Just as she places her hands up to cover her mouth, Michael gets down on one knee and proposes in front of the unsuspecting crowd.

"All of my life, I never believed in true love or love at first sight," he says. "That always seemed to be for the movies and for a privileged few. But from the minute that I laid my eyes on you, I have been in love with you. I'm not sure if it was your mother's contagious wedding talk, or Apsara's special magic, or just seeing you in all your glory tonight. But what I know for sure is that I love you more than anyone in this world. You are the answer to my prayers. Please marry me and make me the happiest man on this planet. I promise to love and take care of you and your family for the rest of my life if you will have me." He looks up at Ravy, who is now jumping up in the air and screaming.

"Yes! Yes! Yes!" she says. "It would be my honor to be your wife. I can't believe this is happening to me! How is this possible? Yes! Yes! Yes!" Michael kisses Ravy on the mouth in the middle of the dance floor, in front of a beaming group of Cambodian guests.

Chas Mai is happy but shell-shocked. Cookie throws a harsh look over at the line of Cambodian bystanders staring intently at the newly engaged couple. They had all been warned earlier by Cookie that they would not be invited to the wedding if she witnessed one misstep or harsh word against Ravy or her fiancé.

Sophea and Adam rush over to congratulate the happy couple. Sophea is wearing the ring Chas Mai and Cookie gave her and she hands it over to Michael. "I know you did not expect to propose tonight, so why don't you go ahead and borrow my ring to give to your fiancée until the two of you can make it over to Tiffany's."

She winks at her future brother-in-law as he proceeds to place the ring on Ravy's finger. "It fits! It fits!" Ravy yells, staring at the block of multicolored stones on her left ring finger. "Thank you, Sophea! We promise to give it back to you soon!"

❦❦❦

Later, as Sophea and Ravy twirl on the dance floor, Cookie turns to Chas Mai and says, "Remember when I used to dance like that at the palace? I was young and beautiful then. I can see they got something good from me."

"It's not just good looks and dance moves that they got from you. You are a kind and loving mother to your girls," Chas Mai says. "Please give yourself a little more credit." Cookie kisses her mother with gratitude. She has been seeking this affirmation for years, and she closes her eyes to cherish the feeling.

Chas Mai continues, "So, I am glad that our prayers to Buddha have been answered. He never disappoints. It just may not happen exactly as we would have imagined. I am very pleased that Ravy will have Michael as her husband. He is a goodhearted man, and we can all probably learn a lot from each other." She tugs at the Buddha necklace around her neck for comfort.

Chas Mai puts her arm around Cookie as the Cambodian band plays a traditional upbeat *Romvong* song. The music is contagious, and before long the entire dance floor is filled with Cambodians and Americans alike. Adam pulls Cookie onto the dance floor, where she outperforms all the younger dancers and is the belle of the ball for one more night.

Chapter 48

The sun peers through the window shades and warms Sophea's face. *It's Sunday morning, and I am sleeping in today.* She nestles into the quilted comforter and closes her eyes for a few more minutes when the phone rings. She lets the machine pick up the call. It is Cookie.

"Sophea, are you there? Sophea, please pick up the phone. It is seven a.m.—time to get up. I am coming over with fresh baked chocolate croissants and coffee. See you soon."

Cookie hangs up the phone before Sophea has a chance to pick up. She prays that her mother was kidding about coming over and falls back to sleep.

"Sophea! Sophea! It's Mommy, please open the door!" Cookie yells through the door. "We need to talk, my love."

Sophea awakens from a very sweet dream and stumbles to the front door. "Mom, really? It's not even eight a.m. I am not awake yet."

"This couldn't wait. Honey, Chas Mai and I talked last night, and I came to a big realization." Cookie hands a steaming latte to her daughter. "We love you and Ravy so much. You two are our whole lives, and I know that's just not fair sometimes."

Sophea's ears perk up as she rubs the sleep out of her eyes. "Keep talking, Mom," she whispers. "I'm too tired to respond, but I definitely want to hear what you have to say."

"My dear love, your need for American independence is one of the hardest things I have ever had to accept," Cookie continues. "But I realize that as a mom, I don't want to be an obstacle in your life. You have a wonderful and beautiful life ahead of you. Chas Mai and I must get out of your way for you to pave your own paths. I had that chance when I left Cambodia. Now I must give that to you. We support you living on your own and will stop trying to make you feel bad about that decision. Chas Mai and I will be okay."

Sophea listens to Cookie's calm and resolved voice. It is like a warm bath that envelops her body. "Chas Mai is getting older. It is my responsibility to take care of her the way she has taken care of me, you, and Ravy all these years. She gets frailer with every passing year, but I just didn't want to see it. I am no longer scared to be the primary caretaker. I want to make my mother's life as happy and comfortable as possible in the years ahead. And I want to help you and Ravy live the lives that you want . . . wherever that may lead you. It's time for me to step up to my role in this family." She smiles.

"Thank you for this, Mom," Sophea says. "I've felt so guilty about moving out. I didn't know if either of you would ever forgive me for leaving the house."

"Well, we haven't quite forgiven you, but we are on our way," Cookie responds. "Moving out was like a slap to our faces. We never thought *you* would move out. I suppose that was rather unfair on our part."

"It's not like you were blindsided," Sophea defends herself. "We talked about the possibility of me getting my own place once I made enough money. I can't be five years old forever, though I know that's what Chas Mai would like."

"In our culture, we believe that parents take care of you for your first twenty years, then you take care of them in their last twenty years," Cookie explains. "We Cambodians don't desert our parents or put them in an old people's home until they die like the Americans do. My sisters and I have decided that we can't expect our children to take care of us in the future, though, so we're making contingency plans to take care of each other when we get old. We cannot expect our Cambodian traditions to be perfectly preserved in this country. We have learned that there has to be some blending...some compromises...so that everyone can be happy."

"All my life, I always leaned on Chas Mai for strength," Sophea explains. "I know that must have made you feel so dismissed at times. You just always seemed more hurt and fragile than the rest of us. I never wanted to take anything from you for fear that you would be upset."

"How can you say that?" Cookie blurts out. "I have been by your side all your life. Are you saying I was not a good mother?"

"No, you've always been a loving mother. But you were closed and distracted at times. I can only assume you hurt so much when you lost Papa that you had to build walls around yourself to stop the pain. As a child, I didn't know any better. I just couldn't feel your love at times, so I went toward Chas Mai."

"Cambodians don't talk about feelings like you Americans do," Cookie replies. "We just keep everything inside and move forward in our own way. And please don't tell me to go see a therapist. That is just not what we do."

"Well, then maybe you can start talking to me more?" Sophea asks. "Everything is always 'fine' with you, so I never really know your true feelings. The most excitement you show is when we are at a buffet and the shrimp cocktail is bigger than normal."

"Please don't blame me for getting excited about shrimp—it's a simple joy. Don't take that away from me," Cookie says, managing a smile.

After a noticeable pause, she continues, "My heart has broken so many times, I think I finally made the decision to stop feeling. I was younger than you are now when Chas Mai and I left Cambodia. In one day, I lost my husband, my country, and the only life I knew. It was all too painful and frightening. I never wanted to hurt like that again. Instead of dealing with the trauma of leaving Cambodia, it was just easier to let Chas Mai take the lead in raising you girls so I could hide my feelings in food, a book, or a television show. Grandmothers can be soft and loving. Mothers have to show they are strong and resilient."

"Mom, you are the best mother I could ever have had," Sophea says out loud for the first time in her life. "I tell you what. We may not be living together in the same house right now, but I have never broken my promise to you and Chas Mai that I will never leave you. You are always in my heart and in my thoughts. Know that I will always take care of the two of you. You, Chas Mai, Ravy, and me—we are family. No one and nothing will ever break us apart."

Cookie reaches out to her oldest daughter with both hands cupping Sophea's face. "So, does that mean that you won't put us in a nursing home when we are too old to care for ourselves?" There is a long pause between the two women.

"Yes, that's exactly what that means." Sophea smiles. "Let me live my life right now with the understanding that one day in the future, we will be together again in the same house. It will be a joy and an honor for me to take care of you and Chas Mai when you are older. That is what we Cambodians do for our elders. I look forward to continuing the tradition. We're family, and we take care of each other. I promise I won't abandon you when you are old."

Cookie takes a deep breath and caresses Sophea's hair, then cradles her in her arms. "I can't remember the last time you held me like this." Sophea smiles. "It feels so nice. And you smell so good. I could fall back asleep."

"Off! Off! You are getting a little too big for this." Cookie pushes Sophea back to an upright position. "I can't breathe."

Sophea clings to her mother and teases, "I'm not letting go! I'm never letting you go! Stay with me here forever!"

"You are a silly, needy little girl! I may not always hug you or smother you with kisses like American mothers do with their children, but know that I have always held you like that in my heart. You and Ravy are my pride and joy." Cookie collects herself. "This is more emotion than I can take for one day. How about if I catch you up on the latest family gossip instead? That is much more interesting than trying to make each other talk about our feelings."

"Mom, I know you have a huge, tender heart that's just waiting for some love." Sophea points to Cookie's chest. "I'm going to peel at it every day like an artichoke until I hit the center. Just watch me." She laughs as Cookie starts to give an update on the royal family back in Cambodia.

Two hours later, Cookie prepares to leave. "Some of your aunts are coming over this afternoon to watch a new movie about the influence of American rock and roll on Cambodian society in the 1960s. They say it could be an Oscar winner. We are having homemade Vietnamese *pho* noodle soup if you want to join us."

"That sounds fun, but I've got a date with Adam this evening," Sophea replies. She kisses her mother gently on the cheek and walks her to a nearby cab.

"Maybe you can buy yourself a new car with all that money they're paying you at the station," Cookie says. "Do you think it's too late for me to learn how to drive?"

"No, but you would be a danger to yourself and others out on the street," Sophea says. "I will look into getting a car. Please call me when you get home." She waves good-bye to her mother.

Chapter 49

"You must wrap the meat filling tightly. It is like swaddling a newborn in a fitted blanket," Chas Mai instructs Adam, who is trying to learn how to make a spring roll. "This is impossible. How I can teach a white man to roll correctly when I can't even get my granddaughters to do it right?"

"Yes, you'd better listen to her." Sophea strokes the back of Adam's head. "If you can't roll right, you'll be demoted to making the turkey and stuffing with me."

"You have done a nice job with your place." Cookie examines the one-bedroom apartment and walks toward the CD collection. "But you could use some better music. It will be hard to digest our food with all this thumping going on." She covers her ears.

"Alright, I'll change the music," Sophea says as she places a new CD into the stereo. "Here's something you will enjoy." The sound of Nat King Cole's buttery voice fills the room.

Sophea returns to the kitchen and marvels at the spread before her. It is a buffet worthy of the royal court, and there's something for everyone: fresh cranberries, blue cheese, and candied walnut salad; garlic mashed potatoes; green bean casserole; Portobello mushrooms, spinach, and Parmesan risotto; roasted beets, cauliflower, and Brussels sprouts; collard greens; corn bread and sausage stuffing; homemade turkey gravy; and three pies—apple, sweet potato, and chocolate mousse. There is also a heaping bowl of Siem Reap noodles, her mom's favorite comfort food. She begins warming up the butter-and-honey biscuits.

Elvis croons "I Can't Help Falling in Love with You" in the background. "That is my favorite song," Chas Mai reminds her granddaughters.

"Perhaps you two can dance to this song at the wedding," Cookie says to Ravy, who is flipping through an album of elaborate Cambodian wedding outfits. "The gold and white jacket will look stunning against Dr. Michael's complexion." Ravy rolls her eyes and blows a kiss toward her fiancé, who's on the phone with the hospital. She glances down at her new, sparkling diamond engagement ring that they recently purchased at Tiffany's.

The doorbell rings, and Sophea opens the door to find Prince Chakra in khakis and a purple polo shirt. "This is my first American Thanksgiving, and I am thrilled to celebrate this special holiday with my family." He gives his niece a warm hug.

"Hello, Uncle." Sophea pauns. "You certainly look very American." She can't help but smile as she offers him a drink. The prince follows her into the kitchen, carrying two unnoticed boxes with him.

"So, how do you like living here in Washington? Of all the places you could have chosen to live, we are honored to have you so close to us," Cookie says. "How are you enjoying the international studies program at Georgetown University?"

"I am enjoying myself very much and meeting lots of new people," Prince Chakra says. "I have become close friends with several ambassadors who live here in Washington. Who knows, perhaps diplomacy will be in my future. It would be an honor to represent Cambodia around the world."

"I think this is cause for a celebration!" Cookies says. "Even if you go out parading in the world, we will always keep a piece of you right here with us. You have become quite the devoted uncle to my girls. Thank you for being so good to them. They need that kind of support from a trusted male figure."

Prince Chakra fidgets with his collar and thinks back to the night when Sophea rejected his wedding proposal and ran out of the house. It was a defining moment for him. Afterward, he decided to focus on his studies and career and put his search for a bride on hold. "Your girls have been very kind to me, too. They have taught me a lot about American culture in the past few months. Look at my shoes! I would never dare to wear these at the palace, but I am obsessed with American shoes at the moment." The prince points down to a pair of red Air Jordan sneakers.

Cookie looks down and shakes her head. "Glad to know my daughters have such a positive influence on your sense of fashion. Please give me a high five." She lets out a high-pitched squeal and raises her right hand in the air. The prince and the princess break out into hysterical laughter together for the first time, very un-royal behavior from these Norodom and Sisowath cousins.

❧ ❧ ❧

"The turkey's ready, everyone," Sophea announces. "Time to eat! Would you like to do the honors?" She hands Adam the carving knife.

Adam cuts through the perfectly golden, deliciously crispy skin. But that's where the perfection ends.

"Honey, you're not going to be happy about this, but I think the turkey's not ready. It's cooked on the outside, but the inside is still raw. Did you thaw the turkey before you cooked it?"

"No," she replies. "I didn't know I had to thaw it first." She looks down at the melted plastic sticking out from the bird's cavity. "Uggh, what's that?"

"That would be the giblets, my sweet." Adam pulls out a bag of uncooked liver and spleen. "Doctor, what do you suggest we do with this?" He passes the bag to Michael, who examines the bag's contents.

"You probably saved us all from food poisoning." Michael laughs. "That's one reason to be thankful today!"

"Who needs turkey on Thanksgiving when we have so much other stuff to eat?" Adam echoes. "I say we go vegetarian today. Who's with me?"

"Stop teasing, guys." Ravy gets up to help her sister. "Sophea's worked really hard on tonight's dinner. Let's salvage this poor turkey. I'm sure we can stick him back in the oven for a couple more hours. We'll be hungry again by then."

Sophea goes on her computer to do some research. "Ravy's right, let me see what I can find. Operation Undercooked Turkey, here we go."

Prince Chakra speaks up, "All is not lost!" He walks toward the kitchen and points out the two boxes he brought, still resting unnoticed on the kitchen countertop. "This is not turkey, but perhaps it will do. The man at the store assured me that this is an American favorite."

195

"I've seen this in a Christmas movie before," Adam remarks. "The day gets saved by Peking duck."

Ravy opens the boxes and says, "Three cheers for Prince Chakra and his roast duck...no, correction, teriyaki Buffalo wings!" Ravy raises her wineglass. "And cheers to Sophea for the most incredible Thanksgiving spread I have ever seen. Who knew you were such a chef?" She gives her sister a tight squeeze.

"Destiny always has the final say," Cookie proclaims. "Tonight we will feast on royal teriyaki chicken wings. Sophea, let this be a reminder to you to never forsake your Asian roots."

"Hallelujah!" Adam carries over a tray of spring rolls he and Chas Mai just fried. "Chas Mai says I wrap shrimp and pork better than either of you." He sticks his tongue out at Sophea and Ravy.

"That's my man." Sophea laughs out loud. "Alright...turkey down. But the rest of the grub is up. Dig in. Cookie won't allow any small plates or dieting tonight."

⋙✣⋘

As everyone is fixing their plates, Sophea places the only photograph she has of herself with her father in the middle of the dining room table. It was taken outside of a house. Cookie looks about twenty and is in a black sarong and green silk tank top. Papa—wearing dark trousers and a light blue button-down long-sleeved shirt—stands proudly next to Cookie. He wears a pair of dark-rimmed glasses and looks directly into the camera. Sophea is two or three in the picture. She is in a striped T-shirt and tight yellow shorts. Her eyes are closed, and she is clutching her heart with her left hand. In the photograph, young Sophea stands in front of her father—small and helpless—his frame towering behind her.

Sophea lights a votive candle beside the portrait on the dinner table to honor her father.

"What's that doing here?" Cookie points to the picture. "Please, not this today. Your father is dead. Why are you trying to make us all sad on Thanksgiving Day?"

"Just let me explain, Mom. A few months ago, I asked Uncle Vito to do some research on what really happed to Papa after that day at the airport." Sophea pauses to assess her mother's reaction. "It's true that Papa made the decision to stay in Cambodia and take care of his elderly parents and younger siblings. Knowing he probably would never see us again, he told us to leave the country without him. He wanted to make sure we survived. The Khmer Rouge sent Papa to a work camp in the Kampong Cham Province. When he tried to escape to Thailand, the soldiers captured him and accused him of being a spy. They sent him to the Tuol Sleng execution center in Phnom Penh, where he was accused of working for the CIA and brutally murdered like millions of other Cambodians."

"Is that supposed to comfort me?" Cookie says, her voice barely audible. "I waited for years for your father to come find us. His choice also left me alone and a widow with two babies to care for. I don't see how he did good by his family. Don't make him a hero, my dear Sophea." She sighs and places both her hands delicately on her left knee.

"The Khmer Rouge kept meticulous records on all the people who came through Tuol Sleng," Sophea continues. "This morning, Pou Vito faxed me the official document that show's Papa's confession and confirms the day of his killing—July 6, 1976. After all these years, we finally have closure. Papa was a good man who tried to do good by his family. And it cost him his life. I know I barely knew him, but I still miss him so much." She hands a piece of paper to Cookie, who glances at the document then closes her eyes.

"Can't you see you are hurting your mother?" Chas Mai says to Sophea. "Why must you constantly dig up the past? Nothing good can come out of it. We need to forget what happened so we can move forward."

Sophea stares at her father's picture. "We can't continue to be silent. We dishonor him by not speaking about his life or talking about his death. I have a right to know about my father. You need to stop being angry, Mom. It wasn't his fault he was killed."

Cookie pierces her fork into a pile of noodles, saying nothing, trying desperately to escape the moment. *All I want is a peaceful meal! Why won't my daughters let me simply enjoy my food?*

"Mom, Sophea's got a point," Ravy interjects. "We all have some responsibility for making sure people don't forget about what happened in Cambodia. A lot of people died, and all we're stressing about today is undercooked turkey."

"We are the privileged Cambodians," Sophea says. "Almost two million Cambodians died during the Pol Pot and Khmer Rouge regime. We're the lucky ones who survived."

"The civil war's been over for twenty years. It's no longer our battle to fight," Cookie says. "Life is hard enough here. It's not our job to give everyone a history lesson about the genocide in our homeland. No one wants to hear about death and suffering. Go make money, then donate to your favorite Cambodian charity. That's enough."

Sophea rubs her two hands together in a nervous gesture. "I have one more thing to tell you. Adam and I are going to Cambodia."

"So, that's your idea of a romantic getaway?" Cookie says. "You're not going to find what you're looking for there. Cambodia has never fully recovered from the war. There are still reminders everywhere—bombed-out buildings, landmines, amputees begging in the street. Young, innocent girls turned into prostitutes. Is this really what you want to see?"

"That's not true! Cambodia has become a premier tourist destination," Ravy says. "People come from all around the world to visit Angkor Wat and the temples. The beaches are beautiful."

"Do not disrespect your mother," Chas Mai gently scolds Ravy. "It's not safe there anymore. The government is corrupt and unstable, and the royal family no longer has power. You could catch malaria the moment you step foot off the plane."

Prince Chakra interrupts in an attempt to avoid another family fight. "Everyone here has strong opinions about Cambodia. I ask that we be thoughtful and respectful in speaking about our country. The king is doing his best to keep the royal family relevant."

"This isn't just about the sights," Sophea says. "There's a part of me that is missing, and I need to go find it in Cambodia. I want to retrace what happened to Papa during his last years. I also want to learn more about the Norodom side of the royal family, as well as meet Papa's living relatives in Phnom Penh. We're excited. We have a whole agenda waiting for us." She smiles at Adam.

An unbearable and long silence falls over the gathering. Cookie stares motionless at her half-eaten plate of food. Chas Mai fiddles with her napkin. Ravy taps her index finger on the table. Michael and Adam pick at their plates, while Prince Chakra adjusts his collar. Everyone is waiting for Cookie to speak.

"Fine, go to Cambodia," she finally says. "But you'll need to lose ten pounds before you go. Cambodians can be cruel to overweight women."

There is a collective sigh of relief. "Well, this is one heck of a Thanksgiving dinner," Adam says. "Anyone who thinks Asian women are soft-spoken and submissive has never known one. Here's a toast to the Norodom women." He raises his glass.

"Please let me know the date of your travels and I will make arrangements for you to visit the king at the palace," Prince Chakra adds. "He is always thrilled to host a member of the family. I also know many people in Phnom Penh and Siem Reap and will be happy to connect you with them. This will be an unforgettable trip for the two of you."

"Wow, maybe we should go on the trip with your sister and Adam," Michael says. "What do you think about getting married in Cambodia?" He looks over at Ravy, who does a double-take at the suggestion.

"If you are serious, I can help with that, too," Prince Chakra says. "Phnom Penh is my hometown and Siem Reap is my playground. It would be my honor to host a huge, traditional Cambodian wedding for you."

"Isn't it presumptuous of you to think that your family and friends would travel halfway around the world to attend your wedding in a third-world country?" Cookie asks. "The idea of flying over twenty hours through several time zones just to see you two get married is exhausting. We can have a very beautiful Cambodian ceremony here at the pagoda in Maryland. I also know a hotel that serves a beautiful buffet dinner."

"Aww, Mom, the prince just offered to throw a wedding for Ravy and Michael. We can't turn down a royal offer like that," Sophea exclaims. "He will take care of all the wedding details and logistics. We can count on our uncle to make this the most-talked about social event Phnom Penh has seen in a while. And you will be the mother of the bride. All you have to worry about is what you're going to wear and who you will dance with at the palace. You will be able to bask in that glory that you miss so much."

Sophea's statement gets Cookie's attention. The women banter a bit more about the pros and cons of having a wedding in Cambodia. This is the most the family has ever discussed about returning to their home country. For once, it is nice to think about future, happy plans in Phnom Penh rather than its association with war and loss.

"I would normally not want to go through all this hassle for a wedding abroad, but for you, Dr. Michael, I would reconsider." Cookie looks at the plate of greens and sweet potato pie in front of her. "Would you like some more food, future son-in-law of mine?"

"Thank you! I would love another piece of that delicious sweet potato pie and a couple more of Chas Mai's spring rolls." Michael reaches toward the nearly empty tray of appetizers. He gazes at Cookie with a loving smile.

"When did you develop such a close relationship with my mother?" Ravy blurts out. "It took awhile, but I guess it's all worth it now." She kisses Michael on the back of his neck.

Cookie pauses, then, shocking her daughters, she says, "Let's have a grand celebration with lots of traditions from both sides of our families. I cannot wait for you to wed my daughter," she says to Michael. "We can have the wedding wherever you two decide." She glances over to Chas Mai for support.

"Did Mom just give in?" Ravy asks. "Unbelievable."

Sophea pulls Ravy from the table, and the sisters begin to dance around the table. "It's time for a party! We're going to have a wedding in this family!" Chas Mai takes a Buddha figurine out of her purse and beckons the girls to give thanks for this wonderful blessing. They all kneel on the floor and proceed to pray together.

Chapter 50

*L*ater that evening, after finishing the dishes, Sophea walks over to Chas Mai, who has been keeping her company in the kitchen for the last couple of hours. Everyone else has left the house, but Chas Mai asked to spend the night with Sophea in her still-new apartment. "What are you thinking about?" she asks her grandmother.

"I'm very proud of you and Ravy," Chas Mai responds. "I pray every night to Buddha that you girls succeed in America but that you never forget where you came from. Tonight, I realized that your mom and I no longer have to remind you to remember our culture and traditions. Our history will always be a part of you. You figured that out yourselves."

Sophea sits down and rests her head on her grandmother's shoulder like she used to do when she was young. "Chas Mai, you're always pushing me and Ravy to fall in love. Finding the right man to spend the rest of our life with is hard to do here in America. It's just not possible to force a man to love you or marry you. Love doesn't work like that."

"Let me tell you a story, *koun,*" Chas Mai begins. "When I met your grandfather, I was still in my very early teens. Back then, no one talked about love or sex, or for that matter, birth control of any sort. Your grandfather was so young and handsome. He struck me like a lightning bolt, and I fell in love with him the moment I laid eyes on him. Your grandfather was literally the prince I had dreamed about all my life. No other man would ever do for me. And I knew that."

"That is so romantic." Sophea looks up at her grandmother. "I want that to happen to me! How will I know if a man is 'the one' for me?" She wonders about Adam.

"Oh, you will know. You will feel it from the inside out," Chas Mai reassures her. "Well, like I said, we were young, inexperienced, and head over heels in love. One thing led to another, and I got pregnant. There was no sex education back then."

Sophea had heard rumors of this story growing up, but she never dared bring up the topic with her grandmother. Still cautious, she blurts out, "Your parents must have been furious with you! What did you do?"

"I did not have many choices back then like you have now." Chas Mai strokes Sophea's hair. "Being pregnant and unwed at fifteen was the worst thing that could have happened to any girl. But my father did not give up on me. On the contrary, he stood up for me right in the middle of the royal palace, right in front of King Sihanouk! My father loved me, and he knew my destiny was bigger than what was before me that day."

"I'm getting chills," Sophea says. "How far will a father go to protect his daughter's reputation? How far will a man go to prove his devotion to a woman he loves? This is better than any reality TV show. And, it's my family!" *And, why have I been saving myself all this time? Poor Adam has been so patient.* "Grandfather was King Sihanouk's cousin, right?" Her grandmother nods her head in agreement.

"My father took me with him to the royal palace and demanded a face-to-face meeting with King Sihanouk," Chas Mai recounts. "He held me tight with his left arm and waved a gun in the middle of the palace with his right hand. This is what he said to the king that day, 'Your cousin, the beloved prince, has impregnated my daughter! He needs to honor her by marrying her and taking care of his child. If the prince does not marry my beautiful daughter, I will shoot him, my daughter, and myself right in front of all of you today!'"

"Now, that must have gotten the king's attention," Sophea says. "Great-grandfather really did that? That's just plain crazy! He could have gotten all of you killed or jailed for life, I imagine."

"You should have seen King Sihanouk's and your grandfather's faces when my father was screaming and waving his gun like a madman in the middle of the royal palace." Chas Mai laughs. "All the guards were ready to pounce on my father, but somehow, it worked. He put down the gun and King Sihanouk and the Queen Mother arranged for a small and formal royal wedding for me and your grandfather the next day in the palace courtyard. I was a happily married bride who gave birth to your mother seven months later. I will never forget that fateful day. It changed the direction of my life. Like we Buddhists believe, destiny will lead the way."

"So, in a way, you did force grandfather to love and marry you," Sophea says. "That's better than any fairy tale."

"You won't need a gun to help you find true love," Chas Mai says. "Back then, my choices and skills were limited. Today, you are a strong, capable, working woman who has earned the right to make the best decisions for your own life. You and Ravy will be all right. Your mother and I have done our job well."

"I'm so glad you are finally spending the night with me in my apartment," Sophea says. "Now that you see me living on my own, hopefully you can relax and stop worrying about me all the time."

"What will I do if you take away my worry?" Chas Mai says. "You three are my world, my personal Apsaras."

"What does that mean?" Sophea asks. "What does Apsara have to do with all of this?"

"At the beginning of the dance, there is a solitary, beautiful female dancer atop the Angkor Wat temples," Chas Mai explains. "She is dressed all in gold, with a giant gold headdress and gold leaves embedded in her long, black hair. Her movements start out slow, timid, and small. But as the dance progresses, she starts to expand her arms more as she explores the world, which is her stage. But, if you notice, the moment when the lead Apsara truly radiates the most is when she is basking in the glow of her fellow Apsaras—who are also dressed in gold from head to toe. Together, they form the most glorious sight—a golden sea of beautiful dancers. Individually, they each still do their soft, graceful hand movements. But, seen together, they are a powerful group of women each lending their light to spotlight the premiere Apsara and each other. She literally glows at the end of the dance because of her fellow Apsaras!"

"You're right," Sophea agrees. "So, you're saying the one beautiful dancer becomes much more radiant once she's surrounded by the other dancers."

"That's exactly what I am saying," Chas Mai finishes. "Your job is to find out who are the Apsaras in your life that will help you shine in your own personal dance. Look for them in your mother, grandmothers, daughters, sisters, and female friends. Once you have this base of women in your life, everything else will fall into place."

"Wow, okay, I'll do that." Sophea reflects on Cookie, Chas Mai, Ravy, and her Wellesley sisters. "I think I'm off to a pretty good start."

"Yes, princess, you are," Chas Mai responds. "Now, I think I need to get some rest. It's been a long day."

Sophea escorts Chas Mai into her bedroom and leads her over to the big sleigh bed, which is covered with a quilted blue down comforter and eight fluffy pillows. "You're only one person. Why do you need so many pillows? Who else is sleeping with you?" Chas Mai points to the mound of pillows. "A bed should be modest. Too many pillows will make the bed look inviting to men. You are sending the wrong message."

"Chas Mai, please don't read into my bedding," Sophea pleads. "I just like a lot of pillows around me. They help me sleep. Trust me, you will fall under their spell, too." She adjusts the pillows and pulls down the comforter for her grandmother.

The women settle into the cotton sheets, and it takes only a few minutes before Chas Mai's soft snoring infiltrates the room. "I promise I won't forget anything that you told me tonight," Sophea whispers into the darkness. "For the rest of my life, I promise to keep your stories and your legacy alive." She kisses Chas Mai's cheek until sleep overtakes her, too.

That night, Sophea dreams of four immigrant princesses surrounded by a hundred dancing Apsaras.

Acknowledgments

This is my first novel and I have so many people to thank. To everyone at Windy City Publishers (Lise Marinelli, Dawn McGarrahan Wiebe, Kristyn Friske, Janet Dooley, Alice Refvik, Shelly Aschkenase, Susan James, and Christy Phillippe) for your guidance and support throughout all the different versions of my book. I always felt that I was in safe and protective hands working with all of you very talented and generous women. Dawn, you have been the captain of this ship who constantly kept me on course and was kind enough to teach me the intricacies of the publishing world. Janet, my gratitude for your editorial brilliance in helping me to integrate Cambodian history into the storyline and for your friendship. Also, I have the most wonderful and big-hearted illustrator, Cynthia Frenette. She is gifted beyond words and created my beautiful book cover and website.

I have many family and friends who gave me valuable insight, support, and love during this book writing journey. Thank you especially to Jason Alderman, Don and Nanette Blandin, Patrick Buechner, Barbara and Bill Cheeks, Dara Duguay, Barbara Graham, Delly Jenkins, Mia Jenkins, Malika Khek Vannier, Vinna Khek, Donna LaFlamme, Laura Levine, Lauren Mullins, Dash Parham, Maryfran Tyler, Richard Vega, Channa Watson, and Rosalind Mays Welch. To my dearest Michelle Mattox and her parents, Warren and Marty Mattox, for their encouragement and lifetime of friendship. Also, a "shout out" to the members of my Berkeley writing groups who have listened patiently to so many of my chapters over the last few years and always provided a safe haven for us writers to share and critique each other's works.

Now, a thank you to the individuals who kept me going every day while I wrote this book. First, to my writing teacher, mentor, and dear friend Derek Green who was the first to believe in my writing, taught me how to tell a story, and encouraged me to pursue my dream of writing a novel. To Mark Wolynn, who helped me honor my amazing and brave father, Youvaing Yim, and who encouraged and guided me to go on this great exploration into my family history. From day one, you have been my editor, collaborator, and "go to" person on all aspects of this book. I could not have done this without you. To my beloved Wellesley sisters Katherine Collins, Michelle Dowling, CB Eagye, Christine White Goldberg, Helen Gregory, Sara Prout, and Dana Sundblad who have devoted so much of their time to push me to finish this book and live out my dream. To my sister Olary Yim Ambrosi and my "G" Ila Kriplani who were my biggest cheerleaders and personal advisors. I love you both so much and am forever grateful for the time, tenderness, and patience you have shown me over the last eight years. This book is as much yours as it is mine.

Finally, I would like to honor my mother Viriyane Norodom Richardson, grandmother Thel Viriya Norodom, and sister Olary. These three women hold me up every day and I am who I am because of them and their unconditional love and understanding. My stepfather Jim Richardson is no longer here with us, but his spirit keeps me going every day. Finally, thank you to my two children, Maile and Napali, who have watched me write and struggle through this book for so many years. Just when I wanted to give up, it was my two little editors who asked the question, "Mommy, are you ever going to finish that book you started?" Well, my darlings, this book is for you. I love you both with every ounce of my heart and soul.

About the Author

VARINY YIM is a first-generation, Cambodian-American author and independent consultant who brings over 20 years of experience and expertise in the fields of communications, nonprofit management, and financial education. Variny has worked as a journalist for *USA TODAY* and *NBC*; public relations executive for companies such as Starbucks Coffee Company, 24 Hour Fitness, and Maxis/Electronic Arts; and nonprofit director for the American Savings Education Council (ASEC) and the Jump$tart Coalition for Personal Financial Literacy.

In addition, Variny has been a public speaker and financial literacy trainer for Visa Inc. and blogged for various websites including *Forbes.com*. She is a graduate of Wellesley College. In 2008, Variny published a book with Jessica Blatt Press titled, *The Teen Girl's Gotta-Have-It Guide to Money* (Watson-Guptill/Random House). *The Immigrant Princess* is Variny's first novel.

Please visit Variny's website (www.varinyyim.com), "Like" her on Facebook, and sign up for her email list.

Made in the USA
Charleston, SC
22 May 2016